Horny Ghost Of

OSAMA BIN LADEN

Rise of the Ghost

P R RESURRECTOR

ISBN: 1490372091
ISBN 13: 9781490372099

Library of Congress Control Number: 2013910437
CreateSpace Independent Publishing Platform
North Charleston, South Carolina

Chapter 1

Did the American military really kill Osama bin Laden? Did the marines catch him alive to take him to America? Are they keeping him alive in a secret prison? Did they just lie that his body was thrown in the sea? If he was killed, was he given a proper burial? Or, was it all just a conspiracy to mislead the American public and international community to justify the wars in Afghanistan and Iraq? Those questions popped up in a lot of suspicious minds and among conspiracy theorists. One of them was twenty-five-year-old John. John, who had lost his job, was interested in making tons of money so he wouldn't have to ever work shitty jobs again. An idea came to his mind: What if he could find bin Laden's dead body? If he found it, he could sell it to bin Laden's sympathizers and followers.

John conducted thorough research to find the area where the marines could have thrown bin Laden's body in the sea. After six months, he had some idea where the American marines could have dropped the coffin. The area covered about fifty square kilometers. An experienced diver and physically very fit, John bought a small boat and other necessary equipment for his mission. He began his adventurous treasure-hunting journey to the marked area with confidence and excitement. He brought enough supplies to last him for more than a year. After reaching the spot, he began the laborious and tiring job of finding the body. He dived every day to look for it, and during the night he slept in his boat. As the days and months passed, his confidence and excitement dwindled. It had been one year without any significant progress.

John was running out of supplies and patience. He decided to give up searching. It was the last day, and he got ready to leave for America. In the afternoon he started sailing back as a very disappointed and poor man. He had wasted a lot of money and one year of his precious life looking for a needle in a hay-stack. The boat was about to sail out of the search area when he had a gut feeling to dive one last time. He dived in and saw something on the ocean floor. As he approached it, his mind exploded with excitement because the item resembled a cof-fin. The coffin had a lot of seaweed around it. He removed the seaweed and immediately was on cloud nine. Grabbing it with a winning smile on his face, he brought it up to the boat. He struggled and finally pulled it in the boat. Daydreaming and feeling like a rich motherfucker, he danced and shouted with excitement.

"Thank you, Jesus, thank you very much. I've done what nobody else could do."

After having a beer, he tried to open the coffin. It was hard to open, but he succeeded after a few minutes. It was still about half an hour before the sun sat on the western horizon. The full moon was ready to illuminate the night. John opened the coffin, and his eyes almost popped out as if he had found a very precious treasure.

"I'm going to be a filthy-rich motherfucker. I don't have to do shitty jobs anymore. I'm going to be my own boss. I'm going to fuck a new bitch every day." He danced and drank beer. All of a sudden, he heard some noise. His eyes turned toward the coffin, and he freaked out. A real and alive-looking bin Laden came out of it. John's happiness turned to despair.

"Please save me, Jesus. He is alive. How it can be? I just saw his remains," John murmured.

"Hi. Thank you for saving me. Where are we?" Bin Laden was naked, and his tiny-looking cock was soft and shrunken.

"Sir, plea…se for…give me. I didn't me…an any ha…rm to you."

"Don't be afraid. I mean no harm to you. I not angry at you. Thank you again." Bin Laden's English was not very good.

John felt relieved and wondered how bin Laden could be alive in the coffin for so long. Unable to understand, he gathered some courage to ask him.

"Sir, please forgive me for asking, but how could you stay alive in that coffin for so long without any food or water?"

"I not alive. I spirit now. The motherfucker Americans gave me no proper burial. They buried me with no clothes. I am ghost now."

John freaked out and looked terrified, almost shitting in the boat.

"No worry. I no harm you. You not answer me. Where are we now?"

"Sorry, sir. We are somewhere in the ocean far from the land." John believed bin Laden's promises not to harm him and felt less scared. He took off his diving suit and had only his underwear on.

"How far America?"

"It will take about twenty days and nights."

"Good, take me there and I let you go when reached there."

"OK sir, no problem. Would you like anything to eat or drink?"

"No, me ghost now. I feel no hungry or thirsty. But I feel only horny, happy, naughty, and angry. Long time I had no sex. Now I feel very horny," bin Laden said.

"Sorry, sir, but you have to wait twenty days, and then I will get you plenty of sexy and beautiful American girls," John assured bin Laden.

"No, I no wait for twenty days. I had so many wives before. I fuck every day. Me cannot survive without sex."

"But, sir, what can we do here in the middle of the ocean? You have no choice but to wait for twenty days."

"I no fussy. You look OK. Your booty is sexy. For twenty days I can fuck your sexy bum." Bin Laden walked behind John, and his lusty eyes checked John's white young butt.

"No, no, no, please, sir. I am not gay. I will do anything for you, but please spare my ass." John's face turned pale, and his hand automatically went to his ass for protection. He was sweating all over. He watched bin Laden's cock growing and becoming hard.

"No worry, I come very fast. My cock not big. Maybe you happy after. Your bum very white and sexy. Me always dreamed about fucking white bum," bin Laden said while caressing and admiring John's butt with lusty eyes.

"Please, sir, don't rape me. Your cock is very big. My hole is tiny, and it will tear. What if I give you a hand job? I am very good at it. I do it every day to myself and enjoy it very much." John held bin Laden's feet as he begged him.

"Shut up, bend over now. I kill you if you not let me fuck you. I no wanker. I like pussy plus assholes and big booty like you have. Take off your underwear now," bin Laden shouted at John.

"OK, ple...ase, don'...t ki...ll me." John immediately bent over in front of him and lowered his underwear.

"Good man, very sexy, beautiful bum. Nice tight hole. Me like tight hole," said bin Laden as he opened John's butt cheeks with his hands so he could look at it properly. "Now, please shake it like a sexy bitch," bin Laden demanded. So as not to make the ghost angry, John obliged and wiggled his ass. As he watched the wiggling sexy ass, bin Laden's cock became big and hard.

"Ohhhhh, my God, you're so sexy and hot. I no wait anymore. My cock going crazy," bin Laden said.

John found an excuse to save his ass. "Sir, I have AIDS. You will become sick."

"Me ghost. AIDS no problem. Before I fucked many women and a lot of men in caves. Sometime no women, I fuck men. I had AIDS before I dead," bin Laden explained.

"Forgive me, sir, but please don't rape me. I will get AIDS." John tried to move away, and his body was shaking violently. He didn't want to get AIDS and forgot what he said before.

"You said you have AIDS. You lie to me. Now bend over and be quiet. You speak one more word, you dead," bin Laden said aggressively.

John didn't say anything and accepted his fate. With no other choice left, he just gave up defending. Bin Laden's dick was already hard and thick.

"Keep your ass up. I promise no pain. I better give you some foreplay first so you want my cock more inside." Bin Laden moved closer to John's ass so he could penetrate his tight hole. He never had sex with a white girl or man before. He had watched a lot of white people in porno movies when he was alive. He always wanted to have sex with them. It was his dream, which he could not fulfill while alive. He spat at John's hole to make it wet. He fingered it first to make John a bit relaxed. John panicked and tried to tighten his hole. He felt bin Laden's warm head on his asshole. Bin Laden started massaging his ass with the warm head of his penetrator.

"Ohhhh, that feels so nice, ohhhh yes, ohhhh no, ohhhh no. Please stop, no come out so fast." The sight and hotness of John's ass made bin Laden feel extremely horny, and he could not control his erupting cock. He came all over John's ass. He felt a bit embarrassed because of premature ejaculation.

"Sorry, this never happened before. Your white ass too hot. Me no able to control."

"It's all right, sir. You will feel better now. Now you don't need to fuck my ass." John felt relived and thought his ass was safe now. He tried to pull up his underwear when bin Laden shouted, "We not finished. Suck my cock to make it hard again. I want to fuck your tight white hole."

"Sorry, sir, I thought you'd finished," John said and immediately started sucking bin Laden's cock in order not to make the already irritated ghost more furious. The taste and smell of bin Laden's dirty poker almost made John throw up. He kept sucking for five minutes, and bin Laden's cock became hard again.

"You very good sucker. See, now it hard again. You very lucky. Now you can enjoy. Come bend over," bin Laden said. John felt disillusioned and that he was the most unlucky person, but he couldn't express his feelings because of the dreadful and horrifying ghost. He quickly bent over to save his life. Bin Laden again spat at his hole. This time he didn't want to do the ass massage because of fearing premature ejaculation again. John screamed with pain when bin Laden pushed all the way inside.

"Ah, very nice, very nice. Your very good virgin and tight hole. No worry, just little pain. After you feel pleasure and maybe you want many times," bin Laden said, trying to calm down John. He spanked John's ass while pumping fast and hard. Enjoying sexual pleasure after so long, bin Laden moaned loudly. John didn't say a word and was wondering what his girlfriend would think if she found out. Tears ran out of his eyes, and the pain got worse. John's ass bled on the boat's floor. Bin Laden didn't stop for twenty minutes. He came two times in John's ass.

"Oh yeah, this my best fuck after long time. Very, very tight and very beautiful white ass. Before I fuck brown and black only."

Bin Laden stopped and John moved over to sit away from him. His body still trembling, he had tears in his eyes and sobbed uncontrollably.

"No cry. It all right. Sorry, I horny ghost, naughty ghost, happy ghost, and angry ghost. I cannot control sex and anger. If no sex, I get very angry. After sex, I very happy ghost. You free after twenty days. You sleep now and we fuck tomorrow again. Maybe you happy tomorrow. Good night, have sexy dreams," bin Laden said.

John didn't answer and turned his face to the other side and pretended to be asleep.

"Why you look for my dead body?" bin Laden asked.

"I wanted to sell your remains to your sympathizers for millions of dollars and become a rich person. I would have never come if I knew my ass would have to pay for it. Now I am raped and left with no money. I borrowed money to find your remains. I am in a lot of debt and with a loose ass."

"No worry. You still can be very rich. You write book. I give you some titles: *Fucked by Bin Laden, Sex Adventures with Bin Laden.* You write this book, you very rich. Americans love reading sex books."

"No, sir, I am a very ashamed, scared, and sad man now. I would never go to sea again," John said.

"No, no give up. You write book, you very rich," bin Laden insisted.

"OK, sir, I will think about it." John did not want to make the ghost angry.

The rapes continued for twenty days. At first it was very hard for John, but as days passed he just let it happen. His pain also lessened, and slowly it became normal. He prayed every day to get rid of bin Laden, and he wanted to reach America as soon as possible to be safe. After twenty days of sailing, they finally came near Miami Beach.

"Sir, if you don't mind, can I ask something?"

"No problem, you my bitch now. You ask anything."

"Sir, are you gay? Did you fuck men in your country? I'm asking because you're fucking me every day."

"No, me not gay. But when I horny, I fuck anything. One time I couldn't find any women or men in Afghan mountains. I was desperate for sex. I saw a male chicken, and I put my cock in chicken's ass. The chicken died. I cooked and ate it. And one time I tried to fuck big rat. The rat very clever. When I tried to put my cock inside his ass, he bite me on my cock and ran away. I tried running after him, but he was too fast. My cock was very painful and swollen. When I slept at night on my tummy, the rat came back. I was very tired. The rat bit off my clothes from my ass and started fucking my ass. I felt tickling on my ass, but I ignored it. I thought my asshole itchy because I not wash it for two days. But when the rat came on my ass, I looked why my ass wet. I saw the rat fucking me. I tried to catch it, but it ran and made fun of me. I tried to shoot it with gun, but it escaped. From that day I never mess with rat. After that I never sleep with my bum up. I never tell this story to anybody. Only you because I like you. Sorry about my English. If you not understand, please ask me again."

"I understood everything. Sorry about the rat raping you," said John while trying to control his laughter. He didn't want to make the ghost angry.

"It is all right. Maybe the rat also feel horny after seeing my ass. I see big buildings. Where are we?" asked bin Laden.

"Sir, we are in America now. This is Miami Beach. Sir, you will find a lot of pussy here. Sir, can I please go now?" Excited to be freed from the clutches of a terrifying and sex-hungry ghost, John kept on talking.

"Oh my God, so many sexy and beautiful pussy. Thank you for your help. You free now, you go. Look for me if you want sex again. I like your tight ass very much." Bin Laden looked extremely jubilant. He scanned the beach from one side to the other, glancing over all the sexy and hot bodies. The ghost had the ability to become more powerful by having sex. But if somebody fucked the ghost in its ass it could lose the energy.

As soon as the ghost allowed John to go, he stormed through the beachgoers, leaving his stuff behind. People stared at him and wondered what was wrong with him. The ghost had the ability to be visible and invisible at will. Once in a visible state, it needed half an hour to become invisible again. It could fly in invisible state but could only run and jump at high speed while visible. People looked at the beach and could not see anything. They got scared, thinking the guy might have seen a shark and was running away. Those swimming rushed out of the water to escape.

Bin Laden was looking at the sexy and hot bodies. Some were sitting and some lying on the sand in revealing bikinis. He saw a male and female couple lying on the sand with their bums up. The girl lay topless and wore a thin bikini bottom. It hardly covered her pussy and asshole. Her magnificently curved, meaty, perfectly round, mouthwatering, hot, and creamy ass made bin Laden go nuts with lust. The sight of a tall white girl's strong, sexy body hypnotized bin Laden. His sexual fantasies and desires overtook his ghostly mind and body. He sniffed the girl's ass and licked her butt cheeks. As he tried to remove her bikini bottom, the shocked girl looked at her snoring boyfriend, who lay beside her. She panicked, thinking somebody was molesting her. Turning around with curiosity, she asked her boyfriend, "Did you just lick my butt and try to remove my bottoms?"

"No, I am lying beside you, and you could see my hands were on the other side. Are you sure?" her boyfriend asked.

"Yes, I'm pretty sure. I wasn't sleeping, and I felt it clearly."

Getting up in a rage, her boyfriend saw a man standing nearby and admiring his girlfriend. Without asking anything and suspecting him, the boyfriend punched the guy in right jaw. Screaming with pain, the guy fell down.

"What the fuck was that for, asshole? I will smash your balls," shouted the guy, and he got up and tried to punch the boyfriend. The boyfriend moved to dodge the punch. Before they could continue fighting, the girl's screams diverted their attention. They couldn't believe what was happening in front of their eyes.

"Someone is taking off my bikini bottom. I can't see him." The girl tried to hold on to her bikini bottom, but something very strong pulled the garment off. The bikini hung in the air, seemingly without any support. It looked as if something was trying to sniff it. After hanging in the air for about a minute, the bikini bottom fell on the ground. By this time a lot of people had gathered around them. Trying to cover herself with her hands, the girl screamed for help. The boyfriend ran toward her to protect her. He could not see anybody and tried to embrace her. As soon as he extended his arms, some invisible force kicked him very hard. His body flung through the air like a soccer ball and dropped in the water. Severely shaking with fear, he screamed from the unbearable pain. Dragging himself out of the water, the boyfriend went back near the screaming girlfriend to help. But the invisible force held him up and kicked in his balls. He flung backward, shouting abuse at something unknown. Brutalized and unable to get up, he couldn't help his screaming girlfriend anymore. Something grabbed the girl from front and laid her down on the sand. The girl's legs opened wide, and her hands seemed to be held by the invisible thing. The invisible thing humped her violently. Her boobs moved as if someone was sucking and squeezing them. The girl screamed and shouted for help continuously.

"Please help. Someone very heavy and strong is raping me. I can't see him, but I can feel his body on me."

People could not see anything and started running away in fear. Some people laughed it off, thinking the girl was pretending to get attention. They got the shock of their life when the girl got carried in the air and something invisible was fucking her violently. They could see that it was impossible for the girl to pretend like that. Terrified, people ran as fast as they could to escape. After raping her, invisible bin Laden dropped her on the ground. He saw a sexy and hot black girl running away. The girl was topless, with big and firm melons. Bin Laden could not resist the temptation and ran after her. He grabbed her by her bikini bottom, which gave her a very bad wedgie. The girl didn't look scared, and she giggled.

"Stop it, horny asshole. I will fuck your brains out. I'm a sex addict, and no one can satisfy me."

"You fuck me. I like girl on top. Come on, please fuck me," said bin Laden. It was his dream to be fucked by a girl on top, so he couldn't stop himself from talking.

"I will if you let me see you and your cock." The girl was really a sexed-up bitch.

"Here, you see me." Bin Laden revealed himself.

"Oh, I know you. You are the guy always on TV. You're bin Laden," the girl said as she moved closer.

"Yes, you right. Now no talk and sex only."

"Ha, ha, ha, ha, ha, ha, your dick is so small and soft." The girl looked down on his tool and couldn't stop laughing.

"No, no, no. It no small. See, I fuck that white girl five minutes before. You suck two minutes, it again big and hard."

"OK, I will try because I want to be a celebrity who fucked bin Laden's ghost." The girl bent down on her knees and sucked him. His cock burst to life and became hard in two minutes.

"See, it standing up now and very big." Bin Laden pointed toward his cock.

"You call that big? That's not very big. I have had some really monster and scary cocks in my mouth, ass, and pussy. I would say it's average," the black girl said.

"Now, please show your pussy. I never seen American black pussy. I hear American black pussy very hot." Bin Laden got very excited and became ready for the action.

"Here, enjoy yourself. Don't burn your mouth or tongue. Handle with care, as it is indeed extra hot." The girl lay on the sand with her legs wide open. She had a lot of big black pubic hair covering her black heaven.

"Oh my God, I see bush. I like bush very much. My dream come true. I love bush. I want to sniff, smell, and lick bush. Thank you, black goddess, for showing me bush. I saw bush first time in porn movie. After I like bush very much and fell in love with bush. It was love at first sight. My fantasy is always sniffing dirty and smelly bush. I also want to shave bush." Bin Laden was over the moon and couldn't stop admiring and talking about bush.

"Will you do something, or do you just want to brag about bush. I always keep bush in my dirty and hot undies. It gets moist and smelly sometimes, but I find a lot of men like smelly bush."

"My whole life I look for bush. Finally I see bush. Oh, baby, American bush smell so nice and yummy. Now I never leave America. I no need visa. Nobody can catch me now."

"Stop talking and fuck. Look at your cock. You kept on talking about bush, and it again became soft and small. Are you scared of bush? I have to suck it again. You better lie down and I will fuck you." The girl sucked and then crawled on top of him. She was really very good at sex.

"Oh, baby, you great at sex. I not scared of bush. I just love bush too much. Oh, fuck me, fuck me. Your big melons very juicy. Oh yes, oh yes. Yes, baby, I like dirty sex." Bin Laden could not stop moaning in pleasure, and he was enjoying the black goddess straddling him and riding his cock wildly.

"You like my ass? Say you like my ass. You want to fuck my black ass? Say yes." The girl became wild and violent. She hit him a few times on his face. She pinched and twisted his nipples. Bin Laden didn't mind because of the extremely hot sexual pleasure.

"Yes, yes, yes, black goddess. I want fuck your ass. I want to lick your yummy ass. I want to put my tongue inside your ass." Bin Laden got really overtaken by the hot and wild sex.

"OK, I'm putting it in my black ass now. Here you go." The girl took his cock out from the front and put it in her back hole.

"Oh, that is very tight hole. Thank you, thank you, thank you." Bin Laden had forgotten everything else. Even those people who were running away scared stopped to watch despite fearing the ghost. They were making videos with their smartphones. Some even used video cameras to capture the unbelievable and unthinkable sexual encounter between a human and a ghost.

"Do you really like it dirty, motherfucker? Tell me how dirty you like it. Say it loudly. I want to hear it." The girl got really wild and abusive. She continued slapping and strangling bin Laden.

"Yes, sexy bitch. I like it very, very dirty. Show me how dirty you can get. Ohhhh. You really very good." Bin Laden didn't mind the abuse and got turned on more. Whenever bin Laden felt sexually excited, he could feel pain and pleasure like humans. Otherwise only other ghosts or supernatural beings could harm him.

"OK, motherfucker, I am coming now. Oh, it feels so great. I'm coming, I'm coming. Oh, baby, I'm coming. I can't stop it now. Oh yes, oh yes, purrrrrrrrrrrrrrrrrrrrrrrr."

"Bitch, what is that? Get off, bitch. What that bad smell? Oh, bitch, you shit on me. You dirty cow."

"Sorry, Mr. bin Laden, but whenever I am fucked in my ass, I always come from my ass, not from my pussy. Oh, it feels so empty now." The girl looked very satisfied and relieved. "Mr. bin Laden, why are you running away now? Come back and fuck me one more time. You said you wanted to lick and put your tongue in my ass. Come back and finish what you desired. Come back, motherfucker, and give my ass a tongue bath." Bin Laden ran away, and the girl followed him.

"Fuck off, you dirty bitch. You so smelly. That was big shit. I not want to lick your shit, bitch. Oh, that feels so dirty," shouted bin Laden as he went in the sea to get cleaned.

"You said you liked dirty sex. Wasn't that dirty enough for you? I thought you don't get dirty because you are a ghost. I love you. I get constipated all the time. Somebody has to fuck my asshole, and then only can I shit. It had been four days since I shit the last time," the girl shouted.

"Bitch, I said dirty sex, not shit sex. I get dirty when you see me." Bin Laden cleaned himself and was coming out of the water when he saw some very fat black and white American women running toward him naked.

"Oh my God, I better run now. Now they see me. I cannot hide." He started running away from the fat ladies. There were about twenty of them. Bin Laden could not be invisible for half an hour after he became visible. That is why he did not want to be visible the first time. The attraction of the black girl made him forget about his invisibility.

"Come on, Mr. bin Laden, fuck me. I can get dirtier than that bitch. I will do a ten times bigger dump on you. This is my fantasy also. It is the first time I've seen a man who likes sex this way," one of the ladies shouted while trying to catch bin Laden.

"Sorry, fat cow, you not understand. I like dirty sex, not shit-on-me sex. You so fat, you kill me my ghostly death," bin Laden replied while running away from them.

"Come on, Mr. bin Laden, fuck my big, round, and sexy booty. I never wash my ass. It's very dirty, and you will love to lick it and fuck my ass with your tongue," another fat woman shouted.

"Please go home. I only have sex two times a day. Now my cock no go hard. He is tired. Fucking American women, no scared of ghost. Go fuck each other."

"Don't worry, we will take turns and suck you. We all want to be famous and celebrities," another one shouted.

"Too much sex kill me. My ghost power no more if you all ugly bitches fuck me."

As they ran, bin Laden saw a lot of police cars coming. The police fired in the air and told the fat ladies to go away. The ladies got scared and ran away for safety. Somebody had called the police. The police officers stepped out from their cars, took out their guns, and ran toward the water, where the girl was lying on the sand shaking with fear. About ten officers approached the girl. They pointed their guns at bin Laden.

"Lie on the ground on your stomach and put your hands behind your back," one of the police officers shouted. "Do as I say, otherwise you will end up with thousands of bullets inside your stinky body."

"Go back, motherfuckers. Me not scared of you. Your bullets nothing for me. I'm a ghost now. If you no go back, you are all dead," bin Laden roared. As he moved toward the police officers, they started firing at him. The officers looked at each other in astonishment, as the bullets didn't do any damage to his body. By that time, his visibility period was over and he became invisible. Some police officers rushed to help the injured girl and her boyfriend. Before they could help the couple, something kicked and punched them hard. Their guns turned on each other, shooting indiscriminately. Police officers' uniforms got pulled from bodies. They tried to resist, but the ghost tore their clothes off. One officer was wearing a G-string underneath and another was wearing sexy red lingerie. Bin Laden laid them naked on the sand in different sexual positions. He pinched their nipples and hurt their balls. When one curled up into a fetal position for protection, bin Laden picked up another officer, took his hand, and inserted the whole arm into the officer's ass. He threw officers down and inserted other officers' cocks into their mouths. He literally tore off some officers' cocks. Instead of shooting, the officers ran wherever they could to save their asses and private parts. Bin Laden made them jump, run, and hit each other. Within twenty minutes, the officers lay on the ground, injured and dead. The beach had been turned into a funny and naked battleground. The black girl also ran away. Some more police cars came, and police officers waited near their cars. Some people informed them what had happened. A girl about twenty years old named Janet came running toward the officers.

"Please stop, don't go near the water. I can see spirits. You wouldn't believe me. It's bin Laden's ghost. He did all this. He is sitting near the girl now, admiring and touching her inappropriatcly. If you go there, he will kill you all. You can't do anything to him with guns. Wait, he is moving now and walking toward us. There he is, coming directly toward us. Everybody, run and save your asses." Janet pointed her finger, and the police officers started shooting. They emptied their guns, but the ghost kept walking toward them.

"Save your life and run. You can't shoot him. He is a ghost now. Please take me in your car also." Janet jumped in one of the cars, and the officer drove away at high speed. Some of the officers could not escape. Turning over their cars, bin Laden bashed them brutally and without mercy. Broken body parts lay everywhere. The fury of the ghost left bloody carnage on the beach. No one was left standing to face the onslaught of a dreadful and horrifying ghost. Panic-stricken people ran as fast as they could to save their lives.

As it was evening, bin Laden went toward the city center to enjoy the nightlife. The police cars and ambulances came after half an hour. The police officer James, who escaped with Janet inside his car, also came back. Janet was still inside the car. Only after confirming from Janet that the ghost had gone, the paramedics took the dead and injured away. They also took the raped girl and her boyfriend to the hospital. The police interviewed people and watched the videos shot by them. Some people risked their lives to record the police officers being killed and injured. The police wanted to speak to the black girl who had sex with the ghost. They broadcast her close-up photo on TV, and somebody informed the police where she lived.

Police officer James, accompanied by another police officer and Janet, went to her house. Janet possessed psychic abilities to see and talk to ghosts. Before the police could get to the black girl, the media were already there. The girl had signed a lucrative deal for interviews with some TV reporters. In order not to scare the public, the police did not announce anything officially. But before they could do anything to control it, videos of scenes at the beach were uploaded on the Internet. The Internet got very busy and slow because of people from all over the world watching those videos. The sexual encounter between bin Laden and the black girl went viral, and the girl became an overnight star. People found it hilarious and entertaining. The world media were after her for interviews, publishers wanted book deals, and even Hollywood filmmakers came looking for her. She had to leave her house in case bin Laden came back to look for her. She was provided police protection and shifted to a secret location. James interviewed her in his office. She told him everything possible she could understand about the ghost. The officers had concluded that the ghost was interested too much in sex. Janet became valuable to the authorities because she could see and talk to ghosts. The police department offered her a permanent job as an undercover officer so they could destroy or do anything else possible to the ghost. Janet accepted their offer and agreed to help. The police identified John, who brought the coffin to America, and were looking for him. He went into hiding so he would not have to reveal anything about his embarrassing and humiliating sexual abuse.

American authorities had no idea about how to deal with an unthinkable and unbelievable weapon of mass destruction roaming free without any fear in America. Even scientists and international experts had no possible solution forthcoming.

Every town and city was put on full alert. The American president and politicians were immediately shifted to a secret location. American soldiers and CIA operatives were shifted to the White House to act as American politicians. The American authorities became certain and convinced that the ghost would attack the White House and target American politicians. Nuclear weapons were also hidden in secret locations.

Bin Laden was not interested in going to the White House. The overwhelming beauty and sexiness of American girls occupied his mind. He just roamed Miami's streets, checking out and admiring hot chicks. By the next evening, he became horny again and needed sex. Janet, the girl who could see him, was transferred to the White House. They expected the ghost to show up there. She was put up in the security control room, watching all the security cameras. No incident had happened since the day before. Bin Laden came to Miami city center and decided to find some hot pussy. He sniffed a lot of girls walking past and made lewd comments about them.

One supermodel-looking girl walked down the central street where all the pubs are. She looked exceptionally hot, and bin Laden followed her. A tall girl with sexy long legs, she wore a short light pink skirt with a revealing pink top. Her big boobs and sexy figure attracted a lot of men's sexual attention. While bin Laden followed her, a tattooed, big-muscled guy blocked her path and started touching her inappropriately.

"Hello, sexy bitch. If you are looking for some extrabig pecker, you have just found it. You want to be fucked at my place or yours?" asked the guy as he grabbed her ass.

"Fuck off, don't touch me," she said, trying to defend herself. The guy with strong muscles almost kissed her when something squeezed his balls and punched him in the face. The guy fell back and was trying to defend his balls as if somebody was kicking there very hard.

"Who the fuck is it? Reveal yourself, asshole. I'm going to make you suck my big cock."

"She is mine. Fuck off, before I kill," somebody whispered in his ears while squeezing his balls tightly.

"You cocksucker, come fight like a man. Show your ass to me," the guy shouted again. Bin Laden got really pissed off. He tore off the guy's clothes, leaving him naked. Then he twisted his arm, breaking it off from the elbow. Bin Laden threw him on the ground and inserted the broken arm into his asshole. The guy screamed in unbearable and agonizing pain while his ass and arm bled profusely. Bin Laden released him. The guy got up and staggered away, screaming to save himself from something awfully dreadful. Everybody around got frightened and wondered what had happened. The girl also froze in fear, wondering who broke the big guy's arm and brutalized him. Horrified and in shock, she started walking away. Bin Laden followed her and sniffed her ass and butt crack.

"Oh, baby, you smell very yummy." Bin Laden got horny and could not control himself as usual. People heard it and wondered who spoke. It was not an American accent. The girl felt something picking up her skirt from behind. She felt two hands opening her butt cheeks apart and sniffing her butt hole. She could not see the thing and got terribly frightened.

"Pooooooooooon." Her stomach was very upset, and she let go a very big stinker.

"Bitch, very bad smell, fucking bitch. Did you eat shit? Fucking American women shit and fart too much," bin Laden said angrily. Everybody heard the horrifying voice. Bin Laden hit the girl on her bum. He got turned off and wasn't interested in that girl anymore.

"I think it's bin Laden's ghost touching her ass. He is going to rape her now," somebody shouted. Horrified people panicked and ran away wherever they could. A lot went inside the clubs to be safe. The girl also disappeared in the crowd. Soon the street was empty except for some fat and sexy girls. They were begging bin Laden to reveal himself and fuck them. They all wanted to be famous like the black girl. Bin Laden didn't like any of them and walked to the next street. A lot of police cars and ambulances came, anticipating some trouble. Somebody had called the police and informed about the ghost. The police had only one gifted person, Janet, who could see him, and she was in Washington. They had advertised for people with similar abilities, but so far nobody else came forward. The police didn't know what to do because bin Laden remained invisible.

Bin Laden decided to search for hot chicks inside the night-clubs. The first one he entered was full of men. They were dancing and kissing each other. From their behavior, he realized that they were all gay. He was interested in only girls that day. He came out and walked to the next club. He looked through the glass window and saw a lot of intoxicated girls dancing erotically. Sexual urges reawakened in his mind, and he walked inside to check out the beautiful girls. He liked a tall white girl with an athletic body wearing a short skirt and blouse. She had an hourglass figure with a big round booty and big, firm, juicy boobs. Her wiggling ass and dancing boobs captured his rising sexual attention, and he waited to follow her home for sex. She drank a lot, and after some time she went outside with a black guy. Bin Laden followed them. They hailed a taxi and sat in the backseat. Bin Laden sat in the front passenger seat. He didn't have to open the door because he had the ability to walk through walls or closed doors.

As the taxi came to a halt, the couple got out and went upstairs to the guy's flat. Bin Laden followed them without creating any trouble. As soon as the couple went inside the flat, they ripped each other's clothes off and the girl pounced on the man's already hard cock. The guy had a very big cock, and the girl was becoming desperate to get it inside her dripping pussy. Bin Laden looked at that enormous tool and then at his little bin Laden. He felt embarrassed and angry because the guy was bigger than him. After sucking it for a few minutes, the girl became desperate and didn't have the patience to wait any longer.

"Come on, big guy, fuck my pussy and ass with that scary cock. Come on, I can't wait anymore. Fuck like a wild animal." She bent down in front of him, spreading her long legs and raising her butt to get his enormous black thickness deep inside her extrawet pussy.

"OK, bitch, you want it hard. You'll be begging me to stop."

"Really, I would love that. Now, don't talk, and show me how hard you can fuck. Blow my mind away. If you make me happy, you can also put it in my ass." The girl shook her big white booty.

The guy held his cock with one hand and spread the girl's pussy lips with the other. He fingered her for a minute, and her juicy cunt started dripping. He tasted her juices from his wet finger and proceeded to ravish her. Bin Laden stood behind the guy, admiring his black ass. The black man was about to enter her when bin Laden inserted his finger in the black guy's butt hole and took it out quickly.

"What the fuck?" the guy shouted, turning his head to see who did it. His attention got diverted, and his cock became soft.

"What is wrong, baby? Why has your cock shrunk?" The girl turned around and looked at his limp dick.

"I think somebody just inserted something in my ass when I was about to enter your pussy. It felt like a finger."

"There is nobody here. You are drunk and imagining things. Come try again," the horny girl said in desperation.

As the guy made it hard again and was about to enter her, the same thing happened again. He got really irritated this time.

"Who is the fucking asshole? You like to play with my black ass, come out and play. You will be screaming for mercy when I put my big dick in your ass."

Watching him going mad, bin Laden was trying to control his laughter. The girl turned again and looked at his cock, which had shrunk too much this time. She also thought the guy was just fucking with her mind and in reality couldn't keep up the erection.

The woman got really pissed off. "OK, I will help you, but this is the last time. If you can't enter me, I will leave and find somebody else to fuck. There is nobody else here, and you are just making excuses." She grabbed the guy's cock and started sucking it.

"I'm not lying. There is really somebody here. I'm not that drunk, and I could feel something like a man's finger penetrating my ass."

"OK, it is very hard now. Try it. Have some confidence and ravish my pussy." The girl didn't want to make him more nervous and encouraged him. She wanted his enormous cock inside her very badly.

"OK, bend over." He got ready to enter her while bin Laden stood behind him with his erect cock. Bin Laden had quietly used some of the Vaseline in the bathroom to lubricate his cock. As the guy bent over a bit to put his dick inside the girl, bin Laden inserted his lubricated dick deep inside the guy's ass and took it out immediately.

The guy went hysterical. "Who is the motherfucker? You think you can put your dick in my ass and hide? You come out now. Otherwise, I am going to tear you to pieces when I find you."

The irritated girl had enough of him and felt like killing him. "Fuck off, asshole. I can't believe you're gay. You can't get it up, and you're imagining another cock in your ass. You are so fucking disgusting. You have wasted that cock. Fuck you. I'm leaving."

"Please don't go. I'm not imagining. Somebody really inserted a lubricated dick inside my ass. Feel the lubrication on my ass." The guy bent in front of her and opened his butt with both hands.

"You are really a disgusting gay. How did you know the feeling of a real finger and a cock inside your ass? You must be used to those things. Fuck off, poofter." The girl kicked him in the ass and went outside, slamming the door shut behind her.

Enjoying the commotion between them, bin Laden struggled to control his laughter. The guy broke a lot of his belongings in a fit of rage. Bin Laden went outside to follow the girl.

The girl came down and walked in the street to hail a taxi. A taxi stopped and she jumped in the backseat. Bin Laden jumped in the front seat. She didn't live far away, and after five minutes she reached her destination. She had a one-bedroom flat, and bin Laden followed her inside. The girl had lost her mood for sex. She took off all her clothes and sat on the bed disappointed and dissatisfied. She took out a scotch bottle and poured herself a big drink. With a grumpy mood, she drank it straight away in one shot. Mumbling abuse at the black guy, she lay on the bed naked with her legs wide open without covering herself with a blanket. Seeing a sexy goddess lying naked in front of him, bin Laden immersed himself in her beauty and sexiness. As he moved his nose around on her pussy, sniffing her bush with eyes closed, he could not control himself any longer. Becoming visible, he immediately covered the girl's mouth with his hand to stop her from screaming.

"Please no make noise. I mean no harm to you. I friendly ghost and if you make noise, I kill you," said bin Laden as he slowly removed his hand from the girl's mouth. With fear running through her body, the girl did not dare to make any noise.

"A...re you b...in Laden's ghost?" With astonished eyes, the girl gathered some courage to speak. The girl had seen and heard stories about the ghost during the day.

"Yes, darling. Me bin Laden's ghost. No worry. I just horny ghost. You very sexy and beautiful. I just have sex with you and no harm you. OK, no get scared," bin Laden assured the girl.

"OK, you can fuck me, but please don't kill me." The girl had watched the video of the ghost and the black girl having sex, and she knew he didn't harm her. In fact, the girl enjoyed the sex and became a celebrity. The girl wasn't afraid anymore and planned to use this to her advantage.

"Good girl. No worry, you and I enjoy fucking. I give you good sex." Bin Laden pounced on the girl and fucked her in ghostly speed. She liked it very much, and then she reciprocated the favor by dancing naked erotically and fucking bin Laden the way he wanted. The sex was amazing, and bin Laden felt very satisfied and relieved.

"That was great fuck. You very expert in sex. I like you very much. If you any problem, tell me, I help you." Bin Laden really liked the girl in a sexual way.

"Oh, dear horny ghost, you also fucked me hard. I didn't know ghosts could fuck so fucking good. My name is Wendy, and I am always here at nighttime. You can come anytime you feel like having sex. I like you very much. Please don't go away." The girl really liked the fast and wild sex.

"Thank you very much. I go now. Take care." Bin Laden kissed the girl and was about to leave when she grabbed his hand.

"Please sleep here tonight with me. I've never slept with a ghost before. You can stay here if you want." She had really enjoyed the sex and longed to keep him there.

"OK, I stay with you tonight. But I go in the morning. Me want new pussy every day. Young and new pussy make me strong ghost."

"OK, baby, but I will miss you very much. Come here and sleep next to me. I want to make a video of you and me."

"No problem, you make video and you make money." Bin Laden felt horny again, and they fucked many times during the night until the girl's pussy and ass became sore. He left in the morning. She uploaded the video on the Internet, and within one hour FBI agents knocked at her door. She cooperated with them and gave all the information.

After collecting information from various sources, the police understood that the ghost was interested only in sex so far. Police knew that they would not be able to fight or kill the ghost with guns. They decided to consult religious priests and psychics. The news spread like wildfire that the ghost was interested only in having sex with sexy and good-looking girls and raping those who resisted his advances. A lot of girls became interested in having sex with him to be famous, but the rest got scared of being raped.

The FBI hid important people and their families whom they suspected bin Laden might target in secret locations. Although the ghost seemed interested only in girls so far, the security forces and CIA didn't want to take chances and compromise any security arrangements. The government had directed scientists to find a way to get rid of the ghost. Foreign governments were also contacted in search of a solution, but none was forthcoming.

Bin Laden's routine of finding new girls and having sex with them continued. Girls who made him happy were allowed to make videos of the sex sessions. He tortured and raped some girls who tried to resist his attempts to have sex. He even killed some of them violently. One day he noticed a very hot black girl in a nightclub. He waited for her to leave and followed her home. Once inside her flat, he revealed himself, but the girl didn't get scared.

"Oh my God, I can't believe you are the horny ghost. I dreamed about having sex with you. Come here, darling; I will fulfill all your wild fantasies. Please allow me to make a video."

"Thank you, thank you, very sexy girl. I want fuck your backside today. You give me good sex, and I make you very happy. It OK, you can make video." Bin Laden always preferred girls who fucked him willingly.

"Come here and lie down on the bed on your stomach. I will give you an erotic massage first." The girl pulled bin Laden on the bed. He liked the idea and lay on the bed anticipating extremely hot sex. The girl took off everything except her skirt. She turned her video camera on and put it over the cupboard to record everything clearly. She poured oil on the ghost's back, legs, and butt and began massaging with her big and hot boobs. Bin Laden closed his eyes and surrendered to the experienced temptress.

"That feel very nice and hot. You very good. Yes, your body is extra hot. Please use your hands." Bin Laden hadn't had that kind of sexual experience before.

The beautiful temptress massaged all his body, and then she started paying more attention to his butt. She spread apart his butt cheeks and poured warm oil on his butt hole. The feeling of warm oil on his butt hole increased his sexual pleasure many fold. She massaged his butt so good, occasionally touching his asshole with her finger. This sent electric sexual shivers through his body. While one hand played with his butt, the other oily hand caressed his balls and cock. She massaged his tool while touching his butt hole lightly and occasionally inserting the tip of her finger inside.

"Oh, baby, that feel so good. No stop. Touch my ass more," said bin Laden. He brought his body up and bent over on all fours. He enjoyed it so much that he moaned with pleasure, and he made circles with his asshole around the tip of the girl's finger. The sensation of her finger in his ass made him more desperate.

"Please put finger in my hole. Feel very good. I like it very much," bin Laden begged.

"Are you sure you want my finger all the way in your ass?"

"Yes, darling, I sure. Come on, put inside. You very good girl. You understand how man feel happy."

"Here you go." She inserted it all the way deep inside him.

"Oh, baby, that feel so good. Fuck me hard. Your finger so big, warm, and thick." Bin Laden got totally overtaken by lust and lost all common sense.

The girl spanked him and fucked him for about four minutes and then pulled out.

"Why you pulled out? Keep inside. That was so fucking good." Bin Laden turned around to ask her and saw the girl had a big cock instead of a pussy. She was already coming and shooting sperm everywhere in the room, including bin Laden's back.

"Bitch, how you have cock? You fucked my ass with your cock. I no like this." He became enraged and started kicking and punching the girl mercilessly.

"Please forgive me. I thought you would be very happy. I asked you before I put it inside. Please don't hit me. You liked it.

A lot of men like it. I'm a tranny, and men always enjoy with me."

"Bitch, I liked finger, not cock. Me not gay. I kill you." He kicked and punched until she became motionless. Thinking she was dead, he left the place feeling furious and violated. Enraged and shocked, he forgot about the video camera. The neighbors had heard the screams and called the police. Police arrived and found the shemale motionless. They called an ambulance, and the shemale was taken to the hospital. After a few days when she gained consciousness and became better, she was released to come home. She had told the officers everything but didn't mention anything about the video camera. Finding the camera still at the same place, she quickly turned it on. A smile returned to her face when she found all the footage intact. In a hurry, she took the camera and packed her important belongings to leave. She moved to her friend's place on the other side of town. Dreaming about being a rich girl, she uploaded the video on the Internet, and in a few days it went viral. People watched it over and over again while enjoying poking fun at bin Laden.

The horny ghost turned into a dreadful and unstoppable monster when bin Laden saw the video being played in a nightclub and people making humiliating and disgusting jokes about his sexual encounter with the tranny. He smashed the TVs and literally tore people in the club into pieces. People ran to save their lives, but nobody in the club could escape his fury. The club turned into a sea of blood with body parts floating in it. Humiliated and disgusted, bin Laden went club to club to find that tranny. Furious and offended, the horrifying creature attacked many places, wherever he found them watching the video, slaughtering people in his path ruthlessly and viciously.

Frightened, the tranny went to the police for security when she heard what had happened. The police shifted her to another city far away, and she disguised her appearance so nobody could recognize her. The police warned people not to watch that video because it would put their and other people's lives in danger. Despite the warnings, it became the most-watched video on social networking sites. Some people even uploaded the videos of people being brutalized and slaughtered in the clubs. The governments of the world tried to ban those, but it was too late. People had already downloaded them to their computers, and the videos kept reappearing under different titles.

Chapter 2

The White House's security was beefed up. The agents became restless and struggled to fall asleep, fearing the ghost could attack anytime. They tried their best not to show it, but they panicked and became jumpy at any noise they heard in the building. The government even grounded the airlines for a few weeks to safeguard the public. The American economy suffered tremendously, and the government had no choice but to let the airlines fly again.

After about two months, the agents in the White House got tired of the fear and playing the waiting game. Some of them even became disoriented and depressed. They clearly understood the stark reality that when the ghost arrived, they would be slaughtered like the people in the clubs. It was their duty, and they had no choice but to obey the orders. Nightmares took over their minds, and they felt angry with the government for asking them to defend a building from something viciously dreadful and undefeatable.

As usual, at about 12:30 p.m. Janet went for her lunch break. Finally, loaded with energy from hot American pussy, bin

Laden arrived near the White House to strike with vengeance. The ghost turned into a more energetic, young, and deadly force from the pussy energy. Visible and proud to be outside the White House, the most feared ghost on this planet walked around calmly and fearlessly to scare the shit out of everybody around. Picking up a bus full of screaming passengers, the ghost roared to announce his arrival to the authorities. Without mercy, he hurled the bus toward the White House. Hearing the roaring and a loud bang, half of the security agents, shaking with spine-chilling fear, rushed outside the White House and took positions to attack the unrelenting creature. Almost crapping in their pants, the agents inside took their positions to stop the unstoppable and horrifying monster. The bus he hurled in front of the White House was smashed into pieces, and there seemed no survivors of the impact. Screaming and disheartened, people ran for cover when they heard bin Laden's horrifying roaring. With his eyes turning fiery red and chest thumping, bin Laden roared thunderously.

"I here, motherfuckers. Get ready. I coming in now. Stop if you can. Ha, ha, ha, ha, ha, ha, ha. You looked for me everywhere. Now I am here. If you want to live, tell your motherfucker politicians to come outside and face me."

A negotiator with a loudspeaker attempted to buy some time and to calm the enraged ghost. "Mr. bin Laden, please speak correct English. We are ready and willing to listen to your grievances. There is nothing to be gained in the unnecessary bloodshed. We can give you money or anything else you want."

"Fuck English. This no Hollywood movie. This real horror action, and I fuck you all now. You want negotiation. Give me all the politicians. Me no want money. You want public safe, you have to sacrifice your politicians."

"Why don't you calm down and we can discuss everything amicably. We are willing to provide all the facilities you need for your comfort and pleasure. We can shift you to a seven-star hotel and provide all the sexy females you want. Please think about it with a cool mind."

"Me want all the American politicians and military leaders to do erotic dances in front of me. Me want them to bend over and let me fuck in their asses. If you accept those demands, I willing to negotiate. If not, I going to fuck you all today. Me know you will not accept that. Me not stupid. Me know you are just wasting my time. Me can shift to any place in America, and you can't stop. I will stay in White House very soon. Try if you can kick me out. Look around, fucking army tanks and helicopters coming. Take your time and get ready. Me not scared."

"Don't make a move. We will blow you up. You will never be able to come near our politicians. We do not negotiate with terrorists." The negotiator changed his tactics as soon as he saw everything in place for the attack. Army tanks moved toward bin Laden, and helicopters flew over with big guns aiming at him. Laser guns targeted his body, ready to shoot.

Bin Laden ignored the warnings and moved at lightning speed toward the army tanks. The guns went off, "boom, bang, boom, bang, boom, boom." He went for the tanks first. Trying to shoot the fast-moving bin Laden, the tanks turned on each other and their own troops. Panicked and frightened, security officers started firing indiscriminately. The agents dropped like flies sprayed with insecticide. Some agents left their guns behind and disappeared into the fleeing people to save their lives. The bullets and lasers had no effect on the ghost. He used the laser guns from the army to shoot down the helicopters. Soldiers, security agents, and guns outside the White House fell silent after about twenty minutes. The vicious ghost then turned his attention to the agents inside the White House.

He stormed inside. Standing without any fear, he stared in every direction. Roaring in a horrific and bone-chilling voice, he announced, "Don't hide, motherfuckers. Come face me." Moving like a twister, he bumped off the terrified agents as if they were toys. Some escaped with their lives by jumping out through the windows. Some hid wherever they could. Fear-stricken, Janet went inside a storeroom. She saw a cupboard and quickly hid inside. She heard strange, nonhuman foot-steps entering the room. To save herself, she started breathing without making any sound. She knew it was bin Laden. The sound of footsteps stopped near the cupboard. Janet held her breath and closed her eyes in fear. Everything went silent. No guns fired, nobody ran around. After looking around for a few seconds, bin Laden walked out slowly. Hearing the sound of footsteps fading away, Janet started breathing normally again. But she stayed still inside and didn't dare to get out of the cupboard.

As all the politicians were already shifted, bin Laden had no interest in staying in the capitol building. He wrote on the wall in big letters, "I miss you, motherfuckers. I will be back." He came outside and vanished. Not hearing anything for about an hour, Janet came out slowly. Bodies of security agents were everywhere. Seeing the unimaginable destruction and loss of human life, Janet felt dizzy, disheartened, and terrified. Crying uncontrollably, she sat in one corner. After feeling a bit better and coming back to her senses, she got up. She walked around slowly to make sure the ghost had gone. She saw the writings on the wall and understood it had left. Only when it was confirmed by Janet that the ghost had gone did the ambulances, army, and police move in to help. Seeing the carnage left behind, tears rained from every eye. Fear gripped their hearts as they helped the injured to be transferred to hospitals. So much bloodshed turned the place into a river of blood. Too many bullet-ridden and torn-dead bodies lay around.

The politicians watched everything live in their secret underground backup office. The government immediately arranged an emergency meeting. Janet was also invited. The army flew her carefully to the president in a helicopter. They made sure that the ghost did not follow them while invisible. Everybody had different ideas, and Janet suggested using ghosts of dead Americans to take on bin Laden because only ghosts would be able to do any real damage to him. She explained that she had seen ghosts killing each other in their ghostly world like humans harm each other in human world. The president also liked the idea, and everybody else in the meeting agreed. Janet was assigned the most urgent task of finding ghosts because only she could see and talk to them.

Janet took with her some CIA agents to find the ghosts. She found many who were mostly criminal ghosts. After communicating with those ghosts, Janet realized that they still possessed the criminal mentality in their ghostly life. They seemed interested only in terrorizing and hurting innocent humans. She found them not to be trustworthy and useful. She had almost given up hope of finding any helpful ghosts, but her hard efforts bore fruit one day. As they drove past an old, rundown church, Janet noticed something. The church building must have been about two hundred years old.

"Stop the car, please," Janet shouted.

"What is it?" asked Sam, one of the CIA agents.

"I saw some ghosts near the church. Go back a bit," Janet replied. The driver reversed the car.

"Stop here. I can see them now. It looks like they are ghosts of some nuns. There are four of them. You all wait here. I'll go and talk to them," Janet said.

"Be careful," Sam cautioned her.

"Don't worry. They don't look dangerous to me." Janet got out of the car and walked toward the ghosts, who sat outside the church building. They stared at Janet and understood that she could see them.

"Hi, I'm Janet."

"Hi, my child, what can we do for you? I'm glad to know that you have this special ability to communicate and see us," one of the nuns said.

"I've had this ability since childhood. You all seem to be very pious nuns. There is a great danger descended on this earth in the form of bin Laden's ghost. He might be the anti-Christ. The humans are defenseless in front of him. We need your help to do something about him," Janet explained.

"Yes, we've heard about it. We've also heard that he has this ability to become more and more powerful by having sex with young women. We're willing to help, but we have heard he is already too powerful. You make a foolproof plan to kill him, and we will do whatever we can. We're always here," the head nun said.

"Please don't take it the wrong way. One question is bothering me. Why have you all turned into ghosts?" Janet asked. She wanted to find out why such pious and helpful nuns ended up as ghosts.

"Very good question, my dear. We knew you would ask that. You know, as humans we all make mistakes. We had committed some sins when we were humans. To pay for those sins, we have to suffer in our afterlife. We're repenting those sins now. That's why we stay outside the church. We don't harm anybody. If we could be any help to humanity now, it will help us to be free from our ghostly lives. We will move on to our next journey of life. So please let us help you. Sorry, I forgot to introduce myself. My name is Margaret. I'm the head nun ghost," the nun answered. As Janet was taking so long, the CIA agents had also come there and heard what the nun had said. Nun ghosts had special ability to communicate and be visible to the humans.

"These are the government security agents," Janet said. "They're just with me to find friendly ghosts to get help."

"Hi, everybody, I think we should become visible because they can't see us," Margaret said, and the nuns became visible to the CIA agents also. They were all young- and beautiful-looking nuns.

"You're all very young. What did you do wrong to deserve a ghostly life?" Sam the CIA agent asked.

"Do you really want to know?" Margaret replied.

"Yes, but only if you don't mind," Sam answered.

"Oh, we don't mind telling the truth. Actually, it will help us repent our sins. About two hundred and thirty years ago, I was the head nun in this church. The church was quite famous, and people came here from all over the country to worship. We used to stay in the building at the back of the church. I was a very religious and pious nurse. I came as a nun first to this church, and these girls joined me later. The priest, Father Joseph, used to live about a ten-minute walk from the church.

As we were all young nuns, sexual urges didn't let us sleep much at night. We used to take cold showers to control ourselves. Sometimes when the cold showers didn't work, we use to stand outside in the freezing cold to calm our bodies and minds down. The young men visiting the church during the day used to add fuel to the fire. The way they looked at us with sex-hungry eyes made our lives more miserable and unbearable. The more we tried to suppress our sexual desires and needs, the harder it became to control. Sex hormones made our bodies burn with desires. Our breasts became swollen and harder. We were surprised how our nipples always remained erect, almost poking out from our clothes. Our panties became very wet all the time. Sometimes we had to change them two or three times in a day. Without telling each other, we all started licking each other's dirty panties from the laundry basket. This added more fuel to the fire. Sometimes at night we sneaked into people's homes while they slept and stole dirty undies of young men. Every part of our body became desperate for sex. The young men noticed the sexual flames arising from our burning-hot bodies, and they all looked very interested in ravishing our virgin bodies. Even the cold weather had stopped helping to control our bodies. Out of all the fruits, we liked only big bananas. We started indulging on homemade hot dogs. We used to take the big pieces of hot dogs out from the bread and passionately lick the sauce off it. It felt so good and tempting. Once the meat was clean, we would suck it before eating it. Our bodies always started craving big bananas, big hot dogs, and ice cream. We used to pour some ice cream over the hot dogs and lick it." Margaret stopped talking for a moment.

"Then what happened?" Sam couldn't stop asking. The CIA agents were all males. Hearing the nuns' story made them horny and their cocks hard like steel. Janet also felt horny, and her pussy became wet.

"Oh, I'm feeling tempted again. Anyway, I must tell you the whole story. All hell broke loose one day. It had just gotten dark. Father Joseph also had gone home. We were all sitting in front of the fire in our building talking to each other. We had taken off our nun costumes and were in just normal clothes. We heard some noise outside. We rushed outside and found a very strong black man lying on the ground. We checked his pulse and found him to be just unconscious. We brought him inside to save him from the cold. His clothes were all dirty and wet from the mud. We covered his body with a blanket and slowly removed his wet clothes. We poured some warm water in his mouth. He gained consciousness quickly. He seemed to be very hungry. We gave him some food to eat. He ate a lot while still sitting with the blanket around him. He told us that he was a slave and ran away to escape from his brutal master. He was tortured and made to work very long hours. His master's henchmen were looking for him everywhere. He begged us to save his life. We took pity on him and promised him to save his life. As he was telling about himself, he again lost consciousness due to the cold weather. We quickly carried him near the fireplace. The younger nun, Jenny, prepared a hot bath for him near the fire. To save his life, we had to remove his blanket and put him in the warm water naked. As the fire and the warm water warmed his body, he woke up. We gave him some wine to drink. When we saw a very strong and naked man in front of us, our sexual desires took over our bodies. When he got out from the water and stood naked near the fire, our sexual emotions made us forget that we were nuns. He also forgot to cover himself up. We noticed him picturing us naked. His penis started rising and growing in size. All four of us just stared at his enormously erect and delicious manhood. We had never seen a naked man before. We had heard some stories about it. We hesitated to cross the line because of shame.

But the youngest of us, Jenny, who was only nineteen years old at that time, pounced on the hardened dick. She grabbed it and put it in her mouth. She started sucking it passionately. We also lost our patience and gave in to our sexual desires. We all looked at each other and pounced on the naked man. We tore the clothes off each other, and in no time we were all naked. We started licking the man's body, his butt, balls, cock, and asshole. We took turns sucking his throbbing cock. The man also sucked our firm and delicious boobs. Seeing each other naked, we couldn't control ourselves and also started licking each other's pussies and sucking boobs. We asked the man to lie on the bed and then took turns straddling him and riding his huge dick. We also took turns sucking the wet cock from each other's pussies. The man also hadn't had sex for a long time. He fucked us the whole night. We didn't let him sleep. When it was daytime, we let him remain in our room, and we locked it from outside. We left more than enough food for him to get strong for the night again. We went to do our daily chores.

We heard from people that the henchmen were still looking for him. But nobody suspected that he could be in our rooms. We waited for the night, desperate to enjoy the man again. After everybody had gone home, we rushed to our place. The man ate and slept the whole day. He was waiting to enjoy our ravishing and gorgeous hot bodies. We didn't wait for anything else and pounced on the man again. We didn't want him to leave, so we just told him that the henchmen were still looking for him. He also didn't want to go. Our sexual marathon kept going for four months. Our behavior had changed. Our face and skin started glowing. Father Joseph and the people noticed the change in us. The young men became suspicious.

One day they hid outside our place to find out what was going on. We were so lost in sex that we had very loud sex that night. There was a knock at our door in the middle of the night. We asked the man to hide under the bed and took some time to open the door. The public had surrounded our place from all sides. Father Joseph and some other prominent religious people pushed their way inside. The henchmen also came inside and found the black man hidden in our room. By that time, all of us had become pregnant also. The enraged public and the henchmen dragged us out of the building by our hair. The henchmen were allowed by the public to take the black man and us with them. We were brutally tortured and raped for many days by the henchmen. Finally they shot us, and our bodies were thrown into the fields. We have been ghosts since then. We pray here every day for forgiveness. We have to spend another five hundred years in the ghostly world. But if we help humanity, this period can be reduced significantly. We don't like this world and want to move on. We're prepared to sacrifice our ghostly lives for humanity," Margaret said.

"Wow, that's a very sexy and sad story," one of the CIA agents said. The CIA agents and Janet got extremely turned on by the erotic story.

"How powerful are you compared with bin Laden?" Janet asked.

"Our combined power might be about twenty percent of his power. If we want to inflict any real damage on him, we have to plan it properly. We are ready to do whatever you will suggest. Don't wait for too long. His ability to get energy through sex will make him more and more powerful," Margaret answered.

"As you're ghosts, do you know any way to get rid of him permanently?" Janet asked.

"We won't be able to hide our ghostly identity from him. He will straight away sense us when we go near him. Use some girls to distract him and make him vulnerable for the attack. We can attack and do our best, but we do not know what will be the end result. We will think about it if there is any way we can end his ghostly terror permanently," Margaret explained.

"What if we find more ghosts to help us? This way we will have extra force to match his might," Janet asked.

"Yes, that will help. We will be here waiting to hear from you. Let us know if you find any others," Margaret answered.

"I'll see you soon. I think we should go and look for others without any delay. Bye for now, and thanks for your help," Janet said.

They left the ghosts in a hurry. It was already dark, and they checked into a nearby motel. The CIA agents and Janet were still feeling horny from hearing the story. After having dinner and drinking a bottle of wine, Janet couldn't control herself and went to the CIA agents' room. She knocked at the door, and Sam opened it.

"Hi, boys, I'm feeling very horny and getting desperate for some real hot sex." Janet didn't beat around the bush and told them what she wanted. They were already talking about her hot body. Two of the boys were white and two were big black guys. They couldn't believe their ears and wasted no time.

"Come on in, sexy, we're also feeling the same about you," Sam answered.

"Turn on some music, boys, and then sit back and watch my erotic dance." Janet staggered inside the big room. Sam turned on the music. Janet started dancing in slow motion in front of the horny guys, her hands moving up and down from her pussy to her extremely sexy big boobs. She slowly removed her top while her body swayed in sexy motion. Watching a sexed-up and horny babe dancing erotically, the guys started undressing themselves. Janet also started removing her other clothes while dancing. She opened her bra and threw it toward the naked guys, who were using their hands to play with their hardened dicks. Janet took off her dirty panties, soaked with her pussy juices and urine. She didn't have time to change them for two days, which made them extra delicious and fragrant. She threw the garment at the sex-hungry boys, and they pounced on it like dogs pouncing on bones. Together they sniffed and licked it clean. The intoxicating smell and taste of her juices and urine fired the boys up more.

Janet covered her pussy with one hand while still dancing. She wiggled her beautiful, firm, and creamy white ass, teasing the already desperate and obviously horny-as-hell guys.

"Come on, sexy goddess, we can't wait any longer to ravish your stunningly hot body," one of the black guys begged. Seeing four big and strong guys begging to fuck her, Janet came to a boiling point from the sexual heat. She put one finger in her wet pussy and licked it to turn up the heat on the boys. The boys' hungry and wet tongues started moving over their lips in response. Putting one finger all the way deep inside her asshole, Janet moved closer to the boys while still dancing. She took out the finger from her ass and offered it to the boys. The boys at once licked it and desperately demanded more. She repeated the process four more times and let each of them taste her asshole. She motioned them to stand, and they obliged immediately. She knelt in front of them. A bunch of enormously hardened dicks dangled in front of Janet's face. They were already wet with precum, and Janet went from cock to cock, giving them a quick suck in her warm mouth. The taste of their precum turned her on more, and then she took turns sucking the huge cocks passionately while playing with the other cocks and balls with her warm hands. Loaded with cum, the guys didn't take long and blew their load in her mouth one by one. She swallowed every bit of the precious and delicious cum. Sam pulled her up and made her stand.

"Now leave the rest to us and enjoy," said Sam. Two guys grabbed her big breasts and started pinching and then sucking her erect tits. One black guy knelt in front of her and started eating her extremely wet pussy. A white guy knelt behind her. Spreading her butt cheeks apart, the guy grunted, "Ah, look at that fucking white yummy asshole. I'm going to tongue fuck and rim that for hours." He buried his mouth in her spread butt and started munching on her magnificently yummy ass. The guy in front inserted his big tongue right inside Janet's wetness. Her juices started flowing inside the guy's mouth. With two tongues fucking and licking her holes, two mouths sucking her hot boobs, and so many hands working all over her body, Janet got overwhelmed by the extraordinary sexual pleasure. The erotic sensation sent shivers through her spine. Moans and groans of Janet and the four guys enjoying sensational group sex echoed through the room, turning the guys and Janet on even more. "Don't stop, please. Ohhhhhhhhh yes, yes, lick and tongue fuck my holes fast. Suck my boobs hard. You're all great lovers. I'm coming, ohhhhhh, my God, ohhhhhh, Jesus, I'm coming," Janet moaned wildly. The guys increased their speed. Electric shocks of pleasure went through her whole body and Janet came, screaming wildly.

The guys didn't stop and continued doing what they were doing. Juices from her pussy filled the black guy's mouth. Swallowing all the juices, he continued the sexual process. Janet's body became tense and she came again. The guys were already hard again. The black guy in front and the white guy at the back got up. They massaged both of Janet's holes with their huge cock heads and then penetrated her holes. The sensation of two enormous cocks in her both holes turned on Janet again. "Come on, guys, pump my naughty pussy as hard as you can. Be as wild as you can, and don't pity my holes." Janet wanted it hard and wild. The guys obliged and picked one of her legs up. She stood on one leg between two strong and huge men. They started pumping her harder and harder. She could see herself being fucked by them in a huge mirrored wall in the room. With her big bouncing melons being squeezed and sucked by two guys and both holes being slammed and pounded violently by two dominating guys, Janet couldn't control her rushing cum anymore. The feeling sent her over the edge, making her convulse with another amazing and out-of-this-world orgasm. The guys didn't stop and kept pounding her holes faster and faster. Her legs trembled and her body shook from the incredible shock waves of pleasure. She continued experiencing multiple orgasms for a few minutes. The guys also came simultaneously inside both holes. Feeling hot cream flowing deep inside both her holes sent Janet over the moon. They held her tightly between their strong bodies until her body calmed down. Her moans must have been heard up to five hundred yards away. It was a small motel, but the manager didn't mind because there were no other people staying there that night. Actually, he enjoyed watching everything through a hole.

"Come on, babe, now it's our turn to fuck you. You like it wild and hard, then you're going to have what you asked for," the black guy who sucked her boobs before said. The guys were not done yet. The two other guys who sucked her boobs before carried Janet to the bed. The king-size bed was exactly opposite the mirrored wall. The white guy, a bisexual, started licking her wet pussy. He buried his mouth in her wet pussy, licking and swirling the black guy's cum from her pussy. The other black guy put his huge dick in Janet's mouth. She sucked his huge shaft while fucking his asshole with her finger. The other two guys who had just fucked her holes started working on her boobs. In no time Janet got ready for another showdown. She occasionally glanced in the mirror. The sight of four strong men enjoying her body turned her on even more. The white guy licking her pussy lifted her bum a bit up and inserted his tongue in her sweet asshole to lick the cum inside from the previous guy who fucked Janet in the ass. The black guy took out his cock from Janet's mouth and lay on the bed. He pulled Janet over him. Janet straddled him, sitting on his enormous hard black cock and facing him. The bisexual white guy moved behind her. Janet moved up and down on the enormous and thick shaft. The bisexual guy started licking her asshole and the black cock coming in and out from Janet's pussy. The other two guys stood in front of Janet with their hardened cocks. She enjoyed sucking the two wet cocks from her pussy and ass and riding on one enormous black cock. Occasionally the bisexual guy took out the black cock from her pussy and sucked on it. Watching him enjoying the cock, Janet became hornier. Then the bisexual guy spread Janet's butt cheeks apart and inserted his huge pecker in her tight ass.

The sensation of two cocks in her both holes turned Janet wild. She started fucking both cocks faster. The extremely fired-up guys also started slamming and pumping her holes faster. Then the bisexual guy pulled the black guy standing in front of Janet behind him. The black guy understood what he desired and wasted no time. He immediately inserted his hard cock into the bisexual guy's ass. "Oh, that's a hell of a cock," the bisexual guy murmured. Janet looked in the mirror and became extremely turned on by watching the black man fucking the bisexual man. This had also turned on the bisexual guy more, and his cock swelled inside Janet's ass. Janet liked it so much while sucking the white cock in front of her. The moans and groans became louder and louder. Suddenly all the cocks swelled and exploded simultaneously, releasing the hot cream in Janet's holes and mouth and in the bisexual guy's hole. Janet again experienced multiple orgasms. The warmth of two cocks exploding in her holes and one in her mouth increased her pleasure tremendously. The white guy's asshole was also filled by hot cream from black cock. Janet felt dizzy and lay on top of the black man. They ordered more drinks and food. After reenergizing themselves, they continued the marathon group sex session through the night in various sexual positions. Tired from the fucking, they slept until 3:00 p.m. the next day. Janet's pussy and asshole became very sore. But she didn't mind because she had the most amazing and wonderful sexual experience ever.

After getting ready, the group drove around to spot any other friendly ghosts. They came back disappointed late at night. Their routine of sexual pleasure and finding ghosts continued for many days. They came across many types of ghosts, but all of the ghosts expressed their unwillingness and inability to confront bin Laden. An old man's ghost suggested to them that they would have to find ghosts of those humans who were loyal to America and were prepared to lay down their lives for it. Janet followed his advice and searched for those kinds of ghosts. Not many patriotic people became ghosts, because they did good deeds and died for others. Only in rare cases when they committed some sins were they sent to ghostly worlds to repent their sins. Finding rare ghosts became an uphill task, and bin Laden's ghost became stronger every day. Janet and the CIA agents gave up the search and came back to devise a plan to take on bin Laden with the help of the nun ghosts. Unable to think of any solid plan, they went back to the nun ghosts. They were already expecting them.

"What took you so long? Did you have any luck finding stronger ghosts?" Margaret asked.

"No, not really," Janet said. "We found many, but they all seemed to be scared of bin Laden's ghost. Have you thought of the best way to deal with him? We thought it out, but so far nothing concrete is coming to our minds. We don't want to do anything stupid and lose you all."

"We also thought about it. There is one way. If we can seduce him to be visible and then stab him in his ghostly heart with a cross, we can exterminate him. One more thing—when he is stabbed, a pious priest who hasn't committed any sin has to say the prayers for two minutes. If we can successfully do that, he will never be able to come back as a ghost to this world or any other world," Margaret explained.

"The arrangement for the girls to seduce him, and the priest for prayers, can be done very soon. If you can hold him down for few minutes after he has been stabbed, it will work. But it will be a suicidal mission. If anything goes wrong, everybody involved could end up dead," Janet said.

"We're prepared to take the risks. We'll have to endure the pain and sufferings he will inflict on us, but we will still achieve salvation even if we're not successful. We're prepared to do that for humanity and to end our ghostly life," Margaret answered.

"OK, we will arrange everything. Humanity will not forget your sacrifices. We'll get back to you as soon as possible. Thank you very much for being so generous and helpful, even though the humans treated you so badly. See you soon. Bye," Janet said.

The preparations began for the mission. The government contacted all the church organizations for assistance, and they wasted no time in finding a priest who was ready to sacrifice his life. Five extremely hot and brave female CIA agents volunteered to seduce him. It was decided to keep Janet at a safe distance from bin Laden during the mission because only she could see him. If anything went wrong, they would still need her later on. The government and the CIA didn't want Janet to be seen or recognized by bin Laden. The nun ghosts and Janet started looking for bin Laden's whereabouts. It wasn't hard to find him, because he always hung around places full of young women. They located him in Washington city center, and the CIA girls came there dressed extremely erotically to seduce bin Laden. He remained invisible and stood leaning against a wall, checking out girls walking past him. The CIA girls were wired, and Janet kept informing them what he was doing. The girls walked past him one by one. The intoxicating beauty of a tall and solidly built girl grabbed his attention, and he started following her. The girl kept walking in front of him and hailed a taxi. She sat in the front seat, and bin Laden followed her inside. He sat in the backseat still invisible. The taxi arranged by the CIA came to a house arranged for the mission. The priest was already hiding under the bed. The girl immediately turned on the music. Hidden cameras were installed in every part of the house. Janet and the other CIA agents arrived outside the house in their well-equipped van. They could see and hear everything going on in the house. The nun ghosts also waited nearby where bin Laden couldn't sense them.

The girl poured herself a glass of wine and started sipping it slowly. She put the glass away and started dancing in a sexy style with the music. Bin Laden couldn't control himself anymore and became visible.

"Oh my God, please don't hurt me. Are you bin Laden's ghost?" the girl pretended.

"Yes, sexy, I bin Laden ghost. No worry. I do not harm you. I want only good time with you. If you give me good sex, I no harm you. You very beautiful girl," bin Laden answered.

"I'll do anything you say, but please don't harm me. I'm very scared." The girl felt a bit nervous but kept acting as planned.

"Good girl, now show me sexy dance. You dance very good. Take off your clothes slowly when dancing. No worry. I make you very happy. I fuck very good. You very hot and sexy," bin Laden said.

"Yes, I'll dance for you. Thank you for saying I'm hot and sexy. I'll make you very happy. I'll blow your mind away with extremely pleasurable hot sex," the girl said. She was well trained in seduction. Even gods could fall for her charming, seductive ways. Dancing erotically, she played with her big juicy boobs. Licking her tits and touching her crotch, she stared in bin Laden's eyes, enticing him to completely immerse in her ravishing beauty. She removed her clothes one by one. Bin Laden's eyes almost popped out, and his throbbing cock became crazy and hard like steel.

"Ohhhhh, my God, I never seen so sexy girl before. Come here and make me happy. Me cannot control anymore."

"OK, baby. Just lie on the bed and let me do all the hard work. I'll make you so fucking happy that you will always want me only," she answered and laid him on the bed. Rubbing her extrahot pussy and boobs all over his body, she played with his balls and cock. With the touch of her hot body, bin Laden lost all his other senses as sexual urges took over. Being careful not to alert bin Laden, the nun ghosts moved closer to the house when signaled by Janet. Sucking his cock and balls, the girl put her pussy directly in his face. The intoxicating fragrance of her pussy juices totally paralyzed his other senses.

"I want to tie your hands to make wild love to you. Are you all right with that?" The girl proceeded as planned.

"Yes, yes. That is my fantasy. Here, please tie my hands and fuck me as hard as you can," bin Laden answered desperately. The girl quickly tied up his hands. Straddling him, she put his cock in her pussy. With his cock deep inside her burning wetness, bin Laden started moaning and moving his hips up and down to enjoy her tight pussy. She moved up and down his shaft, grabbing it tightly in her pussy. The sight of her big bouncing boobs and magnificently carved sexy body blew his mind. Nun ghosts came inside the room and stood where he couldn't see them. The priest hiding under the bed came out with the extrasharp cross held tightly in his hand. The girl looked at him and scratched her nose as planned. The ghosts at once moved at lightning speed and held bin Laden's hands and arms. As the priest moved the cross up in the air to stab his ghostly heart, bin Laden immediately realized what was happening. He saw the sharp cross coming directly toward his heart. His legs moved at once. With all his strength, he hit the back of the girl sitting on his cock with his knees. The girl fell between his heart and the sharp cross. The sharp cross pierced through her back and heart, almost reaching bin Laden's heart.

Everybody panicked, and bin Laden wasted no time to free himself. He had become very powerful. With one pull he broke the bed head and threw off the girl lying on top of him. The priest tried to pull the cross from the girl's body, but it was too late. The mighty ghost broke the priest's neck with one blow. The priest fell down, and bin Laden turned toward the nun ghosts. He didn't let them escape. He injured them to make sure he could suck out their much-needed energy. He raped them first to get the energy and then tortured them throughout the night to set an example. Hearing the strange, horrifyingly loud cries of the nun ghosts, people around the area fled from their homes. Janet and the other CIA agents also fled to be safe. They watched on screen in horror the dreadful and torturous deaths the nun ghosts experienced. As soon as the nuns died their ghostly deaths, lights of their free souls vanished into the sky. Finally they were free from the ghostly lives and achieved salvation. A rain of tears poured from Janet's and the CIA agents' eyes. Disheartened and remorseful, they returned the next day to pick up the dead bodies of the priest and the CIA girl. They had underestimated the power of a barbarian and savage ghost. The unsuccessful operation also made the ghost stronger and more dreadful and lethal. The government and Janet were left without any hope of getting rid of bin Laden. But they couldn't give up, and they continued their search for something powerful enough to eliminate the dreadfully evil ghost, descended on Earth to wreak havoc.

Chapter 3

Bin Laden got bored of the nightclub scene and wanted to find a place always crowded with beautiful and hot girls. He thought for some time and knew where to go. He found a college in Washington with about a thousand students. The college had a big dormitory where a lot of students preferred to stay. He became invisible to avoid scaring the students while entering the college. His eyes moved from one sexy girl to the next. His excitement was evident by his stiff dick, as if his sexual dreams and fantasies had come true. The ghost walked among the sexy girls and smelled the intoxicating fragrance coming from their asses and pussies.

His eyes stopped at a group of white and black girls who were practicing dance. Gifted with exceptional hourglass figures, beauty, and sexiness, the girls danced like goddesses from heaven. The girls were cheerleaders. Bin Laden was about 150 meters away from the group when they suddenly stopped dancing and stared in his direction. The girls sensed the presence of some disturbingly mysterious and supernatural force. Bin Laden also realized that the girls sensed his presence.

There was something intimidating and spooky about those girls. His feet felt heavy moving forward, and he did not go any farther. Already attacked by ghosts once, he decided to be cautious. Other students and the girls' trainer looked surprised and turned their heads to the direction where the girls kept staring as if they had seen something dangerous. They didn't see anything, but the girls continued staring and took positions as if they were ready to attack someone. Bin Laden avoided the confrontation and retreated. He also sensed non-human mysterious forces at the college. He didn't want to enter the untested waters and left the college.

He looked back and noticed the girls still staring at him. He decided to learn more about the girls. He had never seen such beautiful girls before, but there was something more about them than just the beauty. They seemed to possess special powers. Even the other students didn't know much about them. The girls had not shown any sexual interest in any of the college boys and always kept to themselves. They did not entertain any sexual behavior of the boys. The college students thought they were all lesbians. But the girls exhibited a lot of spooky behavior. They avoided mirrors because there was no reflection of them, avoided going into the sun even though sometimes the situation demanded it, and also had retractable fangs. Some students had seen those things accidentally, but the girls denied it and made those students look like liars in front of others. They also scared them not to tell others.

It was 6:00 p.m. and those students living off the campus had gone home. Those staying in the dormitory went to their rooms. Bin Laden waited outside the college until evening. Becoming visible, he cautiously walked toward the dormitory.

He had to walk through the sports field. He got about halfway when the group of girls he had seen during the day came out of the dormitory building and stood in attacking position as if they were guarding the dormitory. Suddenly their eyes turned burning red, and they growled, showing their fangs to warn bin Laden that they meant business. Daring and not frightened from a ghost, the girls walked toward bin Laden with their beautiful, seductive faces turned into creepy, scary faces.

"Go back if you want to live. This is our college, and we will guard it at any cost," one of the white girls called Ruby warned bin Laden.

"Me not scared. Nobody can kill me because I already dead. I very powerful ghost now. I love you all sexy girls. I just want sex with you all, not trouble. If you agree, you happy. If you no agree, I rape you. I know now you all vampires, but me not scared." Bin Laden had figured out that they were all vampires and if he could fuck all of them, his power would increase millions of times. Not wanting to miss the opportunity, he purposely became visible to lure them out of the dormitory. He knew it would be an uphill and dangerous task to take on all of the vampires.

A black girl called Julia came forward and threatened bin Laden. "If you dare to take one more step forward, we will show you what we can do to a ghost."

Bin Laden was in a horny and naughty mood and offered them a compromise. "Look, sexy vampires, me just want sex. You all take off your clothes, we have group sex, you all happy, and me very, very happy. You become my mistresses and live happy ever after. I'll give you all the pleasures, money, anything else you need."

"You can't even touch us. How are you going to have sex? We don't need any pleasure from an old fart. Look at your soft and disgusting dick. You can stick your money where the sun doesn't shine," another black vampire called Mary said.

"OK, bitches, I coming now. Fuck you, vampires. Last warning, bitches, you all make one line and bend over." Bin Laden moved forward, and before he could say anything else, the vampires also marched forward to attack him.

"Are you coming already? Your limp dick didn't even get hard, asshole. How can you fuck us? We like someone who would fuck us the whole night and his dick won't go soft," a white vampire named Rachelle said.

They all laughed and made fun of him.

"Bitches, I mean it. I coming to attack. Wait, I put my cock in your mouths to make you shut up. You try to laugh when my cock in your ass. Take off clothes and fight."

The vampires surrounded him from all sides, their fists clenched to attack bin Laden. He knew there were twelve of them but only ten came to fight him. Surrounded by creepy vampires, he moved around to defend himself. He didn't want to be attacked from behind.

"Where are other two bitches? You only ten."

"Don't worry. They are preparing a big surprise for you. Don't waste time, and fight like a brave warrior," said Ruby. The vampires pounced on him and attacked from all sides. Unexpected thunderous sounds and lightning disturbed the peaceful atmosphere of the college. The students rushed outside, wondering what was going on. Supernaturally powerful forces with extraordinary powers started fighting. The college students watched them with disbelief and astonishment. Some of the students immediately informed the police. Bin Laden was overconfident of his powers and thought he could beat the vampires as easily as he defeated the army in front of the White House. He was wrong. Strong and killing blows came from all sides. He fell backward and realized that his opponents possessed great fighting skills and powers. He got up at lightning speed and started kicking and punching them as hard as he could. The vampires flew in the air and around him, hitting him from all directions. With a bit of luck and quick thinking, bin Laden grabbed Ruby, the sexy and hot vampire, from behind. He put his arm around her neck and warned the others, "Stop, or I break your friend's neck."

"OK, don't kill her," one of the vampires said. Seeing their friend in danger, the vampires stopped, still surrounding bin Laden.

"If you kill her, we will make sure you are exterminated," Mary, another vampire, warned.

"Don't move. She is very hot. My cock is going crazy touching her ass. Don't move, bitch. Oh, darling, very big and juicy melons." The vampire's ass was right on bin Laden's crotch. He grinded his cock in her meaty and firm ass while playing with her big boobs. Bin Laden felt the heat, and his cock was going crazy to enter her burning holes.

Bin Laden's hand slipped in her blouse, removed her bra, and squeezed her firm and sexy boobs. The vampire wore only a short skirt and G-string inside. Bin Laden tore off her skirt and G-string. Placing his hard cock right on her tight butt hole, he became horny and lost his concentration for the fight.

"Oh, baby, so hot ass. I fuck your ass now." As soon as he tried to push it inside her hole, another vampire behind him jumped and kicked his ass. His hard cock penetrated all the way in the vampire's butt hole from the force of the kick. They fell forward with bin Laden on top of the sexy vampire Ruby and his cock still inside her very tight hole. The vampire screamed from the pain.

"Ahhhhh, my ass. You bitch, why did you kick him from behind? His cock is all the way up my ass. It's hurting too much," Ruby screamed and shouted at Nicky, the vampire who kicked bin Laden.

"Oh, baby, it is so tight." Bin Laden's body was overtaken by lust and the feeling of his cock in a very tight and hot ass. He had humped her only a few times when the vampires overpowered him and carried him away from Ruby. Twisting his arms and holding his neck tightly, they rendered him defenseless.

"Why did you kick him from behind, bitch?" Ruby kicked Nicky.

"I saved your life, bitch. Why couldn't you tighten your hole? Maybe you liked being fucked by him in the ass and now you're just pretending to be angry." Nicky turned to kick her and Julia stopped her.

"Stop, both of you. She saved your life, and we have caught him alive. He is very powerful. Control yourself before he kills us all." Julia tried to make them aware of the situation.

"Let me go, bitches. I fuck you all." Bin Laden struggled to free himself. But together the vampires had enough power to control him.

"You wanted to fuck us. Look there and see how we are going to tear your ass into pieces." Bin Laden looked where the vampires pointed and saw the remaining two vampires coming toward him with big strap-on dildos attached, ready to fuck him. He went hysterical and pushed them around to escape but without success. One vampire named Lisa came behind him. She opened his ass cheeks while the others held him down doggy style. She inserted the fourteen-inch dildo all the way deep inside his hole. Bin Laden screamed with unbearable pain.

"You piece of shit, you like to rape women. Now enjoy being raped. Is it big enough for you? Ha, ha, ha, ha, ha," said Lisa. She was enjoying the sexual torture of bin Laden. She humped him for a few minutes.

"You fucking bitches. Women no fuck men in backside. Only men fuck women in backside. You American weird fucking women, you have no shame. I will kill you all."

"We love fucking men doggy style. They like it too much. You're just pretending not to like the fuck. Inside you must be wanting for more, motherfucker."

Bin Laden gathered all his strength and pushed the vampires when their grips loosened on him while they were laughing. It worked and he kicked and punched the ones in front of him. Lisa clung to his back. He also held on to her with his hands and ran as fast as he could to escape. The vampires followed him, but he was too fast for them. While running he opened up the strap-on belt from Lisa's waist and let her drop on the ground. Running continuously with his ass bleeding and the dildo still in his ass, he didn't want to stop and let the vampires catch him again. Laughing their ass off and unable to control themselves, the vampires couldn't keep up with him. Looking back carefully, he stopped when he realized that the vampires had stopped chasing him. He took out the dildo slowly, and his ass bled profusely. Staggering inside a forest to reach a safe place, he rested there for two days to ease his debilitating pain.

With blood boiling in anger, he vowed to rape and exterminate the vampires. Vampires posed real danger to him, and he also needed to have sex with them to get their tremendous amount of energy. He would get the same energy from twelve of them as he would from having sex with millions of ordinary women. This was the first time the dreadful ghost felt scared and had to run like hell to save his life. He would have to be extra careful when going inside the college to take on the vampires. He roamed the city for a few days and had sex every day to get back his strength. The news spread like wildfire that some college girls with extraordinary powers were able to make bin Laden's ghost run for his life. The American government and the military also got some hope to defend America. Within hours, the army moved near the college. They interviewed the girls and offered them whatever help they needed to finish off the ghost. The government and the vampires thought the ghost got scared and wouldn't dare to show up again. They waited for one week, and business became as usual because there was no indication that the ghost hung around the college. The vampires even made fun of his torn ass and thought he must be waiting to get better.

The most powerful vampires were Ruby, Nicky, Julia, Lisa, and Mary because of their age. The other vampires were about 60 percent as powerful as them. The vampires had never revealed their true identity to anybody in the college.

But other students had watched the fight between them and the ghost. The students felt safe in the vampires' presence because they had defeated and abused a very powerful ghost. Even America's powerful army couldn't put a scratch on the ghost. The vampires fed on animal blood and posed no threat to humans. They always visited the nearby forest to feed on the fresh and healthy animals. Being very friendly vampires, they had never caused any problems for the students or public. They were extraordinarily sexy, beautiful, and attractive. Their exceptional talent in dance always made them number one in cheerleading competitions. There was no match for their talent. The college boys tried their luck to have them, but the vampires always politely rejected their advances. After the fight, the boys were careful not to be rude or aggressive toward them, fearing they would get the same treatment as bin Laden.

The vampires revealed in a media interview that they were instructed to be there by their supreme vampire. The supreme vampire had informed them a great danger would descend on America in the form of a powerful spirit. The spirit would become more and more powerful from having sex with young American women. They urged American women to stop offering sex to the spirit in their greed. It would make him the most powerful and lethal force on Earth, and whole armies would be destroyed like toys. He got 50 percent more energy from the women who willingly offered sex. His mission was to fuck as many American women as he could every day to suck their energy out through their pussies. The interviewer was a gay man, and one particular question was bothering him.

"Does the spirit get any energy by fucking the American men in their ass?"

"Yes, he does. He gets fifteen percent of the energy he would get from a willing woman by fucking straight men," Ruby replied. Hearing the answer, a lot of people watching the interview live burst into laughter.

"What about sex with gay men? How much energy does he get?" the interviewer asked.

"If the spirit fucks a gay man in the ass, it is the opposite. The spirit loses fifteen percent of the energy he gets from fucking a young woman. That is why it wants to stay away from gay men," Ruby explained.

"In other words, gay American men can save America if they let the spirit have sex with them," the interviewer stated seriously.

"Yes, that is correct. But how would they attract the spirit to have sex with them?" Julia replied.

"That's the thing they have to figure out to save America," Nicky explained.

"Is there anything else we should know?" the interviewer asked.

"Yes, there is. If somebody fucks the spirit in his backside, it loses energy very fast," Lisa answered. "One fuck in his ass and he loses the energy he gets from one thousand women who willingly have sex with him. That is why we tried to fuck him in the ass. But our cock was a dildo that wouldn't have any effect on his body. He needs to be fucked by a real dick," Lisa answered. The time was up for the interview.

"So here is all the information you need to save America. Please listen to it carefully again on our website and help any way you can to save America and this Earth. Bye for now. We will be back next week to talk about it again." The interviewer concluded the interview.

As a few weeks went past, nothing happened around the college or elsewhere in the city. Bin Laden visited some of the previous girls who offered sex willingly. They did not report anything to the authorities. He chose to stay invisible. He had not forgotten about the vampires and the college. The American government, vampires, public, and even the people and governments of other countries were desperate to know where the ghost had disappeared.

Lisa and another vampire named Paula went to the forest to feed on animal blood. The other vampires had already fed for the day in the morning. Lisa and Paula ventured deep inside the forest and spotted a deer. They went for the kill, and the deer ran as fast as it could. The animals could sense the vampires' or ghosts' presence. As they nearly caught up with the deer, other animals in the vicinity went haywire and made a lot of noise as if they had seen something very dangerous. Even the deer stopped and couldn't move because of the fear of seeing something very dangerous. Wondering why the deer stopped in front of them and didn't run to save its life, the vampires also slowed down. As Lisa's hand touched the deer's body, bin Laden appeared from behind a tree. Then they understood why the animals behaved that way.

"Hello, bitches. Miss me? Long time never see. Are you looking to hunt some real cock today?" The ghost smiled at them.

"You better fuck off. Our other friends are also nearby, and if we call them they would be here in a few seconds," warned Lisa without showing any sign of distress. But inside Lisa and

Paula were very scared and knew that it would be suicide to fight such a powerful ghost by themselves. They didn't want bin Laden to think that the fear of him was making them almost crap their pants.

"I show you today, vampires fucked by a mighty ghost. Nobody come to save you. I know your friends in college now." Bin Laden knew that he could easily take on both of them. He had watched them in the college every day from afar so they wouldn't feel his presence. When Lisa and Paula came out, he followed them. He planned to attack the vampires while they were in small numbers and vulnerable.

"Have you forgotten how you ran for your life with a torn and bleeding ass? We will do worse than that, and this time you won't be able to escape," Paula said in an attempt to scare him. They had no option left except fighting the ghost to save their lives. Understanding clearly that they wouldn't be able to outrun the ghost, the vampires took positions while praying for a miracle.

"I remember all. Now I take revenge from all you fucking vampires. This time you cannot run," bin Laden said with full confidence. Fully prepared, he didn't want to waste any time and leaped toward Lisa. Clenching his right hand, he swung at Lisa. Lisa dodged it while moving backward. Paula attacked him from behind. She jumped on his back and tried to twist his neck. Bin Laden held her arms. Lisa picked up a sharp and thick branch. Aiming for his heart, she jumped at him. Moving aside, he kicked her in the stomach. She was tossed in the air and fell on the ground. Bin Laden quickly pulled Paula by her arms, throwing her in front of him. Seeing Lisa getting up, he picked up Paula by the hair. Turning like a twister, he flung her in the trees. Falling through the tree branches, she dropped on the ground. She became motionless. Lisa again picked up the branch. With full strength, she tried to stab his heart. But it was too late. He grabbed the wood and pulled it with full force. Lisa was no match for him. She couldn't resist. He took the wood in his hands and bashed Lisa mercilessly with it. She begged for him to stop. Bin Laden hit her knees hard, disabling her from getting up again. Paula got up and staggered toward bin Laden, holding another sharp branch. She swung the wood at him with full force. Bin Laden dodged it. With Lisa already disabled, bin Laden grabbed Paula's arms. Twisting them, he rendered her defenseless. Exhausted and injured, Paula gave up resisting. He tore her clothes off. Lisa couldn't get up to help. Making her naked, he held her from behind with her ass right on his crotch. He started licking her and playing with her big boobs.

"You very sexy vampire. I going to fuck you to death," bin Laden said. His hardened cock went crazy from the heat of Paula's sexy ass.

"You'll pay for this, asshole. Our friends will hunt you down, motherfucker," Lisa warned him. But it was too late.

"Me not scared of bitches. I going to rape all of them and torture them to death," bin Laden answered.

He turned toward Lisa and bashed her again. Tying their hands, he raped both of them first to get the much-needed energy. He broke off some thick branches from a tree and inserted them in their pussies and asses. They were unable to bear the debilitating pain, and in a few minutes their horrifying and disheartening screams fell silent. Bin Laden hanged the unconscious vampires on trees with branches still in their holes. He roared horrifyingly, and the whole forest shivered in fear. He became invisible again and disappeared in the woods.

The vampires in the college had an inkling that something terrible had happened. They felt Lisa and Paula were in danger and immediately dashed to the forest to look for them. It didn't take long before they found them hanged on the branches, their bodies brutalized and mutilated beyond recognition. Paula had already died, but Lisa was still clinging to her last few breaths. After telling them what had happened, she also succumbed to her injuries. Seeing their friends dead with unimaginable and heart-wrenching torture, the vampires couldn't stop crying. Enraged and their blood boiling for revenge, they buried their most loved friends and vowed to avenge the killings. They decided to always stick together to be able to fight the ruthless and heartless ghost. They knew their power had lessened with the two killings and the ghost's powers had increased many fold. With only ten of them left now, they couldn't afford to lose any more. They waited many days for bin Laden in the college, but he didn't come inside. Bin Laden would purposely roar outside the college every day to lure them to the forest so he could attack them. The vampires sensed his trick and didn't fall for it. The government provided them with live animals in the college every day to feed.

The ghost became impatient and hungry for their energy. Bin Laden thought that once he finished them off, he would be the ultimate weapon of mass destruction. The vampires were also losing their patience and thought about going outside to avenge their friends' killings. But the government requested them not to take any wrong steps in haste. Finally their wait was over. It was about 6.30 p.m., and most of the students had gone to the dormitory or to their homes. Bin Laden remained invisible and entered the college. The vampires sensed his presence and came outside. There were nine of them, and they couldn't see where the ghost was. Their senses told them that he was somewhere nearby within the college premises.

"Where is Julia?" Ruby looked worried.

"She went to the college library to look for some books on ghosts' powers. I tried to stop her from going alone, but she insisted because she was just in the college premises and bin Laden wouldn't dare to come inside the building," Nicky explained.

"Well, she is wrong. He is here, and I think he knows where she is," Ruby said. They heard a scream coming from the library and dashed toward it. As they entered the door, they saw the ghost carrying Julia and jumping through the window. Julia's hands and legs were tied. Bin Laden made himself visible.

"There she is. He is taking Julia. Get the motherfucker. Don't let him take her away. He will kill her. Everybody be brave and attack," Mary shouted while dashing to save Julia. They jumped through the window to follow the ghost. Bin Laden stormed through the city streets and shopping centers, with the vampires chasing him vigorously and with full force. People ran for cover to get out of their way. Suddenly bin Laden emerged outside the city and headed for the forest. The vampires fell for his trap and followed him in the woods. He was five minutes ahead of them. He had already exhausted them enough. He hid Julia in a cave, her legs and hands still tied. He had planned everything to lure the vampires in the forest.

The vampires entered the forest carefully. Birds and animals went haywire. The ghost roared to entice them to look for him deep in the forest. Advancing carefully together, the vampires reached a place surrounded by big trees. The vampires tried to put on a brave face, but their hearts were beating fast because of their fear of the dreadful ghost. Their friends' bloodied and mutilated bodies flashed in front of their eyes. Fear-stricken and demoralized, the vampires moved forward slowly. Their senses were warning them that the terrifying and merciless ghost was nearby. Suddenly the tree branches moved and made noise from tree to tree as if something was jumping on them. Suddenly the commotion stopped. Everything went dead silent. Only the sound of the vampires' hearts could be heard, beating faster and faster.

"Boom, ha, ha, ha, ha, ha, ha, ha." Bin Laden made a horrific sound and started laughing and teasing the fear-stricken vampires. He started running with lightning speed in circles through the dry leaves around them.

"Don't get separated and stick together. Make a circle so we can fight him properly. He is playing a psychological game with us to scare the shit out of us," Ruby advised them, and they followed. They stood in a circle to cover every direction so they could not get attacked from behind. They could sense him coming near from the moving dry leaves but couldn't see him.

"Show yourself, asshole. Fight like a real warrior, not like a pussy." Nicky taunted him to get him become visible.

"Take off your clothes, everybody, to distract his mind. He might become visible," Mary suggested. The vampires liked the idea and immediately stripped and danced erotically.

Their beauty and sexy dance was so intoxicating that even gods would have fallen for it.

"Here, bitches. I no run today, and if you brave not run to escape. I not fall for your sexy tricks." Bin Laden felt confident and vowed to control his lust. But his mind was getting distracted. He stood there intoxicated by the sight of the gorgeous naked goddesses performing the most erotic dance he had ever seen. Their dancing, big juicy boobs, and extrahot asses overwhelmed him, and he just admired them with lust flowing from every part of his ghostly body. The vampires didn't stop dancing and planned to entice him closer. The ghost felt completely submerged in the sexiness and hotness of the vampires' bodies. He didn't feel like killing them if the vampires could agree to his terms. He just wanted to make love to their sexy and hot bodies every day.

"You all become mine, and we live happy ever after. No need to fight and waste your precious lives. Come on, please try to understand my love for you all."

Mary tried her own negotiations. "If you release our friend, we can reach a compromise. We won't interfere in your life, and you have to leave America."

"Oh no, sexy bitches, I no leave America, I no release your friend. I fuck you all today and then everybody in America. Lust make my brain stupid sometimes, but I not fool. I like your dance. I understand you try to make me horny. Now it is sexy and hot fight. Me naked, you all naked. I no need to take off your clothes to fuck you all," answered bin Laden, and he hit himself many times on the head to come to his senses.

"Asshole, did you forgot the big dick in your ass?" Ruby became frustrated and angry after she realized the ghost didn't fall for their trick.

"You all get this dick in your holes today," bin Laden said and played with his dick to irritate them.

The vampires went crazy and attacked him, breaking their circle. Bin Laden started touching their naked bodies one by one while fighting and making fun of them. He squeezed, sucked briefly, and kissed their butts to irritate them more. Fighting with a happy mood, he molested and teased their sexy bodies. He even humped and touched the pussies of less powerful vampires. Irritated and enraged, the vampires couldn't hit him even once because he moved almost at the speed of light. As they tried to hit him, he was already at a different place. He moved from tree to tree, jumping over them, hitting them. He was just playing with them. With extraordinary luck, Ruby got hold off his cock. She tried to pluck it off. He punched her hard on her face. She flung backward about a hundred meters, hit a tree, and slumped to the ground. She felt how powerful he had become. She knew that fighting separately would make them lose the battle very fast.

"Attack him together," Ruby shouted and got up. Together they put up a good fight, and the ghost had to go on the defensive. They were all over bin Laden. He stopped playing and began fighting seriously. The thought of the dildo in his ass made him fight more seriously. He knew if he was caught this time, they would torture him to his ghostly death. He went for the less powerful ones first to reduce their power and numbers. He severely injured three of them, and they fell on the ground, unable to fight or escape. He also suffered some injuries, but they were not serious enough to take any toll on his abilities.

"Please save your precious lives and escape. Don't worry about us. It's for the American people and America's sake," one of the injured vampires pleaded. Realizing that they were losing the fight and he would kill all of them, the other vampires panicked and started retreating. Ruby was reluctant, but the other injured vampires also advised the same. Watching them retreating while fighting to get out of the forest, Ruby had no other option left. They had to leave the badly injured ones behind to save their own lives. Bin Laden decided not to pursue them because he himself was injured a bit. His strategy was to have sex with Julia and the other injured ones to get their precious energy first. After getting more vampire energy, he would easily be able to deal with the remaining six.

He raped and tortured all of them dreadfully without showing any remorse. Avoiding killing them, he inserted wood pieces in their private parts. He took them while they were still alive and hanged them outside the college on trees. Unable to fight the debilitating and painful injuries, they died a slow and terrible death. The news of the terrifying ghost had reached every part of the world. Fear of the dreadful ghost gripped every human heart on Earth. The surviving vampires took the bodies of the dead vampires from the trees and gave them a proper burial. The vampires knew that bin Laden would soon be coming to the college to kill them because of his increased power after raping the dead vampires.

It didn't take long. Loaded with fresh pussy power from the vampires, the ghost arrived with a bang in the evening. Encouraged and motivated by his achievements, the ghost became visible and knew there would be no match for his power left in America after he killed all the vampires. The vampires understood what would happen and decided to leave the college and go into hiding to plan their next course of action. They didn't want the ghost to become the top force on Earth after killing them. As the terrifying ghost roared, the vampires retreated quietly through the back of the college.

Bin Laden took over the college and stayed there to taunt America. On the first day, he called all the students in the auditorium to hear a speech. Shaking and trembling, the students felt terrified and promptly followed his orders. After the students settled themselves in the chairs, bin Laden stood up to give his speech, which he had already written on a piece of paper.

"Hello, everybody, me ghost of bin Laden. I mean no harm to any of you. You listen properly and obey my all orders. You will be very, very happy in the college. You make me happy, I make you all happy. You entertainment me, and I entertainment you and the whole world. You scratch my backside, and I scratch your backside. You lick my ass, I not lick your ass. You suck my dick, I not suck any dick. I choose new dance group for girls. We have new kind of sports in college. I choose the players and new games. Me very sure you all like new dances, new sports. If any student stay home without my permission, I rape and kill like vampires. If you sick, you must ask my permission. We have party every night in the college. I need sex every day, so I choose two girls every day and fuck. If you say no, you know what I do. When in Tora Bora Mountains and caves, I like playing with my balls every day. Now here also, every day I want one student tickle and play with my balls. Me feel good, I make you all very happy. Me go angry, you all in very trouble. I like America very much. So nice and sexy pussy. See my dick go hard when I think American pussy. You can go now. Tomorrow we start everything."

Listening to his crap and funny English, the students almost burst into laughter. Fear of triggering his anger stopped them. As soon as he allowed them to leave, the students rushed to attend their classes. Checking out every class, he chose two extremely hot girls to fuck for that day.

The authorities had also enrolled Janet as a student in the college. Janet, with a ravishingly hot body, creamy skin complexion, and some extrahot flesh on her booty, could charm any guy to submit to her will. The college authorities were instructed by the government to change the records to show that she was a student there for the past year. Five drop-dead-gorgeous female CIA agents were also registered in the college as students to spy on the ghost. They were trained to be seductive and erotic dancers to control the ghost for as long as they could. The army knew that bin Laden could not be harmed by the humans or their weapons. They needed a ghost as powerful or more powerful than bin Laden to take him on. Their hope of bringing him down with the help of the vampires had vanished. The vampires had disappeared from the city and could not be contacted. Fearing bin Laden, the vampires had decided to leave the city for a safer place.

Janet had tried to convince many ghosts to take on bin Laden, but they expressed their weaknesses and fear. She also tried to find American patriotic ghosts, but her efforts didn't bear any fruit. The authorities and Janet just decided to watch bin Laden from close while continuing their search for the powerful ghost who could take on bin Laden. Janet had herself suggested that the government enroll her in the college because she knew the vampires had planned to run when bin

Laden took it over. The vampires knew that he wouldn't give up his dream of controlling the college. The government agreed with her advice and facilitated her entry as student. Janet and the other female agents planned to use lust, sex, and their charming and seductive acts to entertain bin Laden and keep him from harming the public. This way the government could buy some time to deal with the biggest and most unthinkable threat ever faced by America. The students were also advised to cooperate with the ghost to minimize any harm to them. They had no other choice left and could not afford to anger the ghost.

The next day the ghost selected twelve very hot and busty girls for the dance group to replace the vampires. Janet and the five CIA agents were among them because of their skills and intoxicating beauty. He also selected the fattest girls in the college for funny dancing and wrestling. He decided to conduct real talent shows to keep him entertained and to record everything. He ordered the college authorities to put video cameras everywhere in the college to capture live footage of everything. He planned to put the show online so everybody in the world could watch it. He threatened the authorities to comply with his every demand if they wanted the public to be safe. He made Janet a media adviser and asked her to contact every university and college in America to send their own sexy dancers, wrestlers, and other talent groups to his college. He asked her to send warning letters to the institutions stating that in case of noncompliance with the order, bin Laden would personally pay a visit to punish them. Nobody dared to disobey his orders.

The news of the megalive show became viral. Greedy and unsympathetic American and overseas TV channels sent representatives to negotiate a deal with bin Laden to broadcast his show. They gladly agreed with his terms and conditions. The ghost announced big monetary rewards for the winners. The show was to begin in one month. The preparations to organize everything began. Bin Laden also asked Janet and the CIA girls to teach him proper English. He spent three hours every day learning English. He watched TV and talked to the students to improve. He was a good learner and used his ghostly powers to improve very fast.

Bin Laden announced that all the beautiful girls in the college belonged to him and forbade the male students to have any sexual relationships with them. Anybody caught disobeying his orders would be punished by having their penises cut off. The disobeying girls' boobs and genitals would be burned. This order was hard for the students to obey. A lot of students were involved intimately with each other—some just for the lust, but some really loved each other from the heart. Some of the brokenhearted boys didn't want to take any risks and found sex partners outside the college. The girls were not allowed to leave the college at night. Those girls who lived outside the college were ordered to stay on the campus at night. Every time any girl came back to the college from outside, bin Laden sniffed her pussy to check if she had been fucked. The ghost had a special sniffing ability. The girls also didn't take any risks and out of sexual desperation started having girl-on-girl action, which bin Laden didn't mind. He actually enjoyed watching that, and the cameras were programmed to record everything. The girls were ordered to sleep naked in their beds every night. They were not allowed to turn off their lights. Whichever girl bin Laden liked during the day, he would enter her room at night to fulfill his fantasies.

One boy, Tom, and his girlfriend, Judy, were really in love and wanted to marry each other once they finished their studies. They stayed in the dormitory. It was getting harder for them to obey the order to stay away from each other. The cameras were everywhere in the college, even in restrooms. They were taking the same course and saw each other only during the day in the class. The girls had started sitting separately from the boys in the class to avoid any trouble from bin Laden. There was a gang of boys in the college whose leader was Peter. They always bullied the other students in the college. Peter liked Judy very much but she always ignored him. Peter hated Tom because of Judy's love for him. He was always looking for a way to punish Judy and Tom for it.

The male and female students e-mailed each other but didn't dare to hold hands or become intimate. Tom and Judy also sent regular e-mails to each other in desperation. The more they stayed away, the harder it became. Tom wrote to Judy that he didn't care if he was dead for loving her, but he wouldn't want bin Laden to have Judy. He couldn't sleep at night thinking that bin Laden might fuck his girl. He even started having nightmares about bin Laden fucking her. He couldn't control himself and wrote to Judy that he would dress like a girl and visit her. Judy also got desperate to be in Tom's arms and for his cock. They used to fuck a few times every night before bin Laden's restrictions. She gave the green light to him without thinking about the consequences. Tom went outside the college during the day and had his whole body waxed, including the genital area. He bought sexy red panties, a skirt, a blouse, shoes, and a makeup kit. He also bought a blond wig. He even waxed his beard and mustache area. He wore the skirt, panties, and blouse underneath his usual clothes carefully so nobody could notice them. He hid the makeup kit, shoes, and wig in his bag and brought them into the college. He sat alone at back of the class. When the class was about to finish, he pretended dropping something under the table. He hid there for a few minutes and quickly changed. He put on the wig. Other students and the professor left, turning off the lights behind them. After a few minutes, he came out from the room dressed as a girl. He put two oranges in the bra to make artificial boobs. He went to the ladies' room and stayed there for fifteen minutes pretending to use the toilet. He put on the makeup and came out when he was sure most of the students would have gone. Walking like a sexy girl, he went to the dormitory and entered Judy's room. She was expecting him as planned.

"Hi, Judy." Tom spoke quietly in a girl's voice in order to avoid being caught. They also avoided kissing or embracing each other for a few minutes. Pretending to be talking like two normal girls, they sat on the bed.

"You're really looking like a very hot bitch in those clothes. I'm having lesbian fantasies now," Judy quietly joked.

"Really? Do you want to go between the sheets and eat me out? I would really like that. I'm dying to eat your pussy. Come on, get naked. Let me eat you first," Tom said. They continued pretending to talk like girls.

"All right, darling. I can't resist anymore," said Judy, and she lay on the bed and Tom pounced on her. He quickly removed her clothes but avoided removing his own. Judy was already very wet. As he started sucking her boobs, Judy caressed his back and butt with her warm hands. Unable to control himself anymore, Tom took out his cock from one side of his panties and pushed it inside Judy's burning wet pussy. He started screwing her slowly to avoid detection.

"Oh, baby, I like it when you put your finger in my ass. Please push it more inside," Tom said when he thought Judy slipped her hand in his panties and inserted one finger in his ass.

"What? I'm not fingering your ass. Look, my hands are here. Are you imagining things?"

Tom quickly removed his dick from her pussy and covered himself with his skirt. He looked around in astonishment.

"What's the matter?" Judy asked him. "Are you all right? Why did you stop? Come back here and fuck me. I was about to come."

"Somebody is in this room. Somebody put a finger in my ass. It might be bin Laden." Tom was still in shock and forgot to change his voice.

"Yes, you've guessed right. It is me." Bin Laden revealed himself.

"Oh my God. Sir, I'm very sorry. Please forgive me," Tom begged.

"Sorry for what? You disobeyed my orders, and now you and this bitch have to be punished for it. It is pretty straightforward. I became horny many times and made mistakes. I got punishment for it. The vampires almost ripped off my ass when I lost control," bin Laden said in a calm voice.

Judy got up from the bed and held bin Laden's feet to apologize. "Sir, please forgive us. We really love each other and couldn't control ourselves. We won't do it again."

"I had announced that all pussy belonged to me in this college. You fucking cunts thought you could outsmart me and do anything behind my back. You look very sexy dressed as a woman. Actually, I'm feeling horny now. You fucked my girl, and I'm going to fuck you in front of the whole world. I will make an example of you so nobody else will dare to disobey my orders again." Bin Laden looked at Tom with lust in his eyes.

"Please, sir, it's my fault. I asked him to come here. I will do anything for you if you let him go," Judy begged to save Tom. She was even prepared to die for him.

"No, Judy. Please, sir, let her go, and you can do anything to me. It's my fault. Please punish only me for it," Tom begged to save Judy.

"Both of you come out now. I want to test how much you love each other. Bitch, you don't put on your clothes," bin Laden shouted. Judy and Tom followed him outside into the sports field. He ordered all the students to come out from the dormitory to watch. Without any delay, the students came outside. Peter and his gang of boys started making fun of Tom. They didn't like him because Judy fell in love with him. They were all criminal minded and always wanted to have sex with Judy. Tom had fought with them a few times over Judy. They were the ones who noticed Tom going into Judy's room and recognized him. They had informed bin Laden about it and wanted Tom and Judy punished.

"Look, people, we have a very sexy gay boy here. He likes to be a girl. Now, is it my fault if I feel horny and want to fuck him? He broke rules and now his ass has to pay for it. Now, take off your clothes and leave your panties, bra, and wig on. I want you to moan like a girl when I fuck you. If you don't do as I say, I will ask these boys to rape your girlfriend. Is that understood?" bin Laden shouted.

"Yes, sir, but please promise me you will let her go," Tom requested. "I'll do as you say." He was prepared to die for Judy.

"I promise, but she has to lick my ass first while I'm humping you doggy style," bin Laden said.

"Sir, you can do whatever you want with me, but don't humiliate him like that," Judy again requested.

"Are both you trying to save each other, or are you desperate to be fucked by me?" bin Laden asked.

"Sir, don't listen to her. Come on, I'm waiting. Come ride me like a girl." Tom diverted his attention toward him. Bin Laden mounted Tom doggy style.

"Ah, slowly please, sir," Tom requested.

"Motherfucker is trying to enjoy a rape. Come on, girl, rim my ass," bin Laden said. The girl hesitantly started eating his ass while bin Laden started fucking Tom wildly. Tom started screaming from the pain. His ass bled but bin Laden didn't stop. Becoming scarier and violent, bin Laden spanked Tom's ass harder and harder.

"Don't stop rimming. Otherwise I will kill both of you. His ass is so tight. I will fuck him the whole night." Bin Laden humped him faster and faster using his ghostly powers. Tom's screams could be heard even outside the college. Judy became frightened and didn't stop licking his ass. Peter and his gang cheered bin Laden on. Fear of the violent ghost gripped other students' hearts. After two hours, Tom became unconscious and fell on the ground.

"Motherfucker couldn't keep it up. Come here, girl. Now you bend over. I'm going to fuck your ass," bin Laden said. Judy shivered in fear and without saying anything complied with his demand. Bin Laden penetrated her ass doggy style and humped her. Her ass also bled, and she couldn't stop screaming and crying. Nobody came forward to help. Bin Laden forced the students to stay there and watch. Nobody was allowed to go back to his or her room. The gang of boys still cheered bin Laden on. Other students felt like killing those boys and bin Laden, but they were helpless. Janet and the CIA girls also had to smile and cheer him on unwillingly. Bin Laden had been fucking Judy for one hour when Tom gained consciousness. He heard Judy's screams. He got enraged and attacked bin Laden.

"You motherfucker, you promised me that you would let her go." He jumped on bin Laden's back and tried to strangle him, forgetting that he wouldn't be able to do any harm to him.

"Promises are made to be broken. If I let you go free today, nobody will fear me anymore. Come on, you want to fight?" Bin Laden grabbed him by the neck with one hand while still fucking Judy. He flung Tom in the air, and Tom fell about fifty meters away.

"Oh, she's very nice fuck. Are you jealous that she is getting fucked by someone stronger? Come save the bloody cunt," bin Laden roared.

"Tom, baby, please go away. Let him do whatever he wants. Please, save yourself," Judy cried.

"Fuck you, asshole. Come and fight me. I'm not scared of you, you piece of shit." Unable to tolerate his beloved being tortured, Tom roared and again jumped on bin Laden. Bin Laden stopped fucking Judy and turned toward Tom. He didn't like Tom challenging him like that. He twisted Tom's arms behind his back and held them with one hand.

"Come on, boys, give me a lighter. And you can have that bitch now. I want you all to take turns and rape her the whole night." One of the boys handed over a lighter to bin Laden. They didn't wait any longer to pounce on Judy.

"Watch this." Bin Laden turned on the lighter and started burning Tom's penis. Tom screamed and tried to free himself. He was no match for the ghost.

"Leave him alone, you asshole. Fuck you, motherfucker. I will kill you," Judy roared without any fear. But bin Laden didn't stop. Laughing loudly and without any remorse, he burned Tom's balls and penis. Tom became unconscious, and bin Laden tied him to a pole.

"Fuck her, boys, as long as you want. Tie her to the other pole when you have finished. I want to teach this horny bitch a lesson so no other girl would dare to cheat," bin Laden said.

"Yes, boss. We will," answered Peter. The boys didn't stop the whole night, and nobody was allowed to go inside the dormitory. In the morning, bin Laden burned Judy's vagina and boobs with the lighter. She couldn't bear the torture and fainted. When she regained consciousness, bin Laden poked her and Tom's eyes with burning-hot iron rods. Both of them became motionless and died from the bleeding. The students went back to their rooms, and after that nobody even thought about crossing the line. But in their hearts everybody prayed for a miracle to get rid of bin Laden. The government, army, and the public also felt helpless and disheartened after watching the unimaginable torture of two innocent lovers. They paid the ultimate price for their true love.

The training for the talent show participants began in every college. A lot of greedy and heartless participants were more than desperate to do the show because of the promise of popularity and big rewards. Wanting to be rich stars, they were willing to do anything. Bin Laden ordered a big stage to be built on the sports field, where he could sit like a king. He also ordered the building of a special chair made of gold. Janet and the CIA agents treated bin Laden very nicely because they knew if he suspected anything, he would kill them. He chose two girls from the dance group of the college for the first few days and had wild sex sessions with them. The girls also seemed very happy and enjoyed being fucked by a very powerful ghost who could go the whole night. The mighty ghost didn't need to sleep and was not feeling tired anymore. When he had finished having sex with all the dance girls, he chose two girls from the college every day. Soon the news spread like wildfire among the women that the ghost gave them out-of-this-world sexual experiences, which attracted attention from a lot of sex-hungry women in America.

Bin Laden liked having sex with Janet and the CIA girls because they went to extra lengths to please him. He trusted and promoted them to be his main organizers for the show and other things. They even surprised him one night by getting together and blowing his mind with exceptional group sexual acts and erotic dances. He had forgotten everything else about America and was taken over by the sexual pleasures and lust for the sexy, busty, and experienced girls. Janet and the CIA agents were also enjoying their life to the fullest being with him. Bin Laden chose two new girls every day and then asked the CIA agents and Janet to join them in group sex sessions. The government and the CIA also noticed that Janet and the girls seemed to had forgotten their real duties and were overtaken by sexual pleasures and lust. They were questioned and given warnings. The girls assured the authorities that they had not changed and were prepared to sacrifice their lives for America. One day when Janet and bin Laden lay in bed cuddling each other, Janet tried to get some information out of him.

"Darling, why have you become a ghost?" Janet asked.

"When the fucking Americans killed me, I was put in a coffin and thrown in the sea. There were no prayers held, and my coffin was kicked around and disrespected. I had turned into a ghost. I could get out of the coffin only if somebody opened it. I waited until John (the guy in the boat) rescued me. Sex was my food to get strength. I used him for twenty days. I needed to get a lot of sex to be powerful. The sex from the vampires has made me the ultimate weapon of mass destruction on Earth. I want to avenge my killing from the American government, especially from the American presidents. They are all in hiding, and I am sure one day I will find them. Let them hide. I have all the time in the world to enjoy my life in America. I'm not going anywhere this time. I'm enjoying myself, and they're suffering."

"Why do you hate America so much?" Janet got curious.

"I was with America and liked their thinking that there should be democracy everywhere. I was a very rich guy, and America trained me to fight against the Russians in Afghanistan. I was promised that they would rebuild Afghanistan and help me free the other Arab countries from monarchy rulers. I believed them and fought from my heart and soul. Thousands of my comrades were killed in the war, but we were able to defeat the Russians. Once the war was finished, the Americans left without any promised help. I was promised American citizenship and recognition as a war hero against the Russians. I understood America's true colors after the war and felt betrayed. I was a hero when I fought against the Russians, and then I was declared to be a terrorist. I was furious and decided to attack American interests."

"But why did you kill a lot of innocent people in America? They had nothing to do with it."

"There are a lot of innocent children and adults killed by America in Afghanistan and other countries for their economic interests. The American government calls it collateral damage. I was angry and frustrated, and that's why I did it. I am not very proud of it, but I wanted to show the American government how it feels when you kill innocent people and then call it collateral damage. They kill children and adults attending weddings, which has nothing to do with terrorism. They kill innocent people to control oil, which has nothing to do with terrorism. I attacked them and they attacked Iraq for oil, which didn't even support us in any way."

"But you are still raping innocent women." Janet diverted his attention toward the current situation.

"Now I need energy to be powerful like America, and my energy comes from the pussy. The same way they go to Arab countries to fight for energy, I have decided to pay back the favor. I want to enjoy my life now and live forever in America. Now they can't even kick me out. I am going to be the world power and the mighty king whom nobody can defeat. I will control every country on this earth."

"Can I be your queen?" Janet kissed him and fondled his balls and pecker.

"Yes, baby, you and the other dance girls will definitely be my queens. I will make you the number one queen as long as you take care of me and my kingdom's affairs."

"Can we expect any harm to my mighty king or our kingdom from any unknown forces? I have to know so we could prepare before anybody harms us." Janet tried to be clever in wording the question. She wanted to find out if bin Laden knew whether anybody could take away his powers.

"Yes, we have some threats, which include patriotic female vampires, female ghosts, and even Tibetan monks. We also have to finish off all the gay men because they would drain my power if I fuck them thinking they are straight men. I can get power only once from each woman and man. The second time I fuck them it would be just normal sexual enjoyment but no energy for me. I plan to fuck all the women first and then all the straight men. I am scared to fuck these straight men because they could be gay and lie to me about their sexuality. I wouldn't know whether I am gaining energy or losing it until I become too weak. From women and female vampires, I know I am definitely gaining energy," bin Laden explained.

"What about male vampires and ghosts, Your Highness? Your Highness didn't mention them." Janet noticed that he left them out. She purposely called him Your Highness in order to make him feel that she already considered him a king.

"You are a very smart and intelligent queen. I didn't mention that they are the biggest threats to me. If a male ghost fucks me in the backside for long enough, like the whole day and night, it can take my whole energy and finish me off. It depends how powerful the ghost is. The male vampires can suck out the same energy from my ass as I get from fucking a female vampire." Bin Laden was flattered by Janet calling him a king. He kissed and fondled her in excitement.

"What about Tibetan monks? You mentioned them. How can they be dangerous to you?" Janet was succeeding in getting information out of him.

"Tibetan monks are the only ones who can find and awaken those patriotic ghosts who can fuck me."

"OK, lord of this earth. I better start with the gays first to minimize the threats to you and our kingdom." Janet got up to go, but bin Laden grabbed her by the boobs and laid her down on the bed.

"Not before I make love to my queen." Her flattering words and warm hands playing with his tools of the sexual trade turned bin Laden on. Bending her over doggy style, he pumped her pussy while spanking her meaty buns. They both came in a few minutes. Janet put on her clothes and went outside.

Janet told one of the CIA girls to inform the government and CIA what she had found out. She didn't want to go herself in case bin Laden followed her. She instructed the agent to tell the government to find the Tibetan monks as soon as possible. The government and CIA were satisfied with Janet and the girls' spying. They no longer believed that the women got lost in the sexual pleasures and lust.

In the evening, Janet asked the TV and radio channels to broadcast her warning to the gays.

"As of tomorrow, all the gays in America must register their sexuality with the government as gay, and whenever venturing out from their homes they must wear a T-shirt with the word *gay* written on it. They also must put a sign out-side their house stating that a gay person or persons live there. This order is from the lord of this earth, bin Laden. Anybody found disobeying the order will be severely dealt with. The surgeons will be asked to seal off their assholes and put a tube in their bladders, which would come out from their stomach for their daily business. Their dicks and balls will be burned."

There was panic in the gay men community after the order, but they wasted no time following it. Bin Laden was delighted that his would-be queen was taking steps to safeguard him. The show was to begin in five days. Bin Laden called Janet in the room, away from all the other girls.

"My dear queen, I have to go away for some business for a few days. I will be back a day before the show," bin Laden informed her.

"My lord, where are you going all of a sudden? Is everything all right?"

"Yes, everything is all right. There is just a small matter to be taken care of to safeguard our kingdom. I had ignored it for too long because I was too busy in sexual pleasures. Nothing to be worried about," he assured Janet.

"Can I come with you, my lord?" Janet's curiosity was growing.

"No, dear, you have to look after the things here while I am gone."

"But, please tell me where you are going so I can contact you for any problems."

"There are no phones where I am going," bin Laden explained.

"Please take care of yourself. What about your daily sexual needs? Do you want to take some girls with you?" Janet was not giving up.

"Don't worry, I will find something. OK, take care, my sexy queen." Bin Laden didn't reveal his secret. He kissed her and left immediately. He hadn't looked that worried before. Janet understood that he had gone to eliminate some kind of threat to his power. She did some hard thinking and realized that he must have gone to kill the monks who could awaken the powerful spirits. She immediately contacted the government and the CIA. The authorities were ignorant about the danger to the Tibetan monks' lives. The government contacted the American bases near Tibet to transfer the monks immediately to safer and secret places. There was not much time left, and the helicopters descended on the Himalayan hills to get the monks out. Famous monks were taken away first followed by others from whatever temple they could be found in. Janet grew worried as she waited for news from the government. She thought bin Laden must have reached the temples first and eradicated the threats to his ghostly life. She felt delighted when she received the news that the monks were safe and sound. American spies were placed in all the temples to check if bin Laden showed up there. Nobody reported any ghost sightings or ghostly incidents in or around Tibet. Nothing happened and they all wondered where he had gone. They thought he must be invisible and looking for the monks. It was the last day before the show would be broadcast, and everybody was desperate to know where bin Laden was. Janet worried for her life because she was the only one whom bin Laden had told everything. If he found out the monks were shifted to safer places, he would know who informed them.

Peter and his gang of boys who raped Judy and informed bin Laden about Tom had started terrorizing the other students in the school. Even the police didn't dare to come inside the college and arrest them. They had no fear of the law because bin Laden was protecting and encouraging them. Students didn't dare to utter a word against bin Laden, fearing the gang of boys would inform him. They ruled the college in his absence but didn't make the mistake of sexually exploiting the girls. They raped some of the other male students out of sexual frustration. To fulfill their sexual desires with girls, they went outside the college. They gang-raped a lot of girls outside the college who resisted their sexual moves. The public had seen them raping Judy online and feared them because they had bin Laden's support.

It was lunchtime and bin Laden was still away from the college. The students came out on the sports field to have their lunch. Students' heads turned toward the library when they heard a male student's screams. Peter and his gangsters were dragging a boy toward the sports field. They pulled him near the stage and tied up his legs and arms. Peter went up on the stage and started speaking through the microphone.

"I want all the students to come out here on the sports field and watch the show. This asshole was rude to us and tried to challenge our authority in this college. We had seen him talking to some army officers a few days ago. I think he is giving information about Mr. bin Laden to the army. Mr. bin Laden has authorized us to give any punishment we desire in his absence to those who are conspiring against him. We are going to burn him to death for that."

"They are lying. I didn't do anything. They had never liked me before, and they're finding an excuse to torture me. Please, somebody call the police." The boy begged, but nobody dared to go against Peter's gang.

Peter poured gasoline on the student's body, and he screamed for help. Taking out a lighter from his pocket, Peter shouted, "Look, asshole, I'm going to burn you alive, and nobody can do a damn thing about it. Say good-bye to your little willy first." Peter turned on the lighter. Suddenly something hit him, and he fell five meters away from the student. The lighter also fell on the ground.

"Who the fuck has dared to hit me? I will kill you first, motherfucker," Peter shouted. As he tried to get up, he saw his friends being bashed by something they couldn't see. He jumped to pick up the lighter, but something invisible kept hitting him. The other students looked on with astonishment and disbelief. Within a few minutes, all the gang members lay injured and screaming on the ground. Any of them who tried to get up got bashed without mercy. The students saw the invisible thing tying the gang members' arms and legs with ropes. Janet could see who it was, but she kept quiet in order not to blow her cover and disclose that she could see ghosts. By then the students also realized that they must be some kind of spirits. The ghosts became visible. All the students immediately recognized Tom and Judy. Judy untied the boy who was about to be burned by the gang.

"Thank you very much for saving my life. Please don't let these bastards go free," the boy said.

"Hi, friends, we're back to avenge our sufferings. These wankers won't be able to give any more trouble to you all."

"How can it be possible?" Peter rubbed his eyes as if he was dreaming.

"It's real, assholes. We've come back to haunt you. We know that today your savior is not here," Judy shouted and then tore off their clothes. She had become very powerful in ghost form.

"You pathetic cunts, have you forgotten what happened to both of you? Bin Laden will be here anytime, and you won't be able to escape. You're nothing in front of him. Maybe you enjoyed the fuck and you've come back for more," Peter shouted at Tom and Judy.

"He is not coming to save you, motherfuckers. We will come back for him also when we're powerful enough. We're not scared of that asshole," Judy said with an angry voice.

"We're not going to kill you. We want you to suffer for the rest of your life," Tom warned them. Tom burned their genitals and eyes slowly with lighters. Judy went away for about twenty minutes and came back with a chainsaw. The gangsters begged for mercy while screaming hysterically. Turning on the chainsaw, Judy walked toward them. Ignoring their screams and pleas for forgiveness, she started cutting off their feet and hands. Tom used rope to tie their legs and arms to stop bleeding. He didn't want them to bleed to death. They all became unconscious.

"Somebody, please call the ambulances. I want these assholes to live and suffer the rest of their lives," Tom said. One of the students called the ambulances, which arrived after a few minutes.

"We've got to go now. Once we're powerful enough, we will come back for that asshole bin Laden. Please give him our message," said Judy, and then they disappeared. Students didn't dare to express their happiness because they knew bin

Laden would know everything. The boy who was about to be burned immediately fled the college to escape bin Laden's fury.

It was 10:00 p.m., and the show was to begin at 9:00 a.m. the next morning. Janet stood near the window and saw bin Laden returning. She was careful not to let him know that she could see him when he was invisible. She pretended not to look at him.

She pretended to hear a noise. "Are you back, my lord? Please tell me you are back. I am dying to see you and hear your voice. Please, show yourself to me."

"Yes, my darling, I am back. I missed you a lot." Bin Laden became visible and embraced her.

"I was worried and missed you a lot, my lord. I want your thick and powerful cock inside me now. I will call the other girls also. We are all desperate for your enormous dick." Janet tried to divert his attention toward sex because inside she was terrified that bin Laden might kill her straight away for revealing his secrets. She called the other girls, and together they satisfied his sexual urges. He seemed very happy and not worried about anything. From his excitement and behavior toward her, Janet understood that he didn't suspect her of anything. But she wondered where he had gone.

"I know my lord of the universe must have eliminated the threat to our throne," said Janet, eager to find out something as soon as possible.

"Oh yes, my queen. You know me. I told you not to worry about anything. Now sleep in peace and enjoy your kingdom."

"Yes, my lord, I don't have to worry or fear anybody in your presence and in your kingdom. I better sleep now because tomorrow our whole college will be live on the Internet and TV channels. I have organized everything to be perfect." Janet kept on flattering him.

"I trust you and knew you were a very talented girl. Where did you learn all this? You must be very educated. Where are your other family members?"

"I was brought up in an orphanage since I was twelve years old. I worked hard and finished my master's in business part-time. I tried to find my parents, but I don't know where they are."

"Oh, that is very sad. Come here and sleep in my arms." Bin Laden pulled her in his lap and kissed her good-night.

"There is something else very important you must know," Janet said.

"What is it?" Bin Laden looked worried.

"You know Tom and Judy, whom you had punished to death? They returned as ghosts today and tortured Peter's gang. You can see all that in the video. I couldn't do anything to stop them. They even left a message for you that they will come back," Janet disclosed.

"How dare they do that? Show me the video immediately. I want to find and fuck them to their ghostly death." Bin Laden became furious. After watching the video, he roared in anger. But he didn't know where to find Tom and Judy.

"Don't worry about it, darling. They would be committing ghostly suicide if they came back. I don't think they will ever come back. They know your highness's powers. That's why they fled in a hurry. Please relax now, my darling. Do you want me to call the other girls again and make you happy?" asked Janet.

"No. I'm all right. I want them to come back. How dare the motherfuckers challenge me? You better sleep now in my arms. I'll be fine." Bin Laden kissed Janet.

"OK, good night, my lord."

Janet pretended to be sleeping with her head in his lap. After some time, he carried her and laid her down on the bed and tucked her in a thick blanket. When he left the room, Janet kept thinking about where he could have gone for so long. Why didn't he go to kill the monks? She decided to be extra careful because he might just be acting happy. The government and CIA were also puzzled by his mysterious disappearance for so many days. There was no rape, killing, or any other happenings that they could relate to bin Laden. They told the girls to find out what they could. It must have been something very important. The government and CIA were getting frustrated because the world's superpower was helpless to do anything to the mighty ghost, and he enjoyed taunting them. The politicians felt embarrassed that a live show was going to begin and nothing could be done to stop it. Bin Laden would be mocking Americans in front of the whole world. They consulted scientists, experts, and religious leaders of the world to find a solution, but nothing concrete came out of it. Their last hope, vampires, had disappeared and went into hiding. Judy and Tom were no match for him. As suggested by Janet, the government brought the Tibetan monks to America to awaken the spirits. The government provided them everything they needed, and the monks tried everything in their power, but they weren't having any success.

The day came for the whole college to appear live on the Internet and TV channels. Bin Laden sat like a king on his golden chair on the sports field. The students and competitors for various acts and sports were on the ground. Bin Laden got up and started reading a speech that he had written for the opening ceremony.

"Welcome to our show. We will be entertaining the world live and without any editing or removing any content. We are going to rock your world by showing you live entertainment that you have never experienced before. We are going to have naked sports, naked dancing girls' shows, and much more. I do not want to go into too much detail and bore you. Watch it yourself and enjoy."

First, various sports involving naked sexy girls and big and beautiful ladies began. Then the naked sports were followed by nude dance competitions and live sex competitions between girls. For two weeks the show was well received by viewers. But so far there was nothing special, as promised by bin Laden.

Chapter 4

As the whole college was put on cameras, people watched everything going on in the college. The cameras were never turned off. It had been two weeks, and the viewers began to get bored from the show. The viewers had developed high expectations from the show, but the same stuff every day turned them off. Enough nudity and sex shows were already on the Internet. They longed for something extraordinary, an out-of-this-world entertainment experience—something they had never watched before. Finally, their patience was about to be rewarded.

It was morning and bin Laden sat on his chair in the sports field, watching the big ladies wrestling. He noticed birds on a tree flying away, making noise as if they were giving warning about something dangerous coming. The sky began to get dark as clouds suddenly appeared over the college. The wind changed direction, and the trees swayed in an unusual and creepy way. The participants and the students stood frightened, and they could feel something different from the usual cold or hot weather on their skin. It felt as if something creepy was crawling on their bodies. Janet and the college cheerleaders were sitting on chairs on the stage near bin Laden. He got up and looked around the college, and then his eyes turned to the sky. His face changed, and he looked very worried.

"Get inside the building as soon as you can. Tell the participants and students to also find a safe place and hide."

"Why, what is wrong, my lord? What are you seeing?" Janet asked.

"Do you hear the sounds of galloping horses and firing guns getting louder and nearer?" bin Laden replied.

"No, we don't hear anything, but there is something strange and scary with the trees and clouds," Janet said. "Even birds seemed very scared and flew away. Is the US Army going to attack?"

"No, it is not the army. In fact, it is not humans at all. The army knows it can't even put a scratch on my body. It seems some kind of powerful spirits are coming, because only I can hear them very clearly. No time for any more questions. Go hide in the building. They are already very near," bin Laden said. The girls also noted the wind making strange noises and sounding scarier. They didn't waste any more time and ran for cover. Everybody was panicking and running as fast as they could. Only a few of them were inside the building when galloping horses came from every side of the college, the riders, who were dressed as nineteenth-century cowboys, firing guns in the air while laughing. With a hand on his gun, their dreadful-looking leader spoke in a thunderous and spooky voice.

"Stop wherever you are. We are the friendly ghosts of the old Wild West. We have come to save America from bin Laden.

You people have to watch what we do with him today. Don't run. Stay and enjoy the party. We will not harm any of you."

Everybody stopped where they were and felt delighted when bin Laden got surrounded by hundreds of horse-riding cowboy ghosts. It was the first time they had seen bin Laden looking freaked out, as if he had met his match.

The cowboys' leader sat on his horse about fifty meters from the stage, where bin Laden was standing. "Hey, you piece of shit, you want to surrender without a fight so we can be a bit lenient with you? If you surrender, I will just fuck you and get your powers transferred to me. As a goodwill gesture, I'll apply good lubricant on your hole before I insert my enormous poker inside you. Then I will not harm you if you become my bitch and serve me."

"Tell your motherfucking accomplices to get the fuck out of here if you all want to be safe," bin Laden threatened back. "Otherwise you will all lose your powers when I fuck you doggy style. Today is your lucky day. You'll be getting fucked by the mightiest ghost ever."

"Really, asshole, you think you're powerful enough to fight us? I will count to three, and if you don't surrender, I will make sure all of us teach you what a rape feels like. We're going to put our dicks in every hole on your body and sperminate you," the cowboy's leader roared.

"Don't waste time. Bring it on. I want to finish it fast and show the world live what I will do with your ghostly asses. My show had become boring, but now it will be very entertaining with all of you being brutally raped and tortured by me. You better apply that lubricant on your own asses to endure less pain."

"Boys, get ready for some action. It has been a long time since we had a decent opponent to fight. I want you to teach this motherfucker a fucking terrifying and brutal lesson so that he will never even dream in his ghostly sleep to come back to America. Have no mercy and pump his ass hard." As soon as their leader finished speaking, the ghosts attacked bin Laden with full force. Their leader also joined the fight. People all over the world stuck to their computers and televisions to watch the action. The students and competition participants also moved aside to be safe and enjoy the demise of bin Laden. With so many ghosts surrounding him, everybody expected the end of bin Laden.

The cowboy ghosts fired their guns, which had no effect on bin Laden. They had to resort to hand-to-hand fighting. About twenty ghosts pounced on bin Laden, but he repulsed the attack. Moving like a twister, he punched and kicked them with full force. The cowboy ghosts started falling on the ground everywhere as they were hit by bin Laden. The cowboys thought they could easily overpower bin Laden, but they were wrong.

"I want every cowboy to kick this motherfucker's ass," their leader shouted as he himself attacked bin Laden. "Aim for his asshole. Make your dicks hard and try putting your cock inside his hole. Be brave and once you're inside him, hold him tight from behind so he can't get your dick out from his asshole. Others will keep him busy in the fight." Half of the cowboy ghosts with dicks hard like steel attacked him from behind, aiming to penetrate bin Laden's ass. The fight was not any easier for bin Laden. He got worried because he had to defend his asshole also. He kept it squeezed tightly while fighting the cowboy ghosts. With so many powerful ghosts attacking him from all sides, his strength began to crumble, and his asshole also became a bit loose. One cowboy ghost got a perfect opportunity when the other ghosts attacked bin Laden from the front. While defending himself, bin Laden bent over to punch a ghost. The ghost behind did not miss this chance and jumped on bin Laden's ass. His aim for the hole was perfect, but as soon as the head of his cock touched bin Laden's hole, it bent because it was not hard enough. The leader ghost saw it. Bin Laden immediately squeezed his ass and moved to the other side.

"You motherfucker, you almost nailed him. Why didn't you push all the way deep inside him?" the leader ghost asked angrily.

"Sorry, boss, I never fucked an old ass before. The look of his ugly ass made my cock go soft, and I was turned off," the ghost replied.

"Asshole, you used to fuck pigs, cows, and dogs. You never had a chance to fuck a real human's pussy or ass. How can your cock go soft when you were about to get some real ass? Boys, don't look at his ass. Aim right for his hole and close your eyes. Imagine some hot woman's ass," the leader advised the ghosts.

"Sir, those animal asses looked hotter compared with his ugly butt. If a hot woman's ass looks like that, I will never look at women again," the ghost with the limp dick replied.

"Shut up and fight. Let somebody else have a go now," the leader shouted.

Another guy had the chance, and when he jumped at bin Laden's ass, bin Laden farted loudly. It almost sounded like a bomb going off. The guy flew back with the wind and fell. The fart was so big and stinky that everybody, including the ghosts, had to cover their noses, close their mouths, and stop breathing for some time. The fight came to a halt for two minutes, because even bin Laden had to cover his nose and close his mouth for that long.

"Motherfucker's ass fires like a cannon," the leader ghost gasped.

"Thank goodness it's out. It gave me a stomachache for almost a year," said bin Laden, feeling relieved.

The cowboys' leader announced a new strategy. "OK, listen carefully. Those with the hardest and stiffest peckers move behind him and aim for his ass. The others attack him from the front. This time, don't miss it."

Bin Laden tightened his hole and looked very worried. He didn't want to give up and took to the trees so the cowboy ghosts would not be able to pounce on him together. He fought with his back to a tree trunk so nobody could penetrate his ass. This worked, and he moved from tree to tree and brought many cowboy ghosts to their knees. About fifty cowboy ghosts were lying on the ground injured and unable to carry on the fight. The remaining ghosts, including their leader, were putting up a good fight. Their leader was hundreds of times stronger than the other cowboy ghosts, and he planned to get bin Laden out of the trees. He went on the offensive, joined by others. Bin Laden fought well, but luck wasn't on his side, and he fell from a tree. The ghosts fell upon him at once and overpowered him. They caught him and brought him on the stage. Bin Laden had grown tired fighting the powerful ghosts.

The leader spoke while the other ghosts were holding bin Laden down. "People, watch this and record this. I am going to fuck him now and drain his energy out. Then I am going to make him my bitch and humiliate him every day by having my other friendly ghosts rape him on this stage. Now watch live my big dick entering his ass." The ghosts made him bend over on his hands and knees. Holding his enormous hardened cock in his hand, their leader came from behind to penetrate bin Laden's ghostly hole.

"Oh, that looks like a very tight hole. You will enjoy my big dick all the way inside. I think I better give you a little bit of foreplay so your ass gets relaxed, and then you can enjoy the fuck." The leader ghost tickled bin Laden's hole. Bin Laden became enraged but couldn't do anything. Then the leader rubbed his dick's head on bin Laden's hole. People were glued to their screens. The whole world went silent as people gathered around whatever they could find to watch the spectacle—smartphones, tablets, computers, and TVs. Their screens showed a close-up of the cock's head and bin Laden's tightened hole. As the leader ghost pushed a bit inside, bin Laden gathered his strength in one last attempt to save his ass. The leader ghost turned his attention to fucking bin Laden, and his hold on him weakened. By now, bin Laden was no longer tired and was able to gather his strength. He used his arms' strength and pushed hard on those who held him. The ghosts were flung by the force of his push and fell backward on the ground. The leader ghost's cock was out of bin Laden's hole. He tried to pounce on him again, but it was too late. Bin Laden got behind him and held him by the neck. He inserted his cock all the way inside the leader ghost's ass. The leader ghost's energy started draining. Bin Laden held him with one hand with his dick inside. He didn't let the leader ghost escape as he fought the other ghosts with one hand. He again took to the trees, carrying with him the leader ghost while his cock was still inside, draining the leader's energy. The leader ghost became defenseless. Bin Laden had turned the tables on them, and the other ghosts ran away when they saw their leader down and humiliated. While running, they covered their ass with their hands, fearing bin Laden might try to fuck them also to drain the energy out of them. Bin Laden threw away the leader ghost and then fucked and drained the energy out of the injured ghosts who were unable to run away. Bin Laden got the same amount of energy from the cowboy ghosts as he would by having sex with hundreds of millions of women. He captured all the ghosts who were unable to escape, including the leader, and chained them to the stage.

"How do you feel now, assholes?" asked bin Laden. "Your holes were very tight, and I enjoyed fucking you all." Humiliated and raped, they had no answer and sat there with their heads down. Confident of winning the fight, they had never expected the way their fortunes had turned. The fact that they would have to serve bin Laden for the rest of their ghostly lives demoralized and terrified them more. The show became number one again. People watched again and again.

The government, public, and the army were disappointed when bin Laden won the fight. The threat of bin Laden's ghost was almost eliminated, and the American government was prepared to celebrate it big-time. Janet and her CIA friends were also almost certain that bin Laden was going to be finished. They had not let their excitement show to bin Laden. Disheartened and disappointed, Janet and the girls congratulated bin Laden for his victory. But inside they wished he had been tortured and humiliated to his ghostly death.

Janet and the girls came and sat beside him on the stage. Lost in his thoughts, he didn't realize the girls were sitting beside him.

"What're you thinking, my lord?" Janet asked.

"Nothing much. I am just puzzled how they knew that they could suck my energy by fucking my asshole."

"You know the vampires knew about it, and the stinky bitches even mentioned some things about it in their interviews. I think they must have sent them." Janet felt terrified inside but put up a brave face to ward off suspicion.

"If they had sent them, why didn't they come along to fight?" Bin Laden looked very puzzled.

"Maybe they got scared and knew how they had to run and hide for their lives from my mighty lord," said Janet, trying to convince him.

"Maybe I have to torture their leader ghost and find out." Bin Laden got up and dragged the leader ghost in the middle of the sports field. He started torturing him, and the leader ghost couldn't bear the pain much longer. Brutalized and horrified, he revealed that a very angry ghost knew about his weakness and came to talk to them. That ghost was weak but wanted them to help in eliminating bin Laden's ghost. They agreed after hearing how bin Laden's ghost was terrorizing the Americans. The cowboy leader explained that they were overconfident of their victory and didn't think about getting help from other ghosts. The leader described the ghost as a male. Bin Laden wondered who the ghost was, but he didn't think too much about it. When he told Janet, she wanted to find the ghost as soon as possible because it could be a great help against bin Laden. For a moment she thought about Tom and Judy. But the fact that they didn't come along with the cowboy ghosts to take their revenge made it clear it was somebody else. Janet had to find an excuse to get away from bin Laden and trace that ghost. She thought for a few minutes and then went to bin Laden when he was sitting on the stage.

"Darling, I have to go to the doctor's because I always feel dizzy and tired. There is always a sharp pain in my brain. Even sometimes my eyes can't see properly. I checked the symptoms on the Internet, and it all points to brain cancer."

"Janet, darling, why didn't you tell me earlier? I would have taken you there myself."

"No, dear, I just didn't want to bother you. You have to look after the things around here. It might take a few days, and I will be back as soon as I can. I will miss you very much," said Janet. It seemed Janet's excuse worked.

"OK, take care. But call the girls and tell me if you need any help."

"Yes, my lord, I will. OK, see you." Janet kissed bin Laden and went to pack enough things for a few days. She didn't take long and left immediately. She took a taxi to the city to get far away from the college. She looked back to make sure bin Laden was not following her. As she got down, she noticed a man running toward her. Nobody seemed to notice him running, and she realized he was a ghost. He stopped near her.

"Hi, I am John. I am a ghost now. I know who you are. I have heard a lot about you and also seen you in that asshole bin Laden's live show." John boiled with anger when he mentioned bin Laden's name.

"Sorry, but I didn't recognize you," said Janet, wondering who he was.

"Unfortunately, I'm the guy who brought that dreadful terror on America. I went to look for his coffin in the sea to get rich." John's eyes welled up.

"But you were alive. What happened to you?"

"That asshole raped me for twenty days. When I arrived in America with him inside the boat, I was a terrified and depressed guy. I went to my girlfriend's apartment and didn't tell her what had happened. She was very happy to see me back, but her happiness didn't last long. She got horny straight away and wanted to make love. I tried but couldn't get an erection because of the sexual abuse I suffered in that boat for twenty days. She sucked me and tried everything, but it didn't help. Tears flooded my eyes, and I couldn't stop crying. She wanted to know what was wrong with me. I told her everything, but she didn't believe me. She thought I had become a gay and was making up stupid ghost stories to cover up things. She also thought I didn't love her anymore and was no longer interested in her. She got really pissed at me and told me to get out of the house. After that the government found me and interviewed me. I told the authorities whatever I knew. They tried to send me for counseling and offered me whatever help I needed. But I was too depressed and committed suicide by jumping in the river. As soon as I drowned and died, I was turned into a ghost. From that day

I decided to take revenge on bin Laden's ghost. I am a weak ghost and could not do any harm to him, but I can help the government and you to eliminate this most dangerous threat to our people and America."

"I'm very sorry to hear all that," Janet said. "We all want to finish him off as soon as possible. You will be a very big help. I can see him, but I can't follow him whenever he goes out from the college. He is too fast for me, and if he sees me he would kill me. You are a ghost now and can follow him safely. There is something he is not telling me. He goes somewhere at night also, but he avoids telling me. He thinks I'm sleeping when he leaves. He comes back after about five hours. He becomes invisible when he leaves. One time he went for five days and told me he was going to finish off some very big threat to him. I thought that threat was the monks who could awaken the American patriotic spirits. I informed the government about it, and they rescued them before he could do any harm to them. But the government and I suspect that he went somewhere else because nothing happened in the temples or area around the monks. He told me he had eliminated the threat, but it seems he is still looking for it because sometimes he looks very worried. We must find out about it."

"I will hang around the college every night and day. I will follow him and find out about it. That threat must be something very special," John's ghost suggested.

"Yes, I think that will be our last hope," agreed Janet.

"There is something else: The girls he raped and killed have all been turned into ghosts. They are weak but growing in numbers. They all want to pay him back, but they are very weak compared with him. I have asked them to join together to fight this dreadful evil, and they have agreed. Maybe one day with enough power, we will be able to exterminate the asshole. For the time being, they will also be ready to help in other ways."

"Oh, that will be great. I hope we can find somebody who is more powerful than him. So far everything seems to be a losing battle against his powers. I will be out for a few days, but please get those girl ghosts to help you follow him. If you want to meet me anytime for these few days, I will be here every day around this time. OK, see you soon."

"OK, see you. I will get in touch with you if I find anything new. Take care." John's ghost disappeared in the crowd.

Janet met the CIA and government officials and discussed everything. They informed her that the monks were able to awake a lot of spirits but most of them were reluctant to take on the mighty ghost of bin Laden. They said they possessed minimal powers compared with him. They did agree to help in the event somebody with power comparable to that of bin Laden's ghost was found.

The CIA prepared some blood and doctors' reports indicating that Janet had cancer in her brain and would have to attend regular appointments and get treatment. This was done to convince bin Laden that she was genuinely sick and needed to attend weekly appointments. After a few days, Janet went back and showed the reports to bin Laden. He was happy to let her go for the weekly appointments. He provided her with a checkbook if she needed money. Everything went as usual without any major incidents for two weeks. Janet went for her fake appointments and met John and the other friendly ghosts. The show went on featuring the sexy girls and the fat girls. The cowboy ghosts had to perform despicable and degrading sexual acts on each other in front of the cameras to send stern warnings to any future would-be saviors of America.

After two weeks, bin Laden again decided to go somewhere, this time for ten days. He told Janet about it while he was cuddling with her in the bed.

"Where is my lord going for so many days? Have you found somebody more beautiful than me or the other college girls?"

"No, dear, there is something very important I have to take care of, which I can't tell you." Bin Laden didn't want to reveal anything.

"Can I come this time? I can't stay even one day without you and your enormous tool."

"No, who will look after the show? I depend on you for all that. If you feel horny, you can enjoy some hot lesbian sex with the other girls. You can go and buy any kind of big dildos. But no man is allowed to touch you or the other girls."

"OK. But no dildo in this world will please me like your real, hard, and thick dick. Please try to come back earlier if you can."

"I will."

Bin Laden left at night. John and the girl ghosts followed him. He went outside the city and then through the farms. Occasionally he looked back to see if anybody was following him. John and the girl ghosts were extra careful not to let him discover them. Then he entered the forest and disappeared. They looked everywhere for him without success. They waited there for eleven days, and he didn't come back. When they got back near the college, they saw Janet coming out. She sat in the taxi as usual and alighted about ten kilometers away to the spot where she usually met John and the girls. John and the girls also arrived there.

"Have you found out anything?" Janet was desperate for some good news.

"No. We followed him and he disappeared in the forest and didn't come out," John answered.

"But he was back in the college after only eight days," Janet said.

"But how can that be? We waited there eleven days, and he didn't come out from there. He must have tricked us and came back another way. Did he tell you anything?"

"No, he didn't. It seems the threat is still there because he looks disappointed and frustrated," Janet said.

Everybody wondered where he went and if he knew that they followed him. They informed the government which forest he went into. The CIA brought the monks in the woods to find out whatever they could. The CIA agents and the military also checked every part of the forest. They couldn't find any clue. There were no traces left, and they came back disappointed. After a few days, bin Laden again told Janet that he had to go somewhere for two weeks. He told her to stay there and look after the show in his absence. Janet informed John, and he and the girls' ghosts followed him. Bin Laden went to Afghanistan and Iraq and met a lot of ghosts of dead terrorists and suicide bombers. John and the girls saw him from far away talking to them but couldn't hear what they were discussing. About three hundred ghosts followed him back to America after two weeks. The other ghosts were not powerful like him but were still a force to reckon with. They were all put around the college to guard him from any threats. The terrorist ghosts started keeping eyes on all the students. Bin Laden allowed them to go out in small groups to have sex with American women. They didn't get any energy from the sex. Only bin Laden possessed that ability. The ghost security guards made things a bit hard for John, the girl ghosts, and even Janet. Now they had to be very careful because they could be seen together by any of them. Janet hadn't gone out to meet John since bin Laden came back. She was desperate to find out the details. She could see all the ghosts but carefully avoided giving any indication that they were visible to her. She gave the same excuse to bin Laden as before about needing a medical checkup and went outside. She met John and the girl ghosts.

Janet had so many questions to ask. "What have you found out? Why there are so many foreign-looking ghosts around the college? Where did he go?"

"He went to Iraq and Afghanistan," John told her. "These are all ghosts of dead terrorists. We couldn't go near them to hear what they were discussing, but these ones chose to follow him here. I think he is afraid of something that can threaten his power and is preparing for the defense. There were thousands of ghosts of terrorists who met him there. Two ghosts who followed him here are very funny. One is a ghost of a female dog and the other one of a female donkey. The other ghosts tried to chase them away, but they always came back and followed them here. I think they can see and hear each other. They can't seem to touch, feel, or be harmed. That's why they are so daring and not frightened by bin Laden's powers. They always try to go near bin Laden, but he gets angry and irritated. Their irritating behavior distracts him a lot, and he tries every trick to get rid of them, but without any success. It looks like the other ghosts can't do any harm to them except chasing them. Even when they are being chased, they mock them and laugh at them. We haven't approached those ghosts yet because they might blow our cover that we followed bin Laden. It seems because they are animal ghosts, they are not susceptible to human ghost powers."

"What do they say or do when they go near them?" Janet asked.

"The female dog always tries to dance in front of him erotically, shaking her ass while singing something. Bin Laden gets very irritated by her. The donkey ghost follows him as if she is in love with him. She just wants to be near him. We have even seen him pleading in front of them to go away. Maybe we should talk to the female dog ghost when it is alone."

"Just be careful, and don't tell anything about yourself," Janet advised John.

Janet went back and saw bin Laden and his comrade ghosts chasing the dog ghost and the donkey ghost in the sports fields. Bin Laden was in his invisible form, and Janet acted normal so they wouldn't suspect that she could see and hear them chasing the dog and donkey ghosts. She wondered why bin Laden was going crazy and begging them.

"Please leave me alone. I know I made a lot of mistakes when I was alive. Men do stupid things when overtaken by sexual desires. You must understand that I didn't have any woman around in the mountains for sex. I am very sorry. Please go away and enjoy your ghostly life. If you promise not to bother me, I will make sure you have every comfort here. I will bring some very sexy and handsome male donkey ghosts and male dog ghosts for both of you to enjoy."

"Does that also include sex with you? Will you be willing to have group sex with us? Maybe you can put your cock in my pussy and a male donkey ghost can penetrate your ass. It would be so pleasurable and kinky," the donkey ghost said while getting very excited.

"No, no. Not with me, you stupid donkey. I don't want my ass to be ripped apart by a donkey's big cock. But you can have sex with my other friendly ghosts," answered bin Laden in an irritated and angry tone.

"No, baby, I want it only with you. If you agree I will sit in one corner every day and be very quiet. I wouldn't even want to have any male donkey ghosts," protested the donkey ghost like a loving girlfriend.

"OK, I will if you get the dog also not to disturb me," bin Laden agreed hesitantly.

"Why? I'll be quiet. If the donkey enjoys sex with you, it's got nothing to do with me. I just love making your ass irritated and angry, and I will not agree to anything." The dog ghost turned her backside toward bin Laden and danced, wiggled, and shook like a sexy American female pop star. Bin Laden got angry and ran after it.

"You bitch, why don't you agree and watch me enjoy sex with my darling bin Laden?" The donkey got angry with the dog ghost.

Janet pretended to arrange some things on the stage while watching and listening to everything. She decided to ask John

120

to befriend the dog ghost and ask her what was going on. The next time she went out to talk to John, she saw the female dog ghost already conversing with him.

"Hi, I am Janet. What is your name?" Janet greeted the dog.

"Hi, my name is Naughty Bitch. How can you see me? I thought you were a human, not a ghost."

"I am a human. I have this special gift. I can see ghosts and talk to them."

"I saw you with that asshole bin Laden. He doesn't seem to know that you can see him."

"No, he doesn't know. Please don't tell him about it. I just go near him to know more about him. I have noticed that you don't like him and enjoy bullying and irritating him."

"Yes, I do enjoy it a lot. I despise that asshole."

"But, why do you despise him?"

"Oh, it's a long story. It all happened in Afghanistan. He was hiding from the American forces in the Tora Bora Mountains. He was alone and resting under a tree. I was hungry and went to look for some food. Because I am a bitch, I could smell that he was horny when he looked at my backside with unwanted sexual attention and lusty eyes. There were no women around for him to fuck or rape. He called me to go near him. I was hesitant because I could see the lust in his eyes and his cock growing and becoming hard in his pants. I didn't go and waited about fifty meters away from him. Then he showed me a fresh bone of meat. I was hypnotized by the sight and the delicious smell of the bone and fell into his trap. He caught me and tied the piece of cloth he was wearing on his head around my neck. He held me with one hand and undressed himself. He admired my pussy and ass for a few minutes and then started performing cunnilingus on me. He was feeling so horny that he forgot that I was not a woman. I know I was a very sexy and beautiful bitch. That's why the desire of having sex with me overtook him. He moved from my pussy to my hot ass and started licking it as if it was the most delicious thing he ever tasted. I was enjoying all this and couldn't stop a big wet fart from spreading feces all over his face. He became angry and beat the shit out of me. He still wanted to fuck me and didn't let go. He was completely naked, and when he tried to enter his big cock inside my tight and hot pussy, I freaked out and bit his hand to escape. As soon as his grip became loose, I escaped. I ran as fast as I could, and he followed me, still naked. He begged me to stop. He even said I was very sexy and hot bitch. He said he loved me and wanted to marry me. I couldn't believe my ears that he was so desperate for sex that he was willing to marry a bitch. His headgear was still around my neck. While running to save my ass and pussy from this crazy, lusty old man, I slipped going around a corner and fell from the mountain. I didn't survive and became a ghost. From that day I swore that I would not let him rest in peace even after his death. From that day I followed him everywhere and irritated him. Only he could see and hear me, because he killed me. A lot of people around him thought he became crazy when they found him chasing and shouting at me. They even asked him to consult a psychiatrist because he was imagining things. I lost him when he was killed by the Americans and his body thrown in the sea. I followed him here when I saw him again as a ghost in Afghanistan."

"From where did you learn such a sexy dance?" Janet asked. "I saw you dancing in front of him."

"I was a lap dancer in New York, and a very sexy and hot one. I fucked a lot of men and always behaved like a horny and cheating bitch. I was never loyal to any of my lovers. I took drugs and died from the overdose one day. I was reincarnated as a bitch in Afghanistan. But I still remembered all the lap dance moves. Now I ask bin Laden to marry me, but he doesn't want to because he can choose any bitch in America to fuck. I dream about the wedding dress and having ghostly kids with bin Laden," Naughty Bitch answered.

"Ha, ha, ha, ha," everybody laughed.

"Why are you laughing?"

"We were just imagining you and bin Laden getting married," answered Janet. "What about the donkey? What's the story about her?"

"The day I died and came back as a ghost, I saw him fucking the donkey. The donkey was also lonely and liked when he kissed and licked her body, ass, and pussy. She was used to having a big cock inside from her male donkey partner, and she took his cock easily inside. Although it just tickled her pussy, she liked him performing cunnilingus and analingus on her. She fell in love with him and wanted to marry him. She was turned into a ghost when she died in an American missile attack. Bin Laden was fucking her doggy style when the bomb fell. He survived the attack, but the donkey died. She also doesn't want to leave him. We fought over him for some time but then reached an agreement to get him to marry both of us so we could enjoy threesomes."

"If you hate him so much, then why do you want to marry him?" Janet asked.

"Oh, because when I marry him, I will make his life a living hell. I will be a real bad-ass, nagging wife from hell. I will fuck and suck other dog ghosts and, if possible, men ghosts right in front of him to make his life a living hell. He will be really irritated when he watches his wife being fucked by others," replied Naughty Bitch.

"We need your help. You know he is not interested in you anymore, and you would like to take revenge, wouldn't you?" asked Janet.

"Sure I would. I'm willing to help you anyway you want. John told me he visits some places secretly and they can't find where he goes. I am a bitch ghost, and I will be able to sniff him out in any forest. He can't hide from me anymore."

"Yes, that's what we want. I will tell you the next time he plans to go. He seems to be very scared of something and is preparing to fight it." Some suspicion came in Janet's mind. "What if he agrees to marry you? Will you betray us?"

"If he is dead, I can move forward to another life. I don't want to stay in this ghostly life forever. I wanted to marry him to make his life miserable, not because I love him or something. I can't be freed from this ghostly life until his ghost is eliminated. I am stuck in this life with him. I want to be born in America again and become a lap dancer. I loved that job very much, especially when lusty men looked at me with hungry eyes. I miss all the group sex and sex with other women."

"What about the donkey—can she help us in anything?" Janet asked.

"Yes, we can ask her to just drive bin Laden crazy by always irritating him. That way he will lose some concentration and we can take advantage of his weaknesses," answered Naughty Bitch.

Everybody liked Naughty Bitch's idea, and they started planning bin Laden's end. They waited for him to go wherever he had gone before. Bin Laden had used all the girls in the college and gotten bored. He wanted something different, exotic, pure, and hot to spice up his ghostly life. He told Janet that he wanted to visit the city for some fun and left. Whenever he left the campus, he noticed a big church nearby. About ten very beautiful young nuns were staying there. Their eyes and faces were intoxicating and stunningly beautiful. Bin Laden always imagined them naked, and whenever he walked by he purposely became visible to them. They also looked interested in the mighty ghost. Bin Laden thought they would be very hot fucks because they were virgins and starved for sex their whole lives. His uncontrollable lust for virgin pussy took him there. He saw them sitting outside on the grass talking to each other. With a friendly smile on his face, he approached them to make conversation. He was not interested in forcing them into submission and raping them. He preferred that they participate in his wild sexual fantasies and desires willingly. He longed for the real heat of sex-starved virgin nuns' bodies.

"Hi, ladies, are you enjoying your day?" He stood near them, and his cock went crazy for some virgin pussy. The nuns could see his cock getting bigger, thicker, and harder.

"Hi there, we know you. You are the mighty ghost. We have heard a lot about you," the one who seemed to be the head nun answered. They stared at his enormous hard cock. Bin Laden could see the lust in their eyes and continued the conversation.

"What do you do the whole day and night except pray? You are all very young, beautiful, and sexy nuns."

"We pray the whole day, and when we are free we take cold showers to calm us down from any cravings for hot sex," another answered while licking her lips, desperation showing in her eyes for his enormous dick.

"How can you control that? Don't you feel like sucking and riding some big hot cock?" Bin Laden knew the conversation was going in the right direction and making the nuns horny.

"We do sometimes, but then we go to a special room where we torture each other's bodies with very painful lashes. Then we punish our horny pussies by hitting them hard. We pinch our nipples very hard until the pain is unbearable. Looking at your hard cock, I think we have to stay the whole night in the punishment room," one of them explained while lust flowed from every part of her body.

Bin Laden grew hornier hearing their story, and he couldn't help saying, "You don't have to punish yourself for something that is natural. Why don't you take me to your punishment room and let me give you some naughty, hot, and pleasuring punishment that you would like to have every moment of every day and night. I will beat your horny pussies and asses with my dick. Then I will give you a tongue bath in your holes. I will suck your juicy and big boobs as long as you want."

"We are very pious and holy nuns. We won't let any real or artificial cock go inside our pussies. But because you are a mighty ghost, we can make an exception by allowing you to fuck our virgin assholes. But you have to give us a tongue bath on our asses as you just promised. We can also give you blow jobs. If you agree to these terms and conditions, we are ready to blow your mind with the wildest fantasies we imagine every night," another nun said.

"Yes, that will be great. It doesn't matter. I would love to fuck your tight and sexy ass." Bin Laden's mind was totally overtaken by thoughts of fucking some virgins, and his cock was bursting with cum.

"Another condition is we won't take off all our clothes. We can be topless and let you suck our boobs. We are not allowed to take off our panties in front of a man. You won't be allowed to touch or feel our pussies. You have to move a bit of our panties from our ass to one side to allow your cock to penetrate," another nun explained.

"No problem, no problem. I would love to lick some virgin assholes. Let's not waste any time and fuck," said bin Laden, desperate and unable to wait any longer. The nuns were also desperate by now. They took him in the room and took turns sucking his cock. While some were sucking his cock, the others put their boobs into his mouth. Enjoying sucking those hard and fresh boobs with aroused tits, bin Laden moved from boob to boob. The nuns licked him all over his body with their extrawarm tongues, and they took turns licking his ass. They took turns bending in front of him, and he fucked their holes hard. The loud moans and screams of the fired-up nuns made him hornier, and he slammed their asses harder and faster. While one nun was rimming his hole, he asked her to insert a finger inside to intensify the mind-blowing sensation. After gently massaging his wet hole with the tip of her finger first, she inserted the whole finger inside. The extraordinary sexual pleasure of her finger massaging his prostate sent electric shock waves of enjoyment through his body, and he couldn't help saying, "Oh, baby, please put in two fingers and fuck my hole hard while I pump your friends hard."

The nun listened to him and inserted two fingers inside. The others took turns putting his cock in their asses. The mighty ghost had become powerfully sexual and could go the whole night fucking them all. Their screams and enjoyment made bin Laden go crazier, and he pumped them harder while admiring their sexy butts. He had finished fucking ten of them when he heard some noise outside. Ignoring the noise, he kept on fucking vigorously. The nun at the back fucking his ass took out her fingers and inserted something thick and big inside him. Bin Laden sensed that it was not a finger but was something else he had encountered before. Realizing what it might be, he jumped high and quickly turned toward the nun behind him. He saw the nun had a very big and erect dick inserted in his ass. With lightning speed, he tore off the other nuns' clothes to check them all. To his astonishment, they were all hiding big boners and extralarge balls in their panties. He couldn't believe that he was fucking and getting fucked by trannies. Before he could harm them, the room door burst open and in came a lot of naked male ghosts holding their hardened dicks to attack bin Laden. He understood at once what was going on. It was a setup to drain his energy. The nuns were not real nuns. He pounced on them to save his ass. He fought his way out of the building.

When he came outside, thousands of ghosts hungry for his power were holding their erected peckers to pierce his ass. Bin Laden put one hand on his ass and fought with the other. Being an exceptionally powerful ghost, he put up a good fight. The male ghosts were dropping injured everywhere on the ground. But there were too many of them.

They kept on coming from every direction. Bin Laden saw a way out. On one side were only a few ghosts. He fought toward that direction, and once out of the crowd, he dashed toward the college. While running with one hand on his ass, he saw thousands of ghosts running after him, wielding their stiff dicks and ready to enter his hole. The Naughty Bitch ghost had hidden in the church and saw what had happened. The opportunity to irritate bin Laden too irresistible, she ran beside him.

"What was that? Have you become gay? You were enjoying that big cock in your ass so much, and you liked fucking those men dressed as women. If you wanted kinky sex, you should have asked the donkey ghost and me to wear women's clothes, you cheating son of bitch. I could have worn a strap-on dildo and fucked your ass like a wild dog. But no, you had to have a real dick inside, didn't you? What about your two wives at home? Don't blame us if we find some other cocks to fuck us. You have to stop all the cheating and make love to us," said Naughty Bitch with a bullying smile on her face.

"Shut up, bitch. I will kill you."

"You have already killed me while trying to fuck my hot pussy. Don't call me bitch. Call me hot bitch. I can dress up as a very sexy woman if you want it so kinky."

"I said shut up." Bin Laden tried to hit Naughty Bitch.

"Run faster. They are catching up. I think your ass is very sexy. Look at their hard cocks. I'm jealous. How can they not like my tight ass? Since you're a cheater, I wouldn't mind having some of them in my holes. The sight of a real cock going inside your ass really turned me on."

"Shut up and let me run. Go fuck some dogs." Bin Laden was running out of breath. He looked behind and saw all the ghosts getting closer while brandishing their hardened tools.

"You want me to cover your ass, honey? Tighten it up, baby. They are very near," Naughty Bitch said while laughing and enjoying bin Laden being chased by so many dick-swinging ghosts.

"Fuck off, bitch."

"Squeeze your ass tight like I used to when dogs tried to fuck my pussy. Do you want to hear a real story?"

"Keep your fucking stories to yourself."

"Anyway, I will just tell you. One time I went to the forest and a pack of ten dogs saw me. They were hypnotized by my beauty and sexiness. I got scared and tried to run like you're running now. I squeezed my ass and pussy tight and ran as fast as I could. But the huge, sexed-up dogs quickly caught up with me and encircled me. I was surrounded by wild, huge dogs, and I could see their big, hard dicks almost touching the ground. They took turns sniffing my beautiful and hot pussy and ass, and I could see the sexual lust building up in their huge and scary bodies. I didn't lose my mind and concentrated all my energy around my rear end. I squeezed both holes tightly and stayed calm. I knew they would tear my holes into pieces with their enormous dicks if I loosened up. I told them I would stay still and let them fuck my holes on one condition. They had to promise that if after trying they could not penetrate my holes, they would have to let me go unharmed. Accepting my condition, they took turns mounting me. They couldn't penetrate and ejaculated outside on my pussy. After trying for half a day and ejaculating outside many times, finally they gave up. I made them get tired and ejaculate outside my holes. My pussy lips had become sore from the grinding and hitting by hardened dicks. But I didn't mind a little bit of pain. That's how I saved myself. I think the ghosts will catch you soon and you should do as I did. I am just trying to help you, my honey."

"If I take your fucking advice and stand still, I would end up with thousands of cocks inside my ass and zero energy left. If I survive today, I will make sure I unleash all the sex-hungry dog ghosts on you, bitch. Then I will see how long you can squeeze."

"I know you wouldn't do that to your dream bitch. That day you wanted to marry me to fuck. Now in my heart, you are my husband. Would you let other dogs fuck your sexy and hot wife? I don't think so, honey."

"Don't call me honey, bitch, and you are not my wife."

You proposed that day, and I accepted it. Now we are husband and wife. You want me to lick your ass while you are running, honey? I'm very good licker."

"Fuck you."

"You are welcome to fuck me, honey."

Getting irritated, bin Laden swung at Naughty Bitch, but his fist just went through her body like something going through an empty space. He realized that she was getting on his nerves and if he kept listening to her, he would soon be caught by the ghosts. Seeing the ghosts almost catching up to him, he increased his speed. He felt better and safe as soon as he entered the college premises. His comrades joined the fight and attacked the friendly male ghosts. Bin Laden's ghosts encircled him to protect him from the attacking ghosts. Bin Laden got some time to relax and reenergize.

"OK, some of you cover my ass. I am ready to fight now. Don't let anybody come near my backside," bin Laden commanded as he fought back. With bin Laden reenergized and not worried about covering his ass anymore, the friendly ghosts didn't stand a chance. He went for their dicks first and broke off as many as he could. Seeing their friends falling like dead insects, the friendly ghosts ran and dispersed within half an hour. To minimize the risk of any future attack, bin Laden and his ghosts went after them and killed as many as they could. About five hundred escaped and didn't dare to come back. Bin Laden returned and sucked the energy out of the injured ones.

After the fight, bin Laden wondered how he could be so stupid to fall into a trap again. He was fucked by one tranny before. He decided to take on the trannies first and then punish those who planned the trap. He knew it was the American government behind it. He ordered all the trannies out of the city. Otherwise they would be slaughtered like animals. Trannies had no choice but to follow his orders. The trannies who acted like nuns to trap him had immediately fled the city when they found out bin Laden had survived the attack from the friendly ghosts and slaughtered more than half of them.

Without consulting or telling Janet, bin Laden sent half of his ghosts to find where the American politicians were hiding. The ghosts became invisible to discover any useful information wherever they could. Janet became suspicious when she saw half of bin Laden's ghosts had disappeared, and she immediately informed the authorities. Enraged by the attack and with revenge in mind, bin Laden decided to shift his base to the White House to taunt the politicians and American military. He killed all the cowboy ghosts he had captured and decided to leave the already used college girls behind. He took his ghosts and went in front of the White House to attack. The police and military had already seen his power and fled the White House without a fight. Bin Laden ordered all the security cameras in the White House to be connected to the Internet. He also ordered Janet to install additional cameras to cover the whole building from inside and outside. The White House became the location of his live show, and he recommenced broadcasting to the world. Hundreds of stunningly hot girls were brought to the White House to serve him and his other ghosts. Janet and the other group of dance girls, including the CIA agents, were also shifted to the White House. His tormentors, Naughty Bitch and the donkey ghost, followed them and stayed close to bin Laden. Bin Laden and his men had given up chasing them because it was no use. The American government, military, and public felt humiliated about not being able to do anything about bin Laden taking over the symbol of American pride, the White House. Even the scientists could not do anything about it.

The monks brought to America were also unable to find and awaken any ghost who could retaliate and destroy bin Laden. One monk said that he knew a monk who kept to himself and lived in a jungle in Tibet, away from the general public. He was considered to be very gifted and possessed special powers to deal with the spirits. The government and CIA didn't waste any time and took the monk with them to find the gifted monk. He was traced, and when the CIA agents started to tell him about the situation, he said he knew everything and was waiting for them to contact him. The gifted monk came with them to America and informed them that he needed to be left alone to find a powerful enough ghost to face bin Laden. The CIA agents were worried that bin Laden might find out about the monk and kill him before he succeeded in finding anybody. The monk assured them that bin Laden would not be able to do any harm to him because he could be invisible to ghosts if needed. He also convinced them that he was sure he would be able to find somebody more powerful than bin Laden or with equal power to save America, and that after finding such a ghost he would contact them himself. Trusting the monk, the authorities agreed to allow him to go alone. With full confidence, the monk went outside the city and disappeared.

Chapter 5

A meeting of church high priests was held in secret to discuss the situation in America. After they prayed for and forgave the souls of the dead nun ghosts, it was decided that a priest with a pure soul who had not done any sin should stab bin Laden's heart with a cross and say prayers for two minutes to finish him. As suggested and attempted by the nun ghosts and a priest before, it had to be done when he would be in his visible form. It would be a suicide mission because bin Laden and his ghosts would not allow any Christian priest to go near him. When volunteers were sought, nobody came forward. It seemed that all the priests had committed some kind of sin in their life or they were simply scared to attempt the task because of what had happened to the priest who tried it before. When nobody volunteered, they decided to form a group of twenty-five priests to make a joint attempt, thinking maybe one of them could achieve the goal. It had to be done outside where he would be accompanied by fewer ghosts and the priests could disguise themselves as civilians. They also decided to use the US Army to distract him. The army asked John and other friendly ghosts to help. John and the girl ghosts contacted as many ghosts as they could and persuaded them to join the mission. Janet and the CIA agents around bin Laden were also informed about the mission because they needed to know when he would venture out with fewer ghosts.

Soldiers moved in civilian clothes to the city entertainment area, which bin Laden frequented every week. The friendly ghosts also took positions hiding around the area. The priests also wore civilian clothes and came into the city ahead of bin Laden's expected nighttime arrival. Janet had sent a girl to the CIA who informed them of his plans. A lot of good-looking CIA female agents roamed the city to distract bin Laden. They wore revealing and sexy clothes to seduce him. At 6:00 p.m., when bin Laden was about to go outside, Naughty Bitch and the donkey ghost blocked his way.

"Where are you going, honey?" the donkey ghost asked.

"To the city, stupid donkey."

"Why?"

"Just to enjoy some hot action from hot American pussies, stupid donkey. Who the fuck are you to block my way and ask me these questions?" After answering the questions, bin Laden realized that the other ghosts were laughing because he was answering the donkey as if she was his wife.

"We are your wives," Naughty Bitch answered assertively like a real wife.

"Why are you going to the city when you can have a sexy bitch and sexy ass at home? We can give you all the pleasure you want. Don't you like Afghan bitch and ass anymore?" added Naughty Bitch.

"Fuck off and move out of my way." Bin Laden ignored them and walked.

"Don't forget to squeeze and tighten your hole, honey. Thousands of stiff cocks are wandering around and looking for your tight hole. You know they almost nailed you a few weeks ago. And also remember to check the women to see if they have a cock or pussy. Make them take off their clothes first. Don't get deceived by the big boobs and sexy booties. And one last thing: Strictly don't let anybody play with your ass. You know that you always end up with a cock inside. Sometimes I suspect you're gay and you purposely do it," advised Naughty Bitch with a smile.

"Let's go, boss. Ignore the bitches. Otherwise they will spoil our mood," one of his deputy ghosts said.

"Yes, I think we must. Just shut your ears and walk," bin Laden said, and the ghosts walked outside.

CIA agents immediately alerted everybody involved in the mission when bin Laden left from the White House and came toward the city area. Their hearts beating faster, the priests looked nervous and scared. Bin Laden and his ghosts were in visible form and in great moods to enjoy their night out. The main entertainment street was about three kilometers long, and pubs and lap-dancing clubs lined both sides of the street. The CIA agents had told the civilians to go away to be safe. Bin Laden entered the street with accompanying ghosts from the north side. They walked down the street pinching, groping, kissing, and molesting the girls without suspecting their true identity as Secret Service agents. Seeing the most dreadful and horrifying ghost marching toward them, the agents, priests, and even the friendly ghosts felt scared. Some of the priests and the agents even pissed and defecated in their pants. Seeing bin Laden and his ghosts in front of them frightened and disheartened all the attackers. Hair-raising fear made them sweat heavily despite the night being very cold.

Some of the priests, who were supposed to stab him, chickened out at the last minute and pretended to go to the toilets. Two pious and brave priests thought only about their country and the people. Praying for success in their hearts, they gripped the metal crosses tightly and got ready for the kill. The priests continued saying prayers in their hearts and marched toward bin Laden and his ghosts, who were walking toward them about two hundred meters away. Without any fear in their ghostly hearts from the humans, bin Laden's supernatural gang came roaring. Bin Laden walked in front, his lusty eyes moving from one sexy girl to another. Some female agents saw the two priests marching for the target and distracted bin Laden and his ghosts by flirting with them and flashing their big and sexy boobs. The distance between the target and attackers was now only twenty meters. The priests tightened their grips on the metal crosses. As they approached, a female agent rubbed her big boobs on bin Laden's back. He stopped walking to enjoy the massage. She held his hands and licked his neck while straightening his chest for the priests to attack.

The priests approached him fearlessly. Before anybody could realize it, one of them raised the cross and plunged it deep into bin Laden's chest. The sharpened cross pierced bin Laden's chest like a sharp knife going through butter. Bin Laden's hands went for the cross, and he fell down holding it. The priest started saying loud prayers, but one of bin Laden's ghosts swung at him. The priest's body flung from the impact and hit a wall. The blow was so powerful that the priest's neck broke. The other ghosts attacked the second priest and tore his body into pieces. Hidden friendly ghosts came out in droves to attack bin Laden and his ghosts. Bin Laden's ghosts encircled him and prevented anybody from reaching him. Watching bin Laden falling down with a cross pierced through his body, the friendly ghosts didn't feel scared anymore and pounced on them with full force. Bin Laden's ghosts put up a good fight to stop them from reaching bin Laden. Bin Laden pulled out the cross, which hadn't gone through his ghostly heart. It only scratched one side of it. Seeing his ghosts demoralized and losing the fight, he gathered his strength and got up. Pushing his way out of the circle, he roared. The wind blew like a thunderstorm, and cars and humans flew like leaves. He roared to each direction. Some of the agents and the other priests fled the scene. Even half of the friendly ghosts dispersed in no time, fearing the onslaught of the mighty ghost.

"Don't run. Come and face me. You are all going to pay for this." The thunderous and deafening voice of bin Laden could be heard all over the city. Nobody had seen him previously in that frightening and dreadful avatar. The ghost's anger turned him into a merciless killing machine. Fire poured out of his eyes. Nothing could stand in the way of the monstrous and horrific beast. The remaining friendly ghosts tried to put up a fight but in vain. Bin Laden's fury left the friendly ghosts dropping on the ground, like chickens infected by bird flu. They couldn't last long and fled. Bin Laden's ghosts tried to stop him, but he didn't listen to them either. Going on the rampage, destroying everything whichever way he went, bin Laden spared no one in his path. The entertainment city got turned into a bloody battle ground with dead agents' bodies lying everywhere. Bin Laden's ghosts also joined him and moved street to street, destroying the city center in minutes. He smashed and burned the skyscrapers. He moved from suburb to suburb, killing civilians, police, and soldiers. Nobody could withstand his anger and might. People drove outside the city and fled to every direction as soon as they could. Within a few hours the whole city was turned into a ghost town with unimaginable destruction and dead bodies everywhere. The CIA and the government regretted the botched operation. With so much destruction, they could see that they had awakened a monster who was just interested in sex before. The only survivors were those in the White House. Bin Laden and his men came back to the White House, where Janet and the other agents waited in disbelief. Their hearts poured blood from seeing the destruction and burning smoke coming out from the city. It was a heart-wrenching and agonizing experience for them to put up a brave face and smile. They had no choice; otherwise they would also be slaughtered like sheep.

"What happened to my dearest lord?" Janet asked unwillingly and smiled.

"Nothing. Motherfuckers thought they could kill me, but the poofters underestimated my powers," bin Laden answered and sat on a chair.

"Who did?" Janet pretended not to know anything.

"Motherfucker Americans."

"Maybe they forgot about your mighty powers. How could they do such a stupid thing?" Janet came near him and embraced him in her arms. The other girls followed. Inside they wished to stab him themselves, but they clearly understood their weaknesses in front of him. They wouldn't be able to harm even one hair on his body. Naughty Bitch and the donkey ghost walked in. They had gone outside when they heard bin Laden was attacked. They came in laughing and had a perfect opportunity to irritate bin Laden.

"What happened, dear husband? Did any monster cock plunder your ass today?" asked Naughty Bitch sarcastically.

"Go away. Please don't disturb him," one of his deputies told the donkey ghost and Naughty Bitch. Janet and the girls wanted them to irritate him to death.

Naughty Bitch taunted bin Laden. "I told you to put on panties made of steel. You don't listen. You won't be able to have sex with us if they wreck your ass."

"Fuck off. Can anybody find a way to get rid of these two stupid animals? I will reward him or her with extra powers," said bin Laden.

"Why can't you stay home and enjoy your wives? That way you will be safe. You always get into trouble when you try to look for sex outside your marriage, honey. You know extramarital affairs are bad for your ghostly health and ass. Why do you keep on making the same stupid mistakes? You call us stupid, but actually you are a very stupid ass," said the donkey ghost.

Bin Laden and his ghosts didn't answer them. Knowing them well by then, bin Laden and his ghosts stopped responding and just ignored them. Naughty Bitch and the donkey ghost kept on talking and didn't want to shut up.

"We are going to rest and we will be naked, honey. We know you didn't get any sex today. If you want some hot action, you know where to find us. We could enjoy like old times and also have a threesome," the donkey ghost said to irritate bin Laden again. After nobody answered, they went away.

The other ghosts helped bin Laden to relax by talking to him about sex and girls. On the verge of being killed, his ghosts appreciated what he did when attacked and owed their lives to their mighty boss. Bin Laden also thanked them for protecting his ghostly life. He asked Janet and the CIA agents to follow him into the room. He fucked them hard to take out his frustration, and the girls faked their enjoyment to please him. After he had finished, he sat down and looked puzzled.

"What is the matter, baby?" Janet asked.

"Somebody is giving information about my whereabouts to the government. One question that keeps coming into my mind is how they knew I was going to be in the city tonight."

"Secret Service agents are everywhere, and they must be watching you and following whenever you leave the home. Our building is also online twenty-four hours a day. I think they can hear everything we say here and must be listening to us right now. Friendly ghosts are also helping them," Janet replied. She was scared that she might be the suspect.

"We can feel the presence of other ghosts in the building, but these girls must have been infiltrated by the CIA agents. They were very well prepared and knew what time I was to be there. I was very careless and must be vigilant next time. These sexy girls and my lusty behavior always get me into trouble."

"I will keep my eyes open and check all the girls personally. We must get their phones from them. But I think we must also make the building offline to safeguard our secrets," advised Janet.

"Don't worry too much about it. We will allow only the beautiful and sexy girls to live in this city. Men or any priests will be forbidden to enter. Let them watch. We will turn the whole city into an online show, not just this building," bin Laden told Janet.

"You are a genius. That way we will have full entertainment and less danger," said Janet, thinking of a perfect opportunity for bringing more female agents into the city.

"Get the preparations under way and announce what we want. Bring only the sexy and beautiful girls from other cities." Bin Laden didn't want any time wasted.

"OK, my lord." Janet felt better and relieved. She quickly followed his orders, and by the next day, girls started arriving from other cities. The government also had the perfect opportunity to send as many female agents near him as it could. Girls were promised a very good life and immunity from bin Laden's attacks. The girls knew that those who stayed with him enjoyed it very much and weren't harmed if they followed the orders and didn't break any rules. Furthermore, they all wanted to be famous and watched by billions of people. People were not interested in watching anything else except what was happening with bin Laden and America. The viewers became more curious and desperate to know what would happen next. Will anybody succeed in finishing off bin Laden? Could America find a solution to the biggest danger it faced currently? Who would be able to help America, and who could be strong enough to take on bin Laden's ghost? These questions were being discussed all over the world media and among the general public. Viewers didn't even want to sleep because they didn't want to miss anything about it. After the unsuccessful attacks on

his ghostly life, the American public started praying for a
miracle.

Chapter 6

To make sure bin Laden didn't follow them, after escaping from the college the six vampires, including Nicky, Mary, and Ruby, had gone through farm fields for safety and crossed the border into Canada. After direct confrontation with the ghost, the vampires clearly understood their weaknesses and what extra powers they needed to retaliate. The vampires stayed in a forest to avoid any attention from the general public because bin Laden would want to exterminate them as soon as he could. They settled down there for some time to plan their next course of action. To know whatever was happening in America, Ruby visited the nearby farm just outside the forest to find out the daily news. The farmer, an old man, lived alone and watched TV the whole day. Ruby would visit the farm whenever it was time for the news. Hiding near the window, she could hear and watch everything. As they heard that bin Laden had become very powerful and was living in the White House, they were enraged and wanted to do something about it. Nightmares about their friends' brutal deaths kept them awake at night. Restlessness and anger took over their minds and kept them intent on avenging their friends' killings. One day the vampires were sitting down when Ruby came and told them how bin Laden's ghost was almost killed by the priests. The destruction of the whole city made their blood boil, and they again planned a suicide mission to kill the ghost.

"Who else can help us so we will have enough power to strike?" Nicky asked.

"We need more-powerful vampires who are four hundred to five hundred years old. We can also contact the friendly ghosts. They have tried attacking him many times but failed. There are thousands of them, and they could be a great help. There have also been news stories about two funny ghosts who always irritate bin Laden and his other ghosts. They can't do anything to them because they are animal ghosts. One is a female dog and the other one is a female donkey. Those animal ghosts are always following bin Laden around and know a lot about him."

"But why would they help us?" Mary asked.

"Because the female dog, called Naughty Bitch, doesn't like bin Laden. Apparently she was killed when he tried to rape her in the Tora Bora Mountains. She became a ghost and wants to take revenge. It is also known that it is very hard for bin Laden to hide from her. Because she is a dog ghost, she can sniff him out from anywhere if he is on the land," Ruby explained.

"We must make contact with her. He recognizes us all, and it is very dangerous to go near him," Nicky said.

Mary volunteered. "I will try alone. I will be very careful, and if I'm not back in two weeks, don't come looking for me."

"Are you sure? You know it will be a suicide mission. You can be killed," Ruby said.

"Well, we have to do something. We can't just sit and watch," Mary replied.

"Wait—there is something else I just remembered." Nicky's eyes changed with some hope in them.

"What is it?" Ruby asked.

"Do you remember my vampire brother, Michael? He came to see me once in our college," Nicky said.

"Yes, I do. What can he do for us?" Ruby was curious.

"He once told me about having hundreds of vampire friends living in Mexican jungles. They feed on animal blood also and are friendly toward humans. Maybe we can go and see them. We might be able to convince them to help," Nicky suggested.

"Yes, I think we should. There is no harm in trying. Mary, you go and find whatever you can about bin Laden. We'll go and find the other vampires," Ruby suggested.

"OK, see you. I will meet you here in two weeks. Bye. Come on, guys, give me a hug. It might be my last time," Mary said.

"Don't say that. Come back safe," Ruby said.

"Yes, I'll try my best," Mary replied.

When Mary left, the other vampires went toward the Mexico border. Nicky told them that her brother had said that they were not very far from the border. They spent three days looking around without any luck. On the fourth day, when they tried to hunt for food, about twenty male and female vampires surrounded them.

"Don't make a move. Who are you? And what are you doing here? This is our jungle, and nobody else is allowed to hunt here," a very handsome male vampire shouted.

"We mean no harm to anybody. We come in peace. We were looking for Nicky's brother, Michael, who is also a vampire."

"We have three Michaels and none of them ever mentioned that he had a vampire sister," the male vampire said.

"Can you please take us to them? We would really appreciate it. If you think we are not telling the truth, you can do anything to us."

"I think we should give them one chance to find out the truth," another vampire said.

"My name is Billy. I'm the leader of this clan. I will give you one chance. Please follow us. If you try to play any tricks with us, you will be exterminated."

"Hi, Billy, I am Ruby and these are my best friends. We assure you, we don't pose any danger to you. Maybe you have heard of a fight between bin Laden's ghost and some vampires. Some of our friends were killed in that encounter because he was too powerful. We had to flee and hide ourselves to preserve our strength. We nearly killed him the first time, but he escaped," Ruby said.

"Yes, we heard everything about bin Laden and what he is doing. We preferred to stay out of it. Humans didn't like us much, so we also decided to stay out of their business." Billy explained their position. After walking about fifteen minutes, they reached the place where they all lived. There were about 250 of them. Michael recognized his sister and came running toward her.

"Hello, sis, what are you doing here? I heard about what happened in your college and went to look for you there. Somebody told me you escaped, but I couldn't find you anywhere."

"Hi, bro." Nicky embraced him. "We had to shift to Canada because of the danger to our lives. Our friends were killed and given terrible and agonizing deaths by that asshole."

"Sorry to hear about that," said Michael.

"Sorry to interrupt, but Michael, you never told us that you had a sister," Billy said.

"Just because no one asked and I thought it wasn't important," Michael answered.

"Don't say that. Families are always important. She is our family now. Give them the live animals we caught for food. They must be hungry. They have come a long way."

"Come, everybody, have your food first. I can see you are all looking tired and starving. We will discuss the rest later."

Michael took them inside a wooden room and offered them animals. After they had finished feeding, Nicky explained to Michael the reason for their visit.

"When I went to check on you in the college, I saw whatever bin Laden was doing there," Michael said. "As I was alone and was sure that you were all right, I came back. Half of us felt the need to do something about bin Laden's ghost, but we were advised by Billy to keep out of it. I will try to talk to him and others about it. You better rest now. I will let you know tomorrow what he says."

The vampires held a meeting at night. Those who were in favor of helping convinced their leader and others that they must do something about it. The emerging fact that bin Laden was going to target and eliminate every threat to his power changed their minds. Sooner or later, he would also target them. It was in everybody's interest to unite and fight the horrific monster. In the near future, he would become so powerful that nothing would be able to stop him. Michael informed Nicky and her friends the next day about their decision. Hearing the good news, they felt very confident and powerful enough to attack the ghost. It was decided that all the vampires would wait in the Canadian forest because it was nearer to bin Laden. Nobody wanted to rush things and endanger precious lives. To plan the attack effectively, important information from Mary and the friendly ghosts was needed urgently.

Hundreds of terrorist ghosts from other countries came and joined bin Laden. Getting well prepared for any future attack, bin Laden started fortifying his security. Not being careless anymore, he started eliminating the friendly ghosts and any other threats wherever he could find them. The friendly ghosts also got scared and left the big cities and moved to the countryside. Mary had changed her hairstyle and wore glasses to hide her eyes. She went through farms to avoid detection. She was about one hundred kilometers from the capital city when she heard noises in the crops. As she walked, the steps of somebody invisible were trampling the crops. She couldn't see who it was. The thought of it being bin Laden gave her the creeps. Her skin felt as if it were freezing as the fear of being killed and abused violently sent shivers through her spine. Scenes of her friends being brutalized and killed by bin Laden flashed in her mind. She had no other choice but to keep walking in fear. She got so scared that she didn't dare to turn and look back. The invisible thing came in front and pressed the crops. She realized that some spirit was trying to talk to her. She paid attention as the spirit walked in front of her. She followed the footsteps, and the spirit stopped at an empty field. It started writing on the dirt. Mary read the message. "Hi, I'm a spirit. Please follow me to the nearby service station." Mary followed it and they went into the nearby service station.

The spirit picked up a pen and a paper and wrote "Hi, I am John, please don't be scared. I am a friendly ghost from America. I recognize you. You are the vampire I saw on TV. You gave some information about bin Laden's ghost. I was the guy who brought out his coffin from the sea. I made a big mistake and paid for it with my life and happiness being destroyed. You can't hear me or see me. There is a girl named Janet who is staying with bin Laden. She is one of the many girls the government has sent to be near bin Laden and watch his every move. Janet can see and talk to the ghosts. Bin Laden doesn't know this. I can help you to meet her. It is very risky and dangerous to enter the city. We have to enter the city at night to avoid being detected. They have put cameras every-where around the city, and also his ghosts always roam in and around the city to identify any potential threats. Come, follow my steps. I know a secret way through the tunnels where there is not much security. Janet meets me there every two weeks. We will be meeting her tomorrow." Mary trusted and followed him. They entered the city through the tunnel and hid in one place to wait for Janet. After some time, Mary saw a young woman approaching her.

"Hi, John, how are you? Who is your friend?"

"Hi, Janet, this is Mary, one of the vampires who lived in the college before bin Laden took it over and they had to leave. You remember, don't you?"

"Hi, Mary. How can I forget them? They almost eliminated the bastard. Sorry about your friends. Where are your other friends?"

"Hi, Janet, I've come to gather some information about bin Laden. We want to attack him again. My friend Nicky's brother knows a lot of other vampires. They have gone to ask for their help. We will be very lucky if those vampires agree to help us. They are hundreds in numbers, and I think we might be able to finish him off this time. We will need your help."

"We are prepared to help any way we can. Even if we have to sacrifice our lives, we want these dark death clouds removed from America forever so the American public can have peaceful lives as before. He is scared of something and sometimes goes alone to look for it. He comes back disappointed. It has been a few months since he last went. He has hinted recently that he will be going for two weeks again. He doesn't take anybody along with him. We don't know why," Janet explained.

"Please let John know the next time he goes so he can inform us. I will show him where we stay. If we get help from the other vampires, it will be his last time," Mary said confidently.

"Janet, please inform her that I will talk to all the friendly ghosts also to get together and help. We don't want to leave any chances for his survival," John said.

"John wants you to know that he will be getting all the friendly ghosts to come together once again to help you and your friends."

"Please also keep a priest with a cross ready to stab him," Mary said.

"Yes, we will. There are some priests living in a town about two hundred kilometers from here. They are disguised as farmers and waiting for the occasion to rise again. We will send John with you and you can meet them," Janet said.

"That will be great. Do we need to know any other weaknesses of him and his ghosts?" Mary asked.

"They are easily distracted by beautiful and sexy girls," Janet replied. "I think you already know about that. The other thing is, he has become very powerful now. His energy has increased millions of times. You have to take him outside the city when he is alone. Don't attack him until you are well prepared. We must find the thing that he is looking for. It must be powerful enough to take him on. That is the only thing that frightens and worries him a lot. That could be the death knell for him."

"If we get help from the other vampires and the ghosts, we will be able to get rid of him," Mary said with confidence and certain of the victory.

"OK, I have to go now, otherwise he will wonder where I had disappeared for so long," Janet said. "John will safely get you out of the city. If any of his ghosts come your way, he will try to hold them off to let you escape. Don't try to fight. It is very important that you safely reach your friends and bring back help. We are all counting on you and your friends. In case John has to block a threat to your life, please go to your friends first. The priests are in a town called Virgin Town. If John lives, he will see you there when you come back with your friends. Take care, both of you, and good luck with your mission."

"Bye for now. We will be back soon, and the world will watch his demise," Mary said.

"Bye. See you soon." Janet looked around and hurried out of the tunnel.

John walked in front, and Mary watched his footsteps and followed him. When they were nearly out of the city, Mary heard some noise. She looked at the ground and John wrote, "Go as fast as you can. Somebody is following us. It's one of his ghosts. I will try to stop him. Don't waste any time and go now. Bye."

Mary dashed for the escape. She didn't look back for about a hundred kilometers and didn't have a clue what had happened to John. Her friends were waiting in the forest in Canada. It was getting dark, and she was not back yet. They all looked very worried and were getting impatient. Happiness returned to their sad faces when at last they saw Mary coming toward them. Ruby introduced Mary to the new vampires. Mary told them everything she found out and the help they could expect. Their excitement and confidence increased when they were told that bin Laden would be alone and they could take him when he was far away from the city to decrease his chances of getting any help. For an effective attack, they started planning and preparing for the fight in detail.

They decided to go to Virgin Town and wait there for bin Laden to come out from the city. They left the forest and went through the fields, hunting in the crops for animals to feed on. It took them ten days to reach near the town. They decided to send one person to find out about the priests. Mary volunteered and went to learn about the priests and John. As she entered the town, she noticed a spirit was following her. She knew it was John. He wrote on the dirt, "After you escaped I fought with bin Laden's ghost. It was alone and I was able to escape. I came here and waited for a few days. I will be going back there today, and Janet will meet me in a few days. I hope she will have some good news for us. Just wait outside the town and I will come there to see you when I am back. I will also take you to the priests." Mary came back and informed the vampires about John's instructions.

It was 10:00 p.m., and the night was very dark because of the thick clouds. Bin Laden sat on a rocking chair in a room, deep in thought. Two bodyguard ghosts stood in front of the room.

"Ali, can you please call Janet? Tell her it is urgent and to come straight away," he said to one of the guard ghosts.

"OK, boss," Ali replied and walked to the nearby room, where Janet was in a deep sleep.

"Janet, wake up, boss is calling you," Ali said in a loud voice.

"What is it? He has never disturbed me before while I'm asleep," Janet groggily asked.

"I don't know. He has asked for you urgently, and you must come with me at once."

"OK, let me wash up." Janet got up from the bed and walked toward the bathroom.

"No, no time for washing up. Just come like that. He looks very worried."

"OK, let's go." Janet got worried herself and went with Ali.

"Yes, dear, is everything all right?" Janet asked bin Laden.

"Yes, everything is all right. Sorry to bother you. I have to go somewhere for two weeks. I will leave the day after tomorrow in the evening, and please look after the things around here. As you are my queen, you have to take this responsibility in my absence."

"OK, my lord. But please tell me where you are going so if anything goes wrong I can send the others to look for you. You know you have been attacked many times. There are a lot of power-hungry ghosts and the government looking for any possible way to eliminate you."

"Sorry, babe, I can't tell anybody. Don't worry too much. I will disguise myself as an ordinary human by covering myself with some clothes and a hat. Nobody else knows that I will be leaving except you. I will leave at night in the dark so there is less chance of anybody recognizing me."

"OK, as you say. I won't insist on you telling me. Don't worry about here," Janet assured him.

"Good night. You can go and sleep now. I won't disturb you again. Lock your door from inside if you want to," bin Laden said.

"OK, darling, good night." Janet kissed him and left in a hurry. She locked her room from inside. She went to her bathroom and climbed out through the window. She knew that most of bin Laden's ghosts were busy entertaining themselves with the girls. She was supposed to see John in the morning. She couldn't wait any longer because she knew John always came in the tunnel at night. Rushing outside, she went inside the tunnel. John was already there. They discussed everything and were very excited that they had enough power to face bin Laden. With thousands of ghosts and hundreds of vampires, bin Laden would not have any chance of escaping. They didn't want to repeat the previous mistakes.

"Make sure you tell them to get their force together before attacking him," Janet advised.

"Don't worry. I have already spoken to the friendly ghosts. They are already waiting about fifty kilometers outside the city. Some of the ghosts will follow him without being detected and inform the others. The spy ghosts are everywhere outside the city. They will know which direction he goes," John said.

"I will ask Naughty Bitch and the donkey ghost to follow him. He can't hide from them, and they will know wherever he goes. I think we will let him go all the way to find whatever he is looking for. That way we will know something about the mystery thing that scares him so much," Janet said.

"Yes, that's a good idea. We will attack him when he is coming back. I will inform everybody involved in the mission. That way we will have enough time to plan the attack, and if we are lucky we might get help from that mystery thing if he finds it," John said.

"Yes, clever man. It is his last days now. OK, I have to go now. If somebody suspects that I'm not in my room, I'll be dead. See you, and good luck."

"Bye, see you. I also don't have much time left to spread the news," John said and disappeared in the tunnel. Janet rushed back and went to her room. She felt relieved that nobody had seen her leaving and coming back. John informed the friendly ghosts outside and then left for Virgin Town to get the priests and vampires. As planned, they wanted to assemble around fifty kilometers out of the city. They wanted to let bin Laden go through safely and attack him as he was returning. That way they would know which way he would be coming from. John reached Virgin Town and went straight to the vampires. They all gathered around, and a meeting was held to plan the attack properly. Ruby stood and started explaining.

"I think you all know by now that he is very powerful. His energy can be drained only through his ass. I think all the male ghosts and male vampires should focus their attack on his ass. Those males who have erection problems should focus on fighting him from the front. Those with erections like steel and big cocks should aim to penetrate his asshole. The females will attack him from the front and also distract him by flashing their sexy assets and seducing him with erotic dances. I think we all should get naked before the attack so we don't waste any time getting naked during the fight. Ladies, make him as horny as you can. This will distract him, and his brain will get corrupted with sex. Ladies, come up with some innovative ways to seduce him."

Billy, the leader of the new vampire group, stood up and raised his hand. "I support Ruby's idea. It will make our job easier. There is nothing wrong in letting a dying ghost enjoy its last moments. So do whatever you can and enjoy the sexy fight. I urge the male vampires not to have sex or play with your dicks until the fight is over. Preserve your energy, which will help your dicks stay up like a rocket. Just concentrate on his hole and penetrate it like a rocket."

"But boss, his ass is old and wrinkled. What if the dicks don't want to go in? Or what if he shits?" a funny-looking vampire asked.

158

"Don't worry too much about that. I will be giving erection pills to every male before the fight. If he shits, just imagine it as some delicious pudding."

"Ha, Ha, ha, ha, ha, ha, ha." They all couldn't stop laughing.

"What if he farts? I think he has done that before," another vampire said.

"Don't let him fart twice. As soon as he opens his hole to fart, put the holeblocker inside."

"Boss, what is the holeblocker?" a stupid-looking vampire asked.

"Come over here and bend over. You will know when I block your hole," Billy answered.

"OK, enough jokes for now. Are you ready for the fight?" Ruby asked.

"Yes, we are," everybody answered in a loud voice.

"Are your cocks ready to fuck his asshole?"

"Yes, they are," the males answered.

"Are you ready to take my cock in your tight assholes? I have big surprises for you all," came a thunderous and bone-chilling voice. Everybody looked around. They couldn't see anybody, but the voice sounded like bin Laden's.

"It's him. He is here and invisible. I can sense him. Take your positions. I think John has betrayed us. Remember what I told you. Aim for his ass. Girls, please do what we planned before," Ruby shouted. She suspected John led them there and betrayed them. It seemed he had gone away and didn't write or give any indication to alert them. The panic-stricken and confused vampires had no time to plan any actions. They looked around to fight something that they couldn't see.

"But we can't see him. How can we aim for his hole?" one of the vampires asked.

"Boys, aim for their holes and get some energy," bin Laden instructed his ghosts. "First, take the male vampires with erections. Make sure nobody escapes. I have been looking for them for a long time."

"It's not a fair fight. If you are brave enough, reveal yourself and your friends. Become visible and fight like real warriors. Don't be pussies by hiding yourself. We are not scared of you and have come prepared to die here," Billy the vampire leader shouted in order to entice the ghosts to become visible.

"We will fight like warriors. We want to have fun and record everything on cameras. Get ready to be fucked by ghosts. Here we come." Bin Laden had no intention of remaining invisible while fighting the vampires. Billy and the vampires felt relieved and got ready to fight. Some of the vampires felt scared when hundreds of ghosts and bin Laden became visible. The vampires were surrounded from every side, and there was no escape route. Bin Laden came well prepared, and the vampires knew it was a setup. Feeling betrayed and angry, they were all thinking about finding John and killing him. They had expected help from the friendly ghosts as promised and thought bin Laden would be alone to attack. But now they were left to defend themselves not only from bin Laden but also hundreds of his sex-hungry ghosts.

"Surprise, surprise, I saved you some time and energy by coming here myself. You don't have to travel to kill me. I've become visible to enjoy the fight, and you should also oblige by not running away," bin Laden said as he stood in front of his enemies. He didn't seem scared and in fact looked very delighted to find all the vampires together for killing.

"No one will run away. We won't let you run away either, asshole. We will not repeat the mistake made by Ruby and her friends. This time we will be using real cocks to mutilate your ass. You can squeeze as hard as you want, but today hundreds of real cocks will be penetrating your ass," Billy shouted.

"I heard the girls were going to get naked. Go ahead, make my day, get naked and show some ass and boobies. I don't want you to think that you didn't have a chance to execute your plan to seduce me. I also want to test to what extent I can control my sexual urges." Bin Laden gave the female vampires an opportunity to undress.

"Get naked, girls. Do your best and it might work in our favor," Ruby told the girls, and they quickly took off their clothes. There were more than one hundred of them.

"Wow, it feels like I am in heaven. Girls, I don't want to hurt you. I just want to make wild love to your magnificently sexy and charming bodies. You are all so hot. It will be a waste of so many hot pussies and juicy boobs. As before, I offer you a choice to surrender and submit to my will. As a goodwill gesture, I will let your male friends walk out from here without any harm. You become mine and the males can go home. It's your choice. Otherwise they will also end up being fucked in the ass and dead," bin Laden said.

"Do you think we look frightened and vulnerable? You should be the one surrendering, and we would be very gentle while we fuck your ass. We will even let you live if you just let us suck the energy out of you. The ball is in your court now. Be

161

rational and pity your asshole," Billy replied. All the vampires took positions to attack, and the females flashed their hot assets to make the ghosts weak. The male vampires encircled the females while they started fondling each other as if they were all lesbians. They could see bin Laden and his ghosts drooling over their erotic moves and lusting for their bodies.

"I will be coming for your ass first, lady boy. Boys, don't fall for their seductive ways. Kill the males first, and then as a reward you can keep whichever female you want to fuck. Leave those three bitches for me." Bin Laden pointed toward Billy and then asked his boys to control themselves. He wanted Nicky, Mary, and Ruby for himself. The ghosts marched toward the vampires and attacked. The female vampires' erotic and charming moves had some effect, but the ghosts were able to control their lust. The ghosts attacked the males first while defending themselves from the females. The vampires got overwhelmed by the attack and fought back vigorously to defend their lives. The ghosts pounced on the vampires like lions on their prey. This time bin Laden had about thirty powerful ghosts defending his backside. He didn't have to worry about anybody attacking from behind. He used his power to take on the powerful male vampires first. He went for Billy. "Here I am, lady boy. Defend your ass." Bin Laden overpowered Billy easily and inserted his cock inside his ass. "Don't you want to fuck my ass now? You are a pussy and have no strength to fight." Billy's energy was sucked, and he fell on the ground. Bin Laden picked him up, twisted his neck, and broke it. Seeing their leader down, the vampires felt very vulnerable in front of so many ghosts. The male vampires' cocks became soft from the fear of bin Laden. Some ghosts were also down, but they had managed to take almost all the male vampires first. Seeing this, Ruby decided to tell the females to retreat. She knew continuing the fight would be like committing suicide.

"Run away and save your lives if you can. No point fighting now. They are too many. We must save as many vampires as we can," Ruby shouted. Hearing her, the remaining vampires started fleeing. The ghosts followed them and captured as many as they could. Ruby, Mary, and Nicky fought hard to help the others escape. They were powerful enough to take on the other ghosts, but they were no match for bin Laden's extraordinary power. About forty vampires escaped from one side in a group. Ruby, Mary, and Nicky also wasted no time and escaped. Bin Laden and his ghosts chased them, but they disappeared in the forest. The ghosts came back and raped the captured female vampires and the injured male vampires for hours. After brutally torturing and killing them, the ghosts hanged the dead vampires from trees to warn others. They video recorded everything to broadcast to the world and set an example for others to think twice before making any plans to attack bin Laden. Victorious and loaded with fresh energy from the vampires, bin Laden and his ghosts marched toward the capital city and attacked the friendly ghosts who were waiting for the vampires to join them in attacking bin Laden. The surprise attack left the friendly ghosts panicked and vulnerable. Astonished and demoralized, the friendly ghosts couldn't withstand the terrifying onslaught of bin Laden and his ghosts. Only a few of them were able to escape. The rest got their powers sucked out and were slaughtered like pigs. By dividing the friendly ghosts' and vampires' power, bin Laden almost wiped them out. Jubilant and triumphant, bin Laden broadcast everything to scare the shit out of any would-be attackers in the future. Watching the crushing and humiliating defeat of so many vampires and ghosts, the public and the government felt helpless and disappointed. Every hope of getting rid of the dreadful and horrifying ghost died with their defeat.

The remaining ghosts and vampires couldn't believe that bin Laden knew everything about their attack. They all suspected John and wanted to finish him first.

Ruby and the other vampires went back to the Canadian forest. They were brokenhearted and devastated by the loss of over a hundred vampires' lives. Bin Laden and his ghosts had become too powerful and unbeatable. As the vampires sat, they heard somebody's footsteps on the leaves. They couldn't see anybody and, fearing the ghosts, got up quickly to defend themselves. Mary remembered that only John used to walk like that in front of her.

"Is that John?" she shouted.

"Yes," he wrote on the wet dirt.

"What do you want now? Haven't you caused enough destruction?"

"I didn't do that. They followed me there. I think Janet betrayed us to be his queen. I was caught also but was able to escape when everybody got busy fighting. When I was with you in the meeting, they grabbed me from behind, and because they were invisible, nobody could see it. I saw you escaping and followed you here. If I was with them, I would have brought them here with me. I was very careful this time so nobody could follow me. How can I betray you after what that asshole did with me and destroyed my life? I've got to go back and find out everything," John explained.

"I think we can believe you. Where can we find that girl?"

"She is always with him in the building. She manages his affairs when he is not there. I have to go there using a different way his time. They know about me and will finish me off if they find me."

"How can we get in the building without being noticed? We want to get our hands on that bitch," Ruby said.

"I will find out whatever I can. Please shift to another place and I will meet one of you outside this forest."

"Yes, we will. We don't feel safe here anymore."

John said good-bye to them and left. When he went near the city, he met one of the surviving friendly ghosts and learned about most of the friendly ghosts being wiped out. He felt extremely bereaved and enraged. He vowed to kill Janet himself. He saw a pub outside the city and went inside. The brutal killings of the vampires and friendly ghosts were repeatedly shown on the pub's TV. Bin Laden ordered their broadcast to scare the world to never think about attacking him and his ghosts. In a separate live broadcast, John noticed that Janet was not being shown in the building as she usually was. When he asked one of the friendly ghosts, he told him that since the attack, Janet and some of the other girls had disappeared from the footage on TV. They were no longer shown as bin Laden's favorite girls. John understood that bin Laden must have caught Janet giving his secrets away and killed her.

Chapter 7

In the White House, bin Laden had locked Janet and the other CIA girls in one room. He was busy fighting the ghosts, and his ghosts guarded the room. The girls were tortured and sleep deprived. Being imprisoned without any food and enduring debilitating pain brought suicidal thoughts to their minds. But they were put on suicide watch by bin Laden. Two ghosts always guarded them. They begged for a quick death, but nobody took pity on their unbearable suffering. The time came to interrogate them. Bin Laden went inside the room alone and sat on a chair.

"Hello, bitches. You thought I was very stupid and trusted you. I never trust Americans. I knew from the beginning that you were government agents. I even knew that Janet could see ghosts. But we ghosts can become invisible and go anywhere and hear anything without being noticed. My ghosts always followed you carefully and knew everything you were doing. I gave you only that information that I wanted delivered to the American government. I used you to get to the vampires and the ghosts. How stupid you are to think that I trusted you," bin Laden said and laughed.

The girls felt stupid and didn't utter any word. Their fate was about to be decided by bin Laden. Their eyes were swollen and bodies bloodied from the torture. Bin Laden kicked and slapped them.

Janet begged for mercy. "Please, sir, we're very sorry. We were very stupid to think that we could harm a mighty ghost. Please forgive us and give us a quick death to end our suffering. We have given you great sex. Please, sir, think about those sexual encounters and take pity on us. We're not asking you to spare our lives. We just want an easy death."

"You bitches, I won't kill you myself. I want to make an example of you in public so nobody will dare to cross my path again. You conspired to kill me, and you expect sympathy in return? How can you think that I will have any mercy on you, bloody cunts? Bring the unfaithful bitches outside the building. I want them to be fed to the dogs alive in front of the whole world," bin Laden told the guards and went outside. The guards dragged the screaming girls outside. Bin Laden sat on his golden chair.

"Strip them and take the skin from their bodies, especially from their cunts and boobs," bin Laden ordered. His ghosts quickly followed the instructions and skinned the screaming girls. Viewers screamed in front of their screens. Shivers of fear went through their spines. The world military powers and governments felt helpless and couldn't do anything. The American president and other politicians wept relentlessly. The entire world thirsted for bin Laden's blood while praying for a miracle to make him pay for his brutality and inhumane treatment of the girls. People sulked everywhere in anger, but nobody could do anything to rescue the girls.

"Well done, comrades." Bin Laden ordered their torture level to be increased. "Now rub salt on their bodies. Take your time and do a proper job. We're not in a hurry. I want everybody to enjoy the show. This is just the beginning. I do not want them to die. I want them to be tortured here for weeks." The girls' screams broke every viewer's heart, and a lot of them turned off their devices. His ruthless ghosts followed the orders and enjoyed rubbing salt on the defenseless girls.

"Now bring the hungry dogs. Hang them high enough so the hungry dogs can eat only their feet. Make sure they do not die. We want to feed them alive to the dogs for a few weeks," bin Laden ordered again. His ghosts followed his orders and brought everything needed to hang them high so the dogs could jump to reach only to the girls' bleeding feet. The ghosts tied the ropes on the girls' arms and hanged them. About twenty hungry dogs pounced on them in front of the cameras. The dogs jumped while trying to reach their bleeding feed.

"Bang, boom, bang, bang, bang…bang…bang…" Suddenly the sound of gunfire diverted everybody's attention. Somebody had fired from a rooftop into the hanging girls' hearts. The girls became motionless and died on the spot. Their unbearable cries fell silent. Somebody unable to watch them suffering had the guts to end their plight.

"Go, go, get that bastard who has dared to do this. I want him or her alive. I want the shooter to be tortured like the girls." Bin Laden shouted to the ghosts to capture the shooter alive. His ghosts dashed toward the direction from where the shots were fired. When they reached the rooftop, another shot was heard. The shooter, an army man in civilian dress, had shot himself dead. He didn't want to be captured alive and tortured like the girls.

People everywhere became so scared they didn't even dare to think against the mighty ghost in case somebody read their thoughts. John saw everything live on TV and rushed to the forest to inform the vampires. Now the picture was clear to him what had happened. He met the vampires and explained everything. They also understood and didn't know what to do next. Bin Laden became even more powerful and dangerous after sucking the energy out of the vampires and friendly ghosts. The vampires felt miserable and too weak to confront bin Laden. They didn't have any hope left.

"Did you find out where he goes alone? Maybe we ought to find that out. It must be very important," Ruby said to John.

"No, nobody knows about that. Naughty Bitch and the donkey ghost were supposed to follow him, but he tricked everybody by telling a lie that he was about to go to that secret place. Instead he attacked us. Now, next time we won't be sure when he will be going. I will ask Naughty Bitch and the donkey ghost to always stick to him and find out about it. He can't do anything to them," John wrote on a notebook with a pen that the vampires had provided to communicate with him.

"Can't they kill him? They are always near him, and there must be something they should be able to do."

"No, they can't. Because they are animal ghosts, they can't harm the human ghosts. They can only talk, watch, and listen. They irritate bin Laden a lot but can't really do anything more than that. We can only hope for some miracle to happen. The government and the CIA have brought a monk from Tibet. He has left alone to search for something more powerful than bin Laden. It has been many months, and nobody has heard from him or seen him. The government also has stopped expecting any hope from him. The government was told that he was a very holy and pious monk. He could see and talk to the ghosts also," John wrote.

"Bin Laden might have found about him and killed him," Mary suggested.

"Maybe, but if he had killed him, he would have made it known to the world to taunt the American government. All we can do is sit and watch. It is out of our hands now. I will hang around the city and will let you know if anything happens," John wrote.

"Take care of yourself, and keep a safe distance from the ghosts. You are the only connection we have to the city to get information," Nicky advised.

"I will. OK, I have to go now. I'll be back if I find anything. See you," John wrote.

"Bye. Take care of yourself," they all said in farewell to John.

John left the forest and went toward Virgin Town. The government needed to find out if somebody else had the ability to see and talk to ghosts as Janet did. They had lost any hope of finding the monk alive. Everybody became nervous and scared. The politicians feared for their lives. They knew if bin Laden found out about their secret place, nothing could stop him from assassinating them. It was decided to split the politicians into two groups to keep them at different places. If one group was wiped out, the other one would still be able to govern. The security agencies also kept duplicates of the president to confuse the ghosts. Only a few secret agents knew where the real president was living.

As John reached the forest near Virgin Town, he heard a human voice. He went toward where the voice was coming from. As he approached, it was clear to him that somebody was praying in a different language. He walked farther and saw a monk sitting in a trance state and praying. The monk continued his prayers with his eyes closed. John sat in front of the monk to wait. He knew it was a Tibetan monk but was not sure if it was the one the government believed could do something about finishing off bin Laden. After praying for about an hour more, the monk opened his eyes.

"Hi there, I was waiting for you. You are John's spirit, the guy who woke up bin Laden's spirit," the monk said.

"Yes, but how do you know all this? I have never met you before. I am very sorry. I made that mistake, and now the whole world is going to pay for it. I got greedy and committed this sin. It's my fault," said John. He understood that the monk had extraordinary abilities and could see him.

"It is not your fault. It was meant to be like that. You just did what you were supposed to do. Bin Laden's spirit is doing what it is supposed to do. Humans make mistakes, and sometimes we get punished very badly for that. The ego takes over the mind whenever somebody acquires some extraordinary powers. The politicians get greedy to rule the world and have all the powers. They make mistakes, and the ordinary people suffer. The main culprit is the power. When anybody gets it, they can't control it, and sometimes the sins we commit come back to haunt us. Whatever bin Laden is doing while intoxicated by his powers will destroy him one day. What goes around comes around. It is karma, and we all have to suffer for it in one way or other. Nobody has been able to escape the law of karma, and nobody will be able to escape it in the future. It doesn't matter how powerful you are," the pious monk explained.

"Is Your Holiness the monk whom the American government brought from Tibet?" John asked.

"Yes, I am. It is not the government that brought me here. It's the karma. I was meant to be here and wake up something that is more powerful than bin Laden. I can't tell you what it is, but you have to write the messages on the city walls that it is coming soon. Write a message to bin Laden that he should be well prepared this time. He should get as many ghosts as he can ready to fight it."

"That means it will be the end of bin Laden," John said excitedly.

"Nothing dies. It is all energy. It is converted from one form to another. Like you have become a ghost, and after your ghostly life ends your energy will be converted into something else. It will keep on going forever. I can't tell you what will happen. You will see it with your own ghostly eyes. You can go now, and I have to keep praying for another ten days. Please don't come back here and don't tell anybody about it," the monk said.

"No, I won't. I promise." John said. John rushed out of the forest. He went to Virgin Town and wrote on the walls. Then he traveled to the city. A ghost told him that bin Laden had gone somewhere alone and Naughty Bitch and the donkey ghost had followed him. Bin Laden had tried to chase them away, but they only pretended that they went back to the city.

The ghost saw Naughty Bitch sniffing and going after bin Laden. He was sure that bin Laden was going to the secret place where he went before. It had been a few days since he left. John waited for night and wrote on the city walls what the monk had told him. The next morning, the world read it online and on TV screens. People stopped going to work all over the world and glued themselves to their screens. They didn't want to miss even one moment of the action. Bin Laden's ghosts looked worried, and they had no way to contact him. Nobody knew where he had gone. The ghosts and the people started thinking that he might have known about the threat and chickened out without a fight. The vampires also found out about the news from the old farmer's TV. They didn't want to miss the action, and it was a good chance for them to help and get revenge on bin Laden. They recognized John's handwriting and were confident that he must have found out something important. They didn't waste any time and marched toward the city.

Bin Laden's ghosts covered every corner of the city and went on the roofs of skyscrapers so they could keep an eye out for the coming danger. After one week a little dust storm outside the city scared the hell out of bin Laden's ghosts. If bin Laden was there, they wouldn't have felt so scared. It was afternoon and the ghosts sitting on skyscrapers saw dust rising in the sky from one direction. The dust kept coming nearer. They couldn't tell what was causing it. Somebody had pointed one of the cameras to that direction, and the world's public could also see it. The ghosts knew something fast moving was marching toward the city. The fear of something unknown made them feel as if they were the prey and a fierce lion was coming to hunt them. The dust entered the city streets and then came in front of the capitol building. Everybody was freaking out. The public grew anxious to know if it was the thing bin Laden always feared. The ghosts stood a safe distance away to watch the thing. As the dust settled down, something in red moved like a twister. There was panic among the ghosts, but the public got excited that finally something was scaring the shit out of bin Laden's ghosts. As the dust settled more, it became clear that there were two red things dancing and jumping very fast.

"Hello, people, we are back in a new avatar."

One of bin Laden's ghosts standing nearby recognized them and shouted to inform the others. "Bloody hell, they are the fucking bitches, Naughty Bitch and the donkey ghost." All the ghosts had almost crapped and now felt relieved. Naughty Bitch and the donkey ghost saw the anger and frustration in their eyes and didn't stop irritating them. Because something red was rubbed on their bodies, everybody could see and hear them. The ghosts chased them around but stopped after a while, realizing that it was no use.

"These two bitches must have asked somebody to write on the walls to scare the crap out of us. Nobody else would dare to do that," another ghost suggested.

"Yes, I think you are right," another ghost answered. They all agreed it was just a prank. They became careless and started enjoying the girls. By that time, the vampires had arrived outside the city. They knew it couldn't be a prank because the writing was from John. At night, Naughty Bitch met John and told him the secret everybody wanted to know.

"He is looking for a holy man who is going to awaken a very powerful spirit that can't be beaten by him. This spirit has very extraordinary powers, and some holy man in Afghanistan has told bin Laden that if awakened it is unlikely that he could survive its onslaught. He went town to town in search of the holy man. I think the holy man knows everything about him and knows he is looking for him. I have seen the frustration and fear in his eyes. He wants to kill the holy man in order to stop the spirit from being awakened. It looks as if he is running out of time. He ditched us by crossing a very big river that we were not able to cross. We had to come back, and while returning we found this special substance that can make us visible. It was in a forest. We have brought some with us to try it on bin Laden to see if he could be seen while he is invisible."

"Thank you very much for all your information and help. I have to go and give this information to some of my friends," John said and ran away excitedly with a big smile on his face. Naughty Bitch sniffed out that John was hiding something from her. She didn't say anything and went back. John came outside the city and met the vampires. He didn't tell Naughty Bitch or the vampires that he met the holy man and knew what was coming. As he had promised the holy man, he deflected their questions about it. He informed the vampires of what Naughty Bitch had told him. They all got excited and decided to wait outside the city so they could also join the fight to avenge their friends' deaths. They stayed alert and hidden in case bin Laden came back. They went in small groups to the forest nearby to feed on the animals.

The sky was clear in the morning, and the sun was shining as if it was some special occasion. The ghosts were patrolling in and outside the city for security. A ghost sitting on the tallest skyscraper saw a black cloud moving toward the city. It looked strange because the sky was otherwise clear and this cloud appeared from nowhere. It suddenly was storming toward the city. As it got nearer, it became blacker, bigger, and scarier. The ghost saw a face with two frightening and dreadful eyes in the cloud. He immediately remembered the writings on the wall.

"Get ready. Something very dangerous is coming toward us," he shouted, and all the ghosts became alert and took to the high-rise buildings to see. The vampires outside the city also saw it. It was coming from the same direction Naughty Ghost and the donkey ghost had come. The camera was still pointed to that direction, and the whole world watched the cloud moving toward the city. Soon dark clouds covered the city. A scary-eyed monster emerged and landed in front of the White House. It was visible to everybody. It turned its fiery eyes and scary face in every direction and took notice of the ghosts. It was some kind of spirit in a suit and a tie.

"Hello, assholes, I'm Benjamin, the ex-president of United States of America, and I have come to defend the honor of my country and my people. Where is the motherfucker bin Laden? Has he run away like a pussy?"

The ghosts had realized that the writings on the wall were not a prank. They were the truth, and the president's spirit wanted them to know something powerful was coming. The ghosts got ready to attack the spirit with full force. Hundreds of ghosts descended around the spirit and encircled it. The vampires came in the city and waited on some high-rise buildings to watch. They didn't want to take any risks and wanted to see the power of the president's spirit.

"Listen to me, fucking old man, fuck off if you want to be safe," one of the ghosts warned the president's spirit. "Our mighty boss does not have to fight an asshole like you. We are enough for you."

"Don't run like pussies when I attack. Get ready, mother-fuckers." The spirit went up about fifty meters into the sky and started turning at high speed like a tornado. Then it descended on the ghosts and punched and kicked them with lightning speed. The ghosts didn't know what to do and where to strike. Before they could see anything, they started falling like flies sprayed with insecticide. The spirit was too fast and powerful for them. They couldn't hit it even once. Watching all this from the buildings, the vampires also pounced on the ghosts. In about twenty minutes, half of the ghosts lay injured and dead on the ground. The other half fled wherever they could. The spirit and the vampires took down as many as they could. About sixty of them escaped. The vampires came back and killed the injured ones also. The people danced all over the world and knew that bin Laden's end was near. Even ordinary people came running into the city to attack the ghosts. They cheered the president and the vampires.

"Thanks, and welcome Mr. President," Ruby said and hugged Benjamin. "Finally, America's savior has come. These assholes had ruined America and the lives of its people. They had challenged and taken over the world's superpower." Tears of happiness ran from everybody's eyes, and the fear of bin Laden took flight from their brains and hearts. Military helicopters and the army moved into the city to welcome the president. The White House was empty, and the army generals invited the president's spirit inside. He was offered the president's chair. All the American cities and towns erupted in celebrations. The humiliating defeat of bin Laden's army of ghosts had excited the public so much that they forgot for the night that bin Laden's ghost itself was still alive and kicking. People drank and danced the whole night. They had no fear of bin Laden anymore and were confident that President Benjamin could easily take him out. They even suspected that bin Laden knew about it and fled before the president's arrival. The army was sent to look for the monk who had awakened the president's spirit. The government wanted to honor him. It was decided that the current president and other politicians should remain at the secret locations until bin Laden's threat was removed. Phone calls and Internet messages came from the public. They wanted to hear something from President Benjamin. The government announced that the president would address the public next morning at 9:00 a.m.

The vampires were also invited inside the White House to honor their sacrifices. The remaining friendly ghosts were also invited. They were America's new heroes and celebrities. John didn't feel like coming and kept away from the White House. His old memories came back to haunt him, and he wanted to see bin Laden suffer. He didn't want to celebrate anything until then. The soldiers who were sent to look for the monk came back empty-handed and handed over a note found at the place where the monk prayed. Written on a piece of wood was the message, "Please do not look for me. Dear President Benjamin, please don't overestimate your powers and underestimate your opponent. Ego kills everything. He is no ordinary ghost. He hasn't run away. He will be coming back soon. Be prepared."

The president looked serious and told the army to take all the civilians out of the city. He told everybody that his holiness was right and he respected him very much. The preparations began to evacuate the public from the city. People turned on their computers, tablets, smartphones, and TVs to watch the action live. The public was anxious and desperate to know what would happen. Nobody knew anything and played the waiting game. The cameras were turned in every direction to see bin Laden's ghost coming. The president watched the security cameras because only he could see bin Laden if he was invisible.

In a small town outside the capital, a monk entered a police station. He looked worried and desperate.

"I need to speak to somebody higher up in security. It's very urgent, and please don't waste any time. Connect me at once," the monk said.

The officer recognized the monk. "Yes, Your Holiness, I think I know who you are. All the police stations have been instructed to look for you. Just a moment, please. They have given us a number if we find you." The officer dialed the number straight away.

Somebody on the other side answered the phone. "Hi, this is the CIA chief. How can I help you?"

"Sir, I'm from the Hampton police station. I have the monk you've been looking for with me here. Just a second—I will give the phone to him. He wants to speak to you."

"Hello," the monk said.

"Yes, Your Holiness, I can hear you. What is it?" the CIA boss asked.

"Bin Laden's ghost is not heading toward the capital city. It is heading to Chicago, to a particular hidden place. It has found out that some important politicians are hiding there."

"Thank you very much, sir. Please stay there. I will call you after two minutes. I have to make an important call first." The CIA chief put down the phone and informed the Secret Service agents and the president's ghost in the capital city. There was panic among the security forces, the army, and the police. The president's ghost immediately left for Chicago. The president's ghost also could fly when invisible. It could also jump and run at very high speeds like bin laden when visible. The vampires followed him. There was not much time left, and the army moved in all over the city. People panicked and started fleeing the city to be safe. Rumors spread quickly through Chicago that bin Laden was coming there. The politicians were being brought out of a secret building to be flown to a safe place when all of a sudden dark clouds descended on the city. The current president and some of the ex-presidents were among the politicians being shifted. America's worst fears came true. Bin Laden touched down in front of the politicians to block their escape. His appearance had changed. His eyes and face became so fierce that anybody who looked at him froze in fear. They didn't know what to do, and a lot of them crapped in their pants.

"You motherfuckers, you think you can hide from me? Your last days have come, and there is no safe place in this world for you," bin Laden roared. As he took some steps forward to attack, something heavy landed behind him. The earth shook and bin Laden got a big surprise.

"Stop where you are, cock sucker. One step forward and you're finished." President Benjamin stood behind bin Laden ready to attack.

Bin Laden turned back to face Benjamin. "You were next on my list after I had finished here. It looks as if you want to die first, motherfucker. I'm not like other ghosts you can play with easily."

"I've come fully prepared. You've caused enough destruction. Save your ass if you can," president Benjamin roared.

The two powerful ghosts pounced on each other. They turned into giant and scary ghosts as never before seen. Buildings started to crumble when they hit each other. The army took advantage of their fight and moved out the politicians quietly. The president had killed the other ghosts easily, but bin Laden was a much tougher foe. He was equally powerful and lethal. The fight of two giant ghosts leveled everything around them. People ran for cover. Benjamin was almost winning the fight when bin Laden hit his stomach with the force of millions of ghosts. Benjamin fell backward and struggled to get up. Bin Laden saw the army moving the politicians into a helicopter parked on a skyscraper. As his attention got diverted, Benjamin hit him from behind. Bin Laden fell forward and quickly turned around and kicked Benjamin very hard. They were again at each other's throats. The sound of helicopters flying off took bin Laden's attention away from the fight. Benjamin came to attack him again, but bin Laden dashed for the helicopters. Benjamin ran after him and wrestled him to the ground, continuously kicking and punching him. Bin Laden gathered his strength, threw Benjamin off, and hit him in the stomach again.

"I will see you in the capital city. Wait for me. I have to take care of some other business first. I promise, I will see you soon," bin Laden said and kicked Benjamin three more times. Benjamin fell backward. Bin Laden stormed after the helicopters. About thirty helicopters were in the air. The army's plan was to confuse bin Laden about which one the politicians were in. Bin Laden smashed the tanks and big guns firing at him. The vampires also stepped in front of him to stop him. But they were too weak. He killed a few of them and went for the helicopters. By this time the helicopters were far away and flying to all different directions. Bin Laden went after the two that he thought carried the current and ex-presidents. He caught up to them and brought them down but was disappointed when he saw pigs inside. The pilots had already jumped out with parachutes. Bin Laden went in another direction to follow other helicopters.

The vampires came to Benjamin and helped him up.

"Are you all right, sir?" Ruby asked.

"Yes, I am. The damn thing is very powerful. I thought it would be like child's play to finish him off. His holiness was right—I underestimated my opponent. We have to be well prepared for next time. I'm sure he will turn up in the capital city to fight me."

"We will also try to help you. This time we will not run away," Mary said.

"I think with your help, I would be able to eliminate him. Let's go. We don't have much time. The politicians seem to be safe now. He won't be able to reach the other helicopters now," Benjamin said.

Bin Laden followed the helicopters but failed to capture any more. He became really pissed off at the Benjamin ghost. He had almost succeeded in his mission to finish the politicians, but the ghost thwarted it. He decided to go back to Chicago but was disappointed again because Benjamin and the vampires had already gone. He went inside the government secret building to find any useful information. He tried to turn on the computers, but they were programmed to shut down if somebody entered the wrong password. He saw a lot of files lying around on tables. He went through them, but there was nothing important or useful for him.

President Benjamin and the vampires started making plans to attack bin Laden once he was inside the capital city. Bin Laden didn't turn up for a few days. The wait for him was making everybody nervous. The vampires freaked out hearing any noises, thinking it was bin Laden. His ability to be invisible compounded the extremely dangerous situation. They couldn't relax and stayed alert. One week passed without any action. Everybody wondered where bin Laden had disappeared. The situation got very tense. After about ten days, they finally saw something. Dust clouds were rising from all sides of the capital city. The president and the vampires wondered what it was. The sounds of horses galloping toward the city became louder. As the dust settled and the horse riders came nearer, they could be seen through telescopes. The horse riders looked like Taliban ghosts. They numbered in the thousands and surrounded the city. The ghosts formed a circle about five kilometers outside the perimeter of the city. Then bin Laden appeared among them and went to each side as if he was giving some kind of instructions. The public, the government, and even the vampires looked nervous. Nobody expected him to be so well prepared and accompanied by thousands of ghosts.

"Don't worry," Benjamin told the vampires. "Don't look at their numbers. The other ghosts are weak, and I can finish them myself. It is his strategy to just scare and make everybody nervous. It will make us weak. He wants the fear to take over our minds. I also have a surprise for them, which I can't show now."

Benjamin was right. Bin Laden played the waiting game, and it took a toll on the vampires' morale. They looked a bit scared and nervous. They always wore clothes made of a special material which protected them from the sun. The vampires couldn't rest and had to be alert all the time. On the other hand, the Taliban ghosts were seen enjoying and having fun sitting outside the city. They danced and played games to irritate and taunt the people holed up inside. Naughty Bitch and the donkey ghost came inside to provide information about what was happening in bin Laden's camp.

"They are very relaxed and are not in any hurry to attack. They just want to hold you inside for a long time to irritate you all and make you go without food. He knows that the vampires can't go on for long without feeding," Naughty Bitch explained.

After Naughty Bitch and the donkey had gone, Benjamin called all the vampires to meet him inside the White House. He didn't want anybody to hear the plan. They listened to his well-thought-out plan and agreed. It was the only plan that could save them and kill bin Laden. At about 10:00 a.m. the next day, the sky was clear. Benjamin came outside the city and walked toward bin Laden and his ghosts. He stood halfway between the camp and the city, where he could clearly see bin Laden. Bin Laden and his men wondered why he came out alone.

"Boss, I think he wants to commit suicide," one of bin Laden's ghosts said.

"Come on, fight me, I'm here all alone. Don't be a cunt. Come if you have any guts, you piece of shit." Benjamin shouted.

"Motherfucker, have you lost your brain? If you want to commit suicide, I won't stop you. Get ready. I'm coming. Oh yeah, I'm coming, oh yeah, I'm coming," bin Laden said, making a funny face and ridiculing Benjamin.

Benjamin knew how to answer him. "Come, you poofter. You got turned on by seeing an old man. You are really gay. I'll make you come many times when I put my dick inside your ass."

"Nobody will come in between. This is between him and me. Just watch what I do with this old fart."

Bin Laden got angry and attacked Benjamin. Everybody stood back as instructed by bin Laden and watched the fight. They pounced on, kicked, punched, wrestled, back flipped, and threw each other. They were equally powerful, and it seemed no one was winning. They both got hurt fighting. Bin Laden was overtaken by anger, and he started punching and kicking Benjamin harder. Benjamin fell and bin Laden was all over him. Suddenly Benjamin got up and started running toward the city to escape from bin Laden. Watching bin Laden chasing Benjamin, people lost faith in their hero president. Nobody had expected their hero would turn out to be a chicken. Realizing he was winning the fight, bin Laden's spirits were high, and he followed Benjamin inside the city. Benjamin kept running, and bin Laden didn't give up. Once they were in the city center, the trap was sprung. Thousands of cowboy and other friendly ghosts attacked the Taliban ghosts from all sides. It was a big surprise to them. Laughing sarcastically, Benjamin stopped running and faced bin Laden. Bin Laden realized he made a mistake by coming alone inside the city. The vampires surrounded him. They were all wearing strap-on dildos. John was also among them, and bin Laden recognized him. John, Naughty Bitch, and the donkey ghost put on the red powder brought from the forest to become visible to the public and the vampires. They also wanted to sprinkle it on bin Laden so he couldn't hide himself. John was touching his cock to make it erect in order to fuck bin Laden and avenge his rape. The tables were turned on bin Laden, and the public again cheered up. They understood what Benjamin did was right thing to do. The Taliban ghosts were in a fierce fight to save their own asses, and nobody was able to come to bin Laden's aid.

"I didn't lose my brain, asshole. It's you who lost your brains by following me here. I planned all this, and you are trapped now. Now save your ass if you can because every cock in this country is going to rape you. Nobody is here to cover your ass today." Benjamin looked very delighted as his plan had worked.

Bin Laden just made fun of him and didn't seem scared. "Oh, look, I'm shaking with fear, asshole Benjamin. I almost killed you the other day. I went back to finish you there, but you chickened out. Get your ass ready. I'm going to put my monster cock deep inside your ass to suck your power."

"We will see who puts his cock in whose ass. Don't be so sure. Get ready, I'm coming," Benjamin answered. He attacked bin Laden from the front and the vampires attacked from the back. Bin Laden found it hard to defend from both sides. Whenever he overpowered Benjamin, vampires and John aimed for his ass. Whenever bin Laden felt something trying to go inside his ass, his grip on Benjamin became loose. His attention got diverted between fighting Benjamin and saving his ass. He knew how painful it was the last time the vampires inserted a dildo inside. The vampires and John tried to penetrate his ass and ran whenever he turned to attack them. While he ran after them, Benjamin would attack him from behind. Bin Laden became really irritated and didn't know what to do. The vampires had also sprinkled the red powder on him. It took only a few more minutes before Benjamin and the vampires overpowered him. Nobody came to his aid. His ghosts were slaughtered outside the city. Thousands of cowboy ghosts and other friendly ghosts also sacrificed their ghostly lives. Cheers and celebrations erupted in front of the screens when people saw bin Laden's ghost caught alive. Benjamin and the vampires brought him in front of the capitol building to put on a show for the world to watch. Bin Laden was about to be raped and brutalized. The vampires brought a small table and made bin Laden bend over it. Half the vampires held him down by his legs and upper body. Benjamin had his arms twisted at the back and held him tightly.

"Sir, you must suck his power out," Ruby suggested. "You are a powerful ghost, and it will take only two hours to make him very weak. Just fuck him continuously for two hours. It's very important. We can't do it with artificial dildos. If John tries, it could take him up to three days of continuous fucking. He won't be able to go on for that long. If a human tries, it can take up to six months, which is impossible. He has too much energy inside him. It's only you who can do the job. He is still dangerous, and we do not want to repeat the mistake we made last time. He escaped and became very powerful."

"Sorry, I can't do that. I'm not gay. And look at his wrinkly old ass. It won't turn me on. It would be a different story if his ass were as sexy as you girls'. I would be more than happy to fuck your asses."

"Sir, we promise you can fuck our ass as long as you want after you are finished with him. We will gladly take turns to give you the hottest sex you ever had," Mary said.

"Sorry, but it will be very hard. Can't you ask the public to take turns fucking him for six months?" Benjamin asked.

"Please sir, don't waste any time. Just take your little Benjamin out and fuck him. Don't look at his ass. You can look at our sexy butts and imagine you are fucking us. Girls, take off your clothes. We need to help Mr. President get it up. Come on, sir, please. Let me help you. You keep your grip tight on him," Nicky pleaded and then proceeded to take off Benjamin's pants. Benjamin had no choice, and the thought of fucking the girls afterward stopped him from resisting. Mary opened his pants and dropped them down. The girls could hardly control their laughter. They swallowed the laughter in order not to make the president angry. But the public watching the scene burst into laughter. Benjamin's cock was tiny and very soft. His balls were also soft and hung between his legs.

"Don't laugh. What did you expect? I died an old man. I didn't have much sex in old age, and my genitals lost all feeling. You know the saying 'use it or lose it.' That's why I told you to find somebody else. I didn't want to show it in public."

"Don't worry, Mr. President. we are experts in sex. We can make even a dead man's cock stand if we want. Come on, Nicky. You are very good at it. Come suck Mr. President's doodle. Show the world what you can do," Ruby said.

"I'm not going to suck that ugly and tiny thing, bitch. Why don't you do it? I would prefer to die instead."

"Control yourself, Nicky. If we start fighting with each other, bin Laden could escape. I will make the sacrifice. Move aside. I will suck it," Mary said. She moved near Benjamin's cock and touched it with her warm hands. The other vampires and the sexy-looking female agents of the government forces also took off their clothes. They started dancing erotically and flashed their assets to help little Benjamin wake up. Mr. President couldn't believe his eyes, seeing so many girls dancing naked. All his life he had seen only his fat wife naked.

"It's too cold and without any feeling. I will try sucking it. Oh, that tastes like shit. Didn't you ever wash it?" Mary's face looked disgusted from the taste, and she took it out of her mouth. She almost threw up.

"Sorry, sexy, I was alone with my old male friend just before I died. My wife had died by that time. I knew my time was near, and I wanted to enjoy one last fuck before I died. I put it in my friend's ass. He wasn't able to get up or move from the bed because he was too old. He hadn't washed his ass in months. I was horny and I put it inside his ass, but I died from the smell and the look of his dirty ass. Now that smell has stuck with me. It will never go away. It is a punishment for fucking an old and defenseless man. I have to live with it," Benjamin explained.

Mary threw up and moved away. "I can't suck it. The taste of shit is unbearable. I have given it a go. Now somebody else must try."

"Come on, anybody, for America's sake. Any volunteers please. Be patriotic and love your country," Ruby shouted again.

"Why don't you do it first? Then we will try. Show us how patriotic you are," somebody shouted from the girls' crowd.

"Cowards. OK, I will try." Ruby closed her eyes and went for it. She sucked the awfully dirty and smelly tiny Benjamin unwillingly for five minutes. While she sucked, the naked vampires and girls danced and shook their assets so little Benjamin could rise for the occasion. Some girls even started licking each other and sucking boobs to show Mr. Benjamin something extra.

"I felt something. I think it woke up a bit," said Ruby, and when she took it out from her mouth it was hard but only about an inch long. She again put it in her mouth. Some other very sexy girls also tried. Some girls rubbed their hot boobs on Mr. President's back to help. But his willy didn't grow more in size.

"OK, Mr. President, it looks as if it's not going to grow any bigger. Please just try like that. See if you can suck any energy out," Ruby said.

"OK, move away. Don't be scared, Mr. bin Laden. I will be gentle on your ass. It is not going to hurt. Just relax your ass and make things easy for both of us. Do you remember having any injection on your body? It is just going to sting a little like that." Benjamin tried to put it inside bin Laden's ass, and bin Laden laughed loudly.

"Ha, ha, ha, ha, ha, ha. You are tickling me. It's very funny that you think I'm scared of that tiny cock. Even a mouse has one bigger than that. Ha, ha, ha, ha, ha, ha."

"The asshole is enjoying all this. I think his ass is too tight. That's why it can't go in." Benjamin felt a bit embarrassed and tried to find an excuse. Everything was broadcasting live on Internet and TV channels. The whole world was laughing hysterically.

"I didn't tighten my ass, you motherfucker. I'm not worried anymore, and my ass and body are very relaxed. Maybe the men have to strip in front of him and show him their cocks. Maybe try touching his asshole or fucking him in the ass with a real cock first. I think he is gay. Let me try him in his ass. He might be able to suck my energy through his ass. Ha, ha, ha, ha, ha, ha, ha." For a moment everybody forgot the danger and laughed. Some people fell to the ground and tears came out of their eyes. They couldn't stop laughing.

"Shut your mouth, asshole. Otherwise I will put it in your mouth," Benjamin said angrily.

"Put what in my mouth? You don't have anything. Try to suck mine then you will know what a real cock feels like. Ha, ha, ha, ha, ha, ha." Bin Laden again irritated him. The public couldn't control it anymore. Even the vampires lost control and laughed hysterically. Benjamin became enraged and loosened his grip on bin Laden's arms to free his hands and hit him in anger. Bin Laden was waiting for that moment, and all of a sudden he threw everybody away. He didn't waste any time and went for the president's neck. He moved behind the president and held him from the neck. He inserted his cock in the president's ass and started sucking his energy. The vampires tried in vain to intervene, but bin Laden fought them with one hand while holding the president with the other. As he sucked the energy out of him, the president became weaker and bin Laden grew stronger. After he had sucked all the energy out, he let the president's ghost go free. He was too weak and unable to face the mighty ghost. Bin Laden hit him on the head, and the president's ghost fainted and fell on the ground, motionless. The vampires saw this and fled. He caught a few of them and killed them. The others, including Nicky, Mary, and Ruby, escaped. Then he turned his attention to the military and the public. The humans couldn't outrun him, and there were no survivors. Blood ran through the streets like a river. It was so scary and brutal that people turned their devices off and ran for cover as if he was going to jump out and get them through the screens.

Seeing the bloody carnage, the government and the people were devastated. They lost all hope. Their president's soft cock let them down. The government ordered the CIA to look for the monk. The monk was already with the CIA chief, and they brought him to meet the current president. The president, CIA chief, the army generals, and the monk sat in an emergency meeting room.

"Your Holiness, you have provided us with great help," the president said. "We almost nailed the bastard. Now we have heard that Benjamin's ghost is too weak and bin Laden has imprisoned him in the capital city. Bin Laden's powers have increased and turned him into the most lethal weapon of mass destruction. I have also heard that he has acquired some additional abilities that he didn't have before. We can't do anything else without Your Holiness's help. Please help us."

"I have tried my best. Benjamin's ghost was the strongest I could find. Now bin Laden has his powers also, and I have to find something that is more powerful than him. In my opinion, there won't be anybody that powerful."

"We have heard that he is looking for some holy man who can awaken something more powerful than him. He wants to find the holy man and kill him. He is very worried about it. Could it be that the holy man he is looking for is Your Holiness?" the CIA chief asked.

"No, it's not me. He hasn't come after me even once. If he is looking for me, I would know it. He can't hide it from me. The holy man he is looking for is one of the Native Americans. I do not know who it is. If there is such a holy man, he is your last hope. You have to find him before bin Laden does." As they spoke, the monk gazed in one direction. "Reveal yourself. There is no danger here," the monk said.

"What is it?" Everybody looked around and got worried.

"They are the female ghosts of the girls bin Laden had killed," the monk answered.

The girls revealed themselves. They were Janet and the female CIA agents turned into ghosts.

"Hi, everybody," the girls greeted them.

"How come we can see you?" the president asked.

"They have acquired this ability from bin Laden because they were sleeping with him for a long time. They are not very powerful. To be powerful like bin Laden, a ghost must be five hundred to six hundred years old, or it must have the ability like him to suck the energy out from somebody," the monk explained.

"Yes, Mr. President, his holiness is right. We can keep an eye on bin Laden, but we can't harm him because we don't have enough power," Janet said.

"Can you follow him the next time he goes looking for that holy man? We must find that holy man. We don't have much time left. Bin Laden can come here any time. He has found us once, and he will find us again," the president said.

"Yes, sir, we will not waste any time, and will be around him," Janet answered.

"I will try again to find anything stronger than him," the monk said.

"OK, friends, try your best so we can get rid of the asshole," said the president as he brought the meeting to a close.

Chapter 8

Bin Laden imprisoned President Benjamin and made fun of him and his cock almost every day. He ordered him to stand in front of the camera every day for two hours naked and play with his little Benjamin. It was very humiliating for the president and America. One day, while the president stood naked, bin Laden came and stood near him. He had a stick in his hand. He started touching the president's tiny cock with it.

"OK, Mr. President, I can let you go free on one condition. The condition is that you have to make your cock hard and long enough so it can go a little bit inside your own ass. You fulfill this condition, and I promise that you will be set free. No questions will be asked. To help you, I will ask some girls to perform sexual acts in front of you every day. Let me know if you need anything else. I'll give you two months. If you aren't able to do that after two months, my ghosts will fuck you in the ass and torture you every day in front of the cameras."

"Why don't you just finish me off?" Benjamin pleaded.

"No, Mr. President, you are the biggest prize I have ever won. I can't let you die so easily. I don't want to waste your time, and you can start now."

"Fuck off," the president said angrily. Bin Laden went away smiling. The president thought for some time and then accepted the challenge. Day and night, he massaged his cock with different oils while looking at the beautiful and dancing naked girls and watching porno movies. After one week, his cock started having some feeling in it. After two weeks, it could become hard and also grew a bit in size. This encouraged him more. One month passed, and his cock grew about five inches in size. The president became very delighted and continued his routine. Only two days were left when finally his cock was hard and long enough to enter his own ass. He attempted it in front of the cameras, and his cock went inside about an inch. He was so excited that he ran toward bin Laden, who stood in front of the building talking to his ghosts.

"Mr. bin Laden, I did it. Everybody saw it going in my ass. Do you want to see it now?" Benjamin was so excited that he jumped up and down. For a moment, he forgot that he was the ex-president of America.

"Holy shit, that is unbelievable. That tiny cock is so big now. Come on, show me." Bin Laden was genuinely astonished because he didn't expect the president to find success.

"Look properly now, and don't say afterward that you didn't see it. Here it goes. Oh, that feels very good, my big cock in my own ass. It feels wonderful. Maybe you also should try, Mr. bin Laden." Benjamin was overtaken by the joy and excitement and didn't realize what he was saying.

"That is fantastic. You have done a very good job. How did you manage to achieve that? Tell me quickly. I also want to enlarge my penis. I will reward you."

"That is good. You'll also want to put it in your own ass. You will know how nice it feels. You will really love it. It will be good for your ass's security also. You can always keep your own dick in your ass, and no other dick will be able to penetrate it."

"Shut up, I just want to enlarge it. I didn't say I want to put it in my ass. You didn't answer my question. How did you do it?"

"I massaged it every day for hours with different oils, and it worked."

"Oh, that is great. Now you can massage my cock every day for hours, and I will reward you for it," bin Laden said.

"But Mr. bin Laden, you said I could go free. You're breaking your promise," Benjamin protested.

"Yes, I will let you go free, but you have to do that for me. Just two months. I will provide you with a new bitch every day to use your cock. You have to use it. Otherwise you will lose it again."

"OK, that sounds fair," Benjamin agreed immediately. "I was also feeling bored before. Now I have a job to massage a cock, and I will enjoy sex with a new bitch every day. I had fucked only my boring wife before."

"Good ghost, enjoy your night and start tomorrow. You can choose a bitch for today."

"OK. Thanks very much, Mr. bin Laden. See you tomorrow." Benjamin ran toward a group of sexy girls. He grabbed one and told her that it was bin Laden's order. Bin Laden also made a hand gesture and told the girl to follow him. Benjamin took her inside the room and fucked her for hours. He felt as if he was young again. The girl enjoyed it very much but became tired. Her pussy was sore and swollen from the greatest fuck she ever had. She collapsed in the bed and slept until next morning.

The next day, bin Laden sat on a chair and Benjamin started massaging his cock. Naughty Bitch and the donkey ghost came there.

"Come on, Benjamin, make it thick and large very fast so we can watch bin Laden putting it in his own ass," Naughty Bitch said.

"Fuck off, you two. I was too busy before. I know you provide all the information to my enemies. I have thought of a way to punish you for that and for always disturbing me."

"What is the solution?" the donkey ghost asked while looking at his cock. "You're going to fuck your own ass? Why don't you fuck me like old times in the Afghan mountains? I would love it when it's grown bigger. Oh, baby, I'm horny now. Come on, put it inside me. My pussy is hotter than the ladies'. Don't you remember you used to say that? I loved it when you kissed me and licked my body while fucking." The donkey ghost was really turned on.

"I have to do something about you two. I have had enough of both of you. Jamal, come here." Bin Laden got irritated and called one of his ghosts.

"Yes, boss, what can I do for you?" Jamal asked.

"We had sent some of our ghosts to find something to punish these two bitches. Are they back yet or not? Why have they taken so long?"

"They should come back soon, sir. There, sir, look there. They are coming back. And I think they have found the solution. Look at who is coming with them." Jamal pointed. The ghosts were coming back, and with them was a pack of ten big dog ghosts and four male donkey ghosts with very big dicks almost touching the ground.

"Oh my God, come on, donkey, run to save yourself. They will kill us," Naughty Bitch said and ran in the opposite direction from where the ghosts were coming. The donkey ghost followed. The pack of dog and donkey ghosts ran after them. They couldn't run far, and the male dog and donkey ghosts surrounded them and brought them back in front of bin Laden.

"Hello, boss, do you recognize me? I'm your dog Jack. You had me in your house, but then you had to go away and hide in the mountains," a dog ghost who seemed to be the leader of the pack said.

"Oh yes, I remember you. You have grown to be a very big dog. When did you die?" asked bin Laden, who felt very happy to see his loyal dog.

"When I was about eight years old, I went to look for you in the mountains, but I was struck by an American bomb and died on the spot. I have been a ghost since then. Tell me, what can I do for you? I'm here to look after your security."

"Hi, sir, do you remember me?" one of the male donkey ghosts asked bin Laden.

"No, I can't recall that I know you." Bin Laden tried to remember but couldn't.

"Sir, one day you felt very horny. There were no women, dogs, or female donkeys around. You fucked my ass. I liked that very much, and since then have become a gay donkey."

"Shut up, I never did that. I don't remember ever fucking a male donkey. Who brought this gay donkey? Don't we have enough trouble with those two bitches? Come on, go away, donkey. Don't fabricate stories." Bin Laden tried to avoid the donkey and got angry.

"Sir, you even said my ass was very tight and sexy. I remember you enjoyed it very much and came inside me three times. Don't break my heart, please try to remember. I've never forgotten that and fell in love with you since that day. I missed you so much after that encounter. When I couldn't find you, I committed suicide. Finally I have found you again," the donkey said with a bit of disappointment and started crying.

"Fuck off, don't talk rubbish. How can a donkey fall in love with a human?" shouted bin Laden.

"When a human can fuck a donkey, why can't donkey love him back? Sir, you try my dick inside you and maybe you will fall in love with me," the donkey said.

"He, he, he, he, he, he, he." Naughty Bitch and the female donkey ghost couldn't stop laughing.

"Take this donkey away before I kill him. Leave him where you got him. Ask the other donkeys to kill him if he doesn't go away. Jack, tell your pack to fuck Naughty Bitch twenty-four hours nonstop. Take turns and never stop. She told me before she is very good at squeezing her holes so no cock can penetrate. I want to see for how long she can keep squeezing. Fuck both her holes."

"OK, sir. Come on, boys, bring her in front of the cameras. Make sure she doesn't run away."

"Donkeys, you take this female donkey ghost and do the same. I will ask my ghosts to bring some more donkey ghosts because one of you has turned out be a poofter. Make sure nobody fucks its ass. I know he will enjoy that."

"OK, sir," one of the donkeys said.

The orders were followed, and Naughty Bitch's and the donkey ghost's screams could be heard everywhere. They tried to stop them, but the male dogs and donkeys were hungry for sex. They collapsed on the ground, but the fucking didn't stop. Bin Laden and his ghosts had finally solved the Naughty Bitch and female donkey ghost problem. But they had a new problem now. Whenever they chased away the gay donkey, it always came back. It followed bin Laden everywhere and flashed its ass to bin Laden to make him horny. When this didn't work, he just cried and cried. Bin Laden was cursing himself for fucking those animals in Afghanistan. Now they had come back to haunt him. He couldn't think of a solution for the gay donkey himself and asked Jamal and the other ghosts to find one.

When bin Laden and his ghosts went inside the White House, Naughty Bitch started playing tricks on the dogs. The dogs were still fucking her and enjoying it. There were ten of them, and the wait for each turn was about four hours. It was Peter's turn. Peter was a large dog with a big cock. He was the most powerful dog ghost among them. Jack was second to him. The other dog spirits were too weak to fight him. He could easily take on the other dogs, but he didn't have many brains. Peter was humping Naughty Bitch.

Naughty Bitch played her card to control Peter. "Come on, big boy. Oh, that feels so nice. You are the greatest. You don't have to stay in line to wait for your turn. I can be all yours if you want. You are so strong and handsome. You should be the leader. That Jack is nothing in front of you. Why do you have to take orders from him?"

"Really, you think I should be the leader? Are you sure that you will be only mine?" Peter immediately fell into her trap and had no brainpower to understand her cunning tricks.

"Yes, baby, why would I want those weak and ugly-looking dogs? You are the most powerful dog spirit. You are the alpha dog. You will be the king, and I will be the queen. With my brains and your power, we can control all the dog spirits in the world. Imagine every dog spirit bowing in front of you as other ghosts do for bin Laden. No human spirit can face him now. Don't you want to be the king of kings? And if you agree, I will give you the most passionate and hot sex a dog ever had from a bitch. I will suck your cock, lick your ass, and have sex with you in every possible position. I'll even not get jealous if sometimes you feel like fucking other bitches. I will be the perfect queen for you."

"OK, if you are willing to do all that, I won't let any other dog touch you now. You just give me ideas to rule because my blood always gets more circulated to my cock than my brain. That's why I'm always horny and not thinking properly," Peter said. He was ready to be the king.

"Get off now, Peter. That's enough. You should let the others also have their turn," Jack came near them and ordered.

"Fuck off, Jack. She is my bitch now. If any of you even come near her, I will tear you all into pieces."

"Grrrrrr. Get down now or face the consequences," Jack growled.

"Grrrrrr. I said fuck off. Don't disturb me. I'm about to come, and you are ruining my pleasure," Peter growled back.

"Come on, baby, you're so good. Your cock is so big. Oh yes, oh yes, oh yes, fuck me hard. I love your cock, oh yes." Naughty Bitch didn't want him to dismount in order to make sure they fought each other.

"Don't you see? She wants us to fight each other so she can escape. Maybe you should use your brain more than your dick," said Jack.

"Come on, Peter, don't listen to him. I'm only yours and he can't order you like this. Ask your brain: Do you want to be the king or not? Ignore him and keep on fucking my hot pussy. Please don't take it out. It feels like an out-of-this-world experience. No other dog can fuck like you." Naughty Bitch added more fuel to the fire.

"She is right. Fuck off and tell the others also that I'm the leader now. I should have used my brains more. You were the leader because I didn't use them. She is a beauty with brains. With my power and her brains, I will take over the dog spirit world and then the other species. Are you going away now or not?" Peter warned.

Jack wasn't scared. "If you want it the hard way, come and fight like a dog,"

"Go, baby, I will give you hot sex later. First make him shut up. He is ruining my pleasure." Naughty Bitch had succeeded in playing her cards right.

Peter pounced on Jack, and within minutes Jack fell to the ground, injured and defeated. The other dogs didn't intervene and became scared of Peter. They accepted him as their leader. Bin Laden and his ghosts came out to see what was going on when they heard the dogs fighting. They all looked puzzled and confused when they saw Jack lying injured on the ground. They wondered what had happened.

"The bitch must have played some trick. Come on, boy, get up. Jack, come on. What happened here?" Bin Laden had an idea what had happened but was not sure.

"Naughty Bitch has instigated and lured the most powerful dog ghost, Peter. He is on her side now and wants to take over the dog spirit world. The Bitch is very smart and has turned the tables on us. Only I was powerful enough to challenge him. No other dog spirit will be able to bring him down. He has become power hungry now and wants to be like you," Jack explained.

Naughty Bitch egged Peter on. "Come on, Peter darling, suck the energy out of Jack. Fuck him in the ass. Nobody can stop you now. You have the same ability as bin Laden the asshole. Come on, baby, don't give him a second chance to challenge your authority." It worked and Peter proceeded to wreck havoc with Jack's life.

"Don't you dare come near me. She is corrupting your mind. Kill me if you want, but don't do this," Jack growled and warned Peter. But he knew it was too late. He shouted, growled, and screamed for help, but nobody could help him.

"I will find a way to make you pay for all this. I promise it won't be long. You have a last chance to save your life. Turn back now." Bin Laden tried to punch and kick Peter in uncontrollable anger. As expected, it didn't do anything to Peter. It was as though he punched and kicked through the empty space. He could only give warnings to Peter, which Peter ignored.

"Come on, get up and bend over. I'll give it to you doggy style, baby. Maybe you will enjoy it. You might want to become my bitch later on." Peter inserted his powersucker inside Jack's ass and fucked Jack for half an hour. Peter became stronger and Jack weaker. Even the mighty bin Laden ghost couldn't do anything. Within half an hour, Jack's dignity and power was taken away from him, his asshole torn and mutilated by Peter's enormous doggy dick. He lay on the ground crying and humiliated.

"Come on, baby, finish him off. We don't want any trouble from him later on." Naughty Bitch was unforgiving. Peter listened to her and grabbed Jack's neck in his mouth and bit it off. Jack didn't resist because of the humiliation he had gone through. Bin Laden and his ghosts went hysterical.

"I'll make sure you suffer worse than Jack every day. You motherfucker, you watch out now. Both of you are my main enemies now. Don't worry, I will find something. There is an end to everything." Bin Laden couldn't stop his anger.

"Yes, bin Laden, there is an end to everything, and that includes you. I think your end is coming near. If humans can't do anything about you, I will make sure I make Peter so strong that one day we will find a way to make you massage Peter's cock. I will also make sure Peter sucks power from your ass with his powersucker. Fuck you, asshole." Naughty Bitch became daring and dangerous. Proud and victorious, she walked off, moving and shaking her ass in a sexy way. Her walk was so sexy that Peter ran after her and the other dog ghosts followed them.

"Oh my beautiful darling, you're so sexy and hot." Peter got turned on while walking with her.

"Come, my king, I will give you such hot sex today that even bin Laden will get jealous. I want to make love to you in front of him. You just lie down and enjoy. Come, follow me, we have to go near him." Naughty Bitch came back to irritate bin Laden. She started performing extraordinarily hot sexual acts on Peter. Peter moaned with pleasure, and Naughty Bitch made purposely loud noises to irritate bin Laden more. She had become an even bigger problem for bin Laden. He wished he hadn't become horny when he saw the bitch in Afghanistan. One small mistake was producing a big headache in his afterlife. He couldn't time travel and undo this. It scared him when he thought the dog ghost Peter could really become powerful like him. The dog seemed to have the same abilities but less brains. But Naughty Bitch was extra smart and could teach him the tricks of the trade.

After a few days, the dogs disappeared and nobody knew where they had gone. Bin Laden didn't want to take any chances and asked his ghosts to find and spy on them. He also asked all the ghosts to find a solution to deal with them.

The donkey ghost stayed there. It hurt her first day, but after that she liked having three cocks to herself. She enjoyed having group sex with the three male donkeys and didn't disturb bin Laden anymore. Bin Laden was delighted that at least she was minding her own business and became busy with the male donkeys. But the gay donkey was still a headache. To solve his problem, he asked his ghosts to find some gay donkeys. Benjamin was enjoying his life with a new girl every day, and he didn't mind massaging bin Laden's cock for it. Bin Laden also felt satisfied with Benjamin's job because his cock became stronger, harder, thicker, and double in length. The girls loved having sex with him. It was a win-win situation for everybody involved. Benjamin posed no danger because he was weak compared with bin Laden. Bin Laden's ghosts arranged for another male gay donkey to join the one already there. It solved the gay donkey problem.

Bin Laden's spy ghosts came back with bad news. They informed bin Laden that Peter and Naughty Bitch had already recruited thousands of ghosts in their army of dog ghosts. Peter was having sex with female dog ghosts to become powerful like bin Laden. They were moving place to place, finding new dog ghosts and increasing their power. Peter was even fucking the living bitches to get more energy. It would be only six more months and Peter the dog ghost would become so powerful that he could easily take on bin Laden if he found a way to come into the human ghost world. Naughty Bitch had been seen consulting the old and intelligent dogs to find a way for it. Bin Laden looked worried and ordered his ghosts to find a way to enter the dog ghost world so they could eliminate them before Peter's power threatened their existence.

Bin Laden again went away to search for the holy man. Janet and her female ghost accomplices met Naughty Bitch and Peter. They discussed ways to bring down bin Laden. But no way seemed to lead to his destruction. Naughty Bitch took them to the place where bin Laden was looking for the Native American holy man. Janet and her accomplices decided to stay in that area and look for him. They found out from some local Native American ghosts that they had seen the holy man going into the forest to be safe from bin Laden. The holy man knew that bin Laden was looking for him desperately. Janet asked one of the ghosts about the holy man.

"What is he like? How do we recognize him?" asked Janet.

"He is a very old Native American man," a ghost explained. "He prays most of the time. You will always see spirits around him trying to get his blessings to leave the ghostly world to be born again. He allows only those spirits who do good deeds and don't use their power to harm others to cross over. He has helped thousands of spirits. The spirits have to pray with him for some time before they achieve their salvation. He wears a hat with a lot of feathers in it. He is in contact with some very powerful ghosts. I think he is the one who can help America."

"Thank you very much. We need to find him very urgently," Janet said. As they finished talking, they heard some noise not far from them. They saw a ghost that looked like one of bin Laden's ghosts. The ghost had heard everything. Janet and her friends dashed toward the ghost to kill it. But the ghost was too fast and disappeared in seconds. Janet and her friends looked very worried. They knew the ghost would inform bin Laden in which forest the holy man was. It wouldn't take much time for bin Laden to find the holy man. They sent one ghost to the nearby police station to inform the CIA. They needed to find the holy man before bin Laden did and take him to a safe place. They didn't waste any time and went into the forest. Within hours CIA helicopters came, and the army also joined the hunt in the forest. Janet met John and the vampires, who had moved in the same forest to be safe from bin Laden. They all went along to help to protect the holy man. They knew bin Laden would be there soon.

Janet saw an American Indian man sitting near a lake surrounded by a lot of spirits. He matched the description given by the ghost. They hurried toward the holy man. Seeing the army and Janet, he understood what was going on. A helicopter landed near him. Without saying anything or wasting any time, he rushed inside. Janet saw about thirty of bin Laden's ghosts running toward the helicopter. Bin Laden was not among them. Janet, her friends, and the vampires blocked their way. They attacked the ghosts to stop them from reaching the helicopter before it could fly away. After the helicopter had gone, the fighting continued. Janet and the vampires were winning the battle when suddenly a spine-chilling and frightening voice came.

"Don't let any one of them escape." It was bin Laden. "I'm here. Sorry, I got the news a bit late. I came as soon as I could."

"Retreat and save your lives. You won't be able to fight him. The holy man is safe now," Janet announced.

They ran wherever they could to escape bin Laden's fury. His ghosts also attacked them from behind. Only Janet, John, Nicky, Mary, and Ruby were able to escape. The rest were slaughtered like animals. Bin Laden didn't have time to come after them. He went to look for the helicopter with the holy man in it. But the helicopter was nowhere to be seen. Enraged and disappointed, bin Laden roared in a terrifying and dreadful voice. The forest became gripped in fear. The animals dashed for safety. Janet, John, and the vampires ran out of the forest as fast as they could.

Furious and worried, bin Laden came back. He asked his ghosts to attack every government building and any other place they suspected to find the holy man. He was running out of time. He realized that the holy man could really put an end to his ghostly existence. He couldn't imagine what kind of monster he was going to wake up. The prophecy told by the holy man in Afghanistan had come true. It was the first time that he felt so scared and worried. He became restless and extremely disturbed. He and his men burned down buildings and attacked the army wherever they came across them to find the holy man. The CIA didn't take any chances, and only a few agents knew the whereabouts of the holy man. Aircraft were ordered to the ground because bin Laden and his men would have attacked them. The holy man began his prayers at a secret place to wake up the monster. He had informed the CIA that it would take ninety days of uninterrupted prayers to wake up the monster. He had already prayed in the forest for a month. But his prayers were interrupted, and he had to start all over again.

It was no more fun for bin Laden. His days of happiness were over. He ran pillar to post to find the holy man. He asked his ghosts to think deeply and thoroughly to figure out where the holy man could be hidden. But no one knew. Bin Laden's brain was affected by the anger. It was the first time the public saw him fearing something unknown. The public also started praying for the thing to wake up and teach bin Laden a humiliating lesson. Everybody wondered what it could be, how it looked, and what powers it possessed. People started guessing. The CIA had tried to ask the holy man what the thing was that bin Laden feared so much. But the holy man said he couldn't give any information. It would jeopardize the operation, and bin Laden might get a clue about it.

Chapter 9

After they were unable to find the holy man in the government and army places, bin Laden sent his ghosts to all the forests in the country. He decided to go to Afghanistan to see the Afghan holy man who had told him about the prophecy. He had informed his ghosts that he would come back within a few days. He went to the mountains where the Afghan holy man resided. He was in luck—the holy man was already expecting him.

"Come in, Mr. bin Laden. I've heard what happened," the holy man said.

"Yes, Your Holiness, whatever you said seems to be coming true. I looked everywhere for that American Indian holy man, but when I finally found him, they snatched him right out of my hands. I do not know where he is now. I need your help to find him," bin Laden said.

"You're wasting your time trying to find him now. It has been forty-five days, and he needs forty-five more days to wake up the monster. Even I can't use my powers to see where he is.

He has some special kind of energy around him that is making him invisible to everybody. He could be anywhere. He could be right in front of you in the capital city, but you will not find him now. You should be concentrating your energy to face the monster. You will not be able to hide anywhere from that monster. It will sniff you out even from caves. Your best bet is to face him in the capital city with all your might. Even I can't see what it will be like and what powers it will possess. You should gather as many powerful ghosts as you can to face it. There is another danger coming your way from the dog ghosts. You must curtail their power. Otherwise in a few months they could be a bigger trouble for you. I think they will figure out a way to cross over to your ghostly world."

"Can you please suggest any way to cross over to the dog ghost world so at least I can deal with that threat first? I would really appreciate it," bin Laden said in desperation.

"You remember you had a dog named Jack," said the holy man.

"Yes, he came to me in spirit form but was killed by Peter the dog ghost. I want to avenge his death and punish Naughty Bitch and Peter."

"That dog has been born as a human. Soon he will die as a human child from a sickness. He will return as a human spirit and come to see you. Jack hasn't forgotten what happened to him. He will tell you the way to enter the dog spirit world. His pain won't ease until Naughty Bitch and Peter are made to suffer. You don't have to look for him. Go back and wait in the capital city. Jack will come and see you there. The monster will come there also. You have to be well prepared. Another thing to remember is to control your anger. Do not underestimate this monster. It won't be coming to you invisible. It will be visible to even humans. It will not come in silence. It will come with a bang. It will want you be to be well prepared. It will not be scared of you. It is the only one who could put an end to your existence."

"Thank you very much, Your Holiness. You have been a great help. I will do as you say. Bye for now," said bin Laden as he got up to go.

"Bye, take care."

Bin Laden came back to the capital city after three days. Thousands of warrior ghosts followed him from Afghanistan for the ultimate showdown. Bin Laden recalled all the ghosts to the capital city. He felt disheartened and frightened but had no other choice. He preferred to face the monster in the capital city instead of chickening out. He didn't divulge much to his ghosts because he didn't want to scare the shit out of them. He needed whatever extra help he could get to fight the most dreadful, fearsome, and unknown monster he ever encountered.

Naughty Bitch was eager to show her growing strength to bin Laden. She missed teasing and irritating him and decided to pay him a visit to show off the dog ghost army's strength. It had grown to about thirty thousand, and she knew it would irritate and terrify him. The dog ghost army marched toward the capital city. Bin Laden was counting the days before the monster would wake up, and there were only thirty days left. People everywhere got excited to see the extinction of bin Laden and his ghosts. There was a spooky peace everywhere. Everybody was busy watching the devices to hear any news about what was going to happen. Even the criminals and the thieves had forgotten about committing crimes. No longer interested in having fun, he got serious about planning how to defend himself and kill the unnerving monster. He felt frustrated because he didn't know what it looked like and how it fought. President Benjamin enjoyed his life quietly with the girls. Bin Laden had even stopped him from massaging his cock. Even his dick felt the effects of bin Laden being frightened and unnerved. His cock became soft and developed erectile dysfunction. Benjamin had all the time for himself and waited for another opportunity to strike bin Laden. He hadn't forgotten the humiliation he suffered in bin Laden's hands. But he knew he was too weak and he needed a way to get back the power he had lost. This time his cock was ready to strike, but no idea was coming in Benjamin's brain to restore his energy.

All of a sudden, bin Laden's ghosts standing on skyscrapers started shouting. Panic was everywhere in bin Laden's camp. They saw black clouds and dust coming toward the city. Everybody thought it was the monster.

"Boss, there is one month left. How can the monster come early?" one of ghosts standing next to him asked.

"I don't think it's the monster. It must be something else. Tell them to calm down. Why in the fuck are they so scared? I'm here. Tell them not to worry," bin Laden said and then went on top of a building to check what was going on. The clouds and the dust entered the city.

"It's not the monster. It looks as if there are too many things coming, like an army or something. It can't be the humans. They wouldn't dare do that. You all wait here. I will go and check," bin Laden said. Then Naughty Bitch, Peter, and dogs became clearly visible.

"It's the bitch and her fucking dog army. Don't worry about it. She is just here to do some bitching as usual," bin Laden said loudly.

"Hello, honey, did you miss me? Don't crap in your pants. I won't do anything to you today. When I'm ready, I will announce beforehand that we are coming to ravish your ass, and my Peter will put his powersucker inside your hole," Naughty Bitch said. She walked around bin Laden in a sexy style while flashing her backside to him.

"I'm not scared of bitches. You take your jokers out of here. Don't start having any dreams about becoming powerful like me. Soon I'm going to come and find you. You won't have a place to hide. I will personally burn and annihilate that backside of yours that you are so proud of."

"You find my backside too sexy, don't you honey? You must have fucked me in your dreams. I still remember how you ran after me to fuck me. I know I'm a very hot bitch. Your tongue must be dying to lick my pussy and ass."

"Fuck off. You are repulsive and an ugly bitch."

"Then why were you willing to marry me that time for a fuck? I know you are lying, and you must have masturbated many times while imagining me."

"I think he is jealous that I'm fucking you now. He wouldn't even be able to satisfy you. Look at his extrasoft dick," Peter interrupted.

"Yes, baby, you're right. Your cock is the greatest. I will make sure one day bin Laden will have it in his ass. I know he would enjoy it too much. I want to film it personally when you penetrate his ass."

"You wait for a few weeks, I will show you whose powersucker goes into whose ass. Promise me that you won't run away."

"Why, do you have some kind of magic thing to enter our world? I'm also looking for it. The day I find it, you will be running with your hands on your ass to protect it from Peter's dick. I promise I won't run away. You also promise me that you won't run away either," said Naughty Bitch, suspecting that he might have found something. She wanted to find out about it.

Bin Laden sensed her fear. "Why are you looking scared now? Do you want me to tell you what it is? Just wait—you will see it very soon."

"Oh, I've heard somebody is coming to fuck your ass before we do and you're crapping in your pants every day. How many more days to go before the big occasion? I want to come and watch. That will be the best, most entertaining show ever."

"Don't worry—your show is not far away now. Go gather enough energy to defend your asses. Both of you don't have enough time. Don't complain that I didn't warn you. Don't crap here. Run, you're running out of time, bitch. I think you look very scared."

Peter notices the fear on Naughty Bitch's face. "I think he's just bullshitting. Don't worry about it. I'll be there to defend my darling," he said.

"You should worry about your own ass. My cock is three times bigger now. Don't scream when my powersucker tears it like paper," bin Laden warned them.

"Let's go, baby. I think he looks serious about it. His face tells me he knows something. I can sniff it," said Naughty Bitch and turned to go back. Peter and their army of ghost dogs followed. It was the first time Naughty Bitch got irritated and angry. She was worried that their power was no match for bin Laden if he found a way to come into their world. Bin Laden was right—the dogs needed to accumulate much-needed energy as soon as they could. They went back, and she didn't let Peter rest for even one day. One week passed and their strength grew to forty thousand ghosts, and Peter's energy was still around 50 percent of bin Laden's.

Bin Laden and his ghosts sat in front of the White House while discussing the plans for the war with the monster. A child ghost appeared flying in front of them. Bin Laden got excited.

"Is that Jack?" Bin Laden was expecting him desperately.

"Yes, master, nice to see you," Jack said. He died as a child as predicted by the holy man in Afghanistan and came back in the form of a human ghost.

"Nice to see you, Jack. I'm really happy to see you. You're a very loyal friend. Even families betray, but you haven't forgotten me. I was expecting you."

"Yes, master, I know it. I've come back to avenge the betrayal and humiliation I suffered. I can't rest in peace until I punish those assholes with your help."

"Just show me how to enter into their world. Leave the rest to me. I will punish them the way you want. Don't leave me again, and stick to me. The holy man in Afghanistan told me that you would know how to cross into their world. Just tell me how to do it."

"Master, when Peter murdered me here in front of you, my spirit traveled through many dimensions. I saw so many worlds of different creatures separated from other worlds by dimensions. As the science on Earth is figuring out now, there are different universes and worlds, each living in its own dimension. Some are two-dimensional, some are three, some are four, and some even more. Sometimes we are close to another world, but we can't notice it. Sometimes we can hear them and see them, but we can't touch them. The dog spirit world and human spirit world are like that. We can see and talk to each other, but we can't cross into each other's world. The human spirit world and real human world also behave this way. That's why humans can't see ghosts. Only a few have the gift to cross over to either side."

Bin Laden didn't grasp all that and became desperate to know if Jack knew the way. "Sorry, Jack, you're talking like a scientist. I can't comprehend all that. Just let me know how we can cross over to the dog spirit world."

"Yes, master. There is a thing called a wormhole between two worlds. We have to find this wormhole between our world and the dog spirit world."

"Where can we find it, and how long it will take? We don't have much time left," bin Laden said.

"Master, we are in luck. I have already found it. That's why I was late. We don't have much time left. We must get them while they're still weak. I have seen the dogs. They are getting very powerful. Master, I have a request that you will spare those dog ghosts who will choose not to fight us. There are a lot of them who were forced into submission. They don't have any enmity with the human spirit world. Please give them the option to surrender first. Our enemies are only Naughty Bitch, Peter, and those who will choose to side with them."

"Yes, Jack, I promise. My enemies are also just those two. We won't harm anybody else if they surrender," bin Laden assured Jack.

"Come on then, master. The wormhole is about one hundred and fifty kilometers from here. We should be there by this evening. Once we go through it, we will start looking for the dog ghosts."

"We need to take only half of our ghost army with us. The other half will stay here," bin Laden said.

"Are you sure, master? Never underestimate your opponent," Jack said.

"Yes, I'm sure. Don't worry about it too much. They came here last week. I have seen their strength. I think they can't even fight me alone. I'm taking half of our ghosts just as a precaution. They were already scared last week and left in a hurry. Let's go now. I don't want them to run away and hide," bin Laden said.

The mighty ghost and his army marched out of the city. Naughty Bitch had already planted her dog ghost spies around the capital city. Her spies followed bin Laden's ghost army. The spies sent one of them to inform Naughty Bitch. Upon hearing the news, Naughty Bitch's anxiety and worries became clearly visible on her face. She immediately called a meeting of all prominent dog ghosts. Peter as king and Naughty Bitch as commander in chief of the dog ghost army sat on higher ground.

"Dear respected generals of the dog ghost army, we have become so powerful that the human ghost world is gripped by the fear of our king's and his army's growing powers. In two more months, our King Peter the Great will overtake bin Laden. Fearing his onslaught and extermination of their human ghostly world, bin Laden's army is marching toward us. A human child ghost is guiding them to some secret place. Our spies are following them. I'm one hundred percent sure that the march is to eliminate our dog ghostly world. They can't digest the fact that one day dog ghosts will rule all the ghost worlds, including the human's. I could smell it that he knew something about entering our ghostly world when we paid him a visit a few weeks ago. Soon our spies will confirm my suspicions. My plan is to divide our army in six different combat groups. Three groups will stay here with Peter and face their forces. Once they engage in fighting, the other three groups in my command will surprise and attack them from behind. This way we will have the upper hand. We will give the human ghosts a taste of dog ghosts' power and supe-riority," Naughty Bitch said.

"Why don't we disappear for two or three months until Peter and our army are equal or more powerful than bin Laden?" one of the prominent and wise dogs suggested. "Then we will be sure of our victory and won't have a lot of causalities from our side. We can see how they will come to our world, and then we can use the same way to go into their world to attack them. I think we must retreat this time. If we don't, we will be committing suicide."

"We won't be able to hide anywhere from him," Naughty Bitch replied. "He will find us and destroy us. At least now we know he is coming to attack us and we will be ready for him.

Don't you all believe in the mighty Peter the Great? We don't want bin Laden to think that we are cowards and ran away without a fight."

"Yes, generals, she is right. I'm not a coward, and she is always right. Because of her brain, we are very powerful today. We should be grateful to her because she has organized us into a mighty force. We were just some wandering dog spirits before."

"But sir, sometimes it's wise to retreat and save everything we have. We know we will be powerful enough in two to three months' time. That's why he is coming to attack us. He knows he can be victorious now," another wise dog ghost suggested.

"No, I don't want to hear anything else. I trust her, and it's my order that we will do as she says. Is there anybody here who doesn't want to follow my orders?" Peter growled in anger, and nobody dared to question him anymore. Naughty Bitch's face lighted up because she was calling the shots.

"OK, go now and start doing the preparations for the war," Naughty Bitch ordered the wise and prominent dogs. They all left and didn't show their anger to them. In their heart they knew that Naughty Bitch was asking them to commit suicide. Peter didn't have much brainpower and always listened to her. As they were leaving, another dog ghost spy came in scared and worried.

"Your highness, I've very bad news. The human ghosts have found a way to come into our world. Not far from here they are entering something from one side and coming out on the other side. They caught one of our spies, which they couldn't do before. They are torturing our spy to get information out of him. I immediately left to warn you all. I think their army won't be far away now. Get ready for whatever your highness wants to do." The spy looked totally in shock.

"Tell everybody to take positions. Your highness, you wait in the front to keep them united and strong. I will take my three groups and hide. I will attack from behind as we discussed. We don't have enough time left. I will go now. See you soon. Victory will be ours. My Peter the Great will show them his mighty skills of war and power," Naughty Bitch said and left in a hurry. By now their army had grown to ninety thousand dog ghosts. She divided them in six groups of fifteen thousand each. One general was appointed for each group, including her and Peter. She left three groups with Peter and took three with her. Her nightmares came true. She saw dark clouds and dust storms coming toward them. Bin Laden's mighty army came roaring. Peter didn't get scared and waited for them to arrive. He wanted to fight head-on and to his last ghostly breath. The rest of the dog ghosts with him felt scared. They felt the war was being imposed on them unnecessarily. In their heart they despised Peter for doing everything Naughty Bitch told him to do. The human ghost army drew nearer, with bin Laden in the lead. The child ghost was also flying in front. The two armies stood about fifty meters apart, awaiting orders to pull their enemies' hearts out.

"Listen to me, my dog friends. My enemies are only Peter the Asshole and Naughty Bitch. I've no problem with the rest of you. You let me take them peacefully, and your lives will be spared. After that, you can live peacefully in your ghost world and we in ours. I promise you that I will never interfere in your lives again. Humans and dogs have always been friends. Because of that bitch and asshole Peter, we have become enemies. What for? We can live in peace and harmony again. You know your brother Jack. This child ghost is him. He has come back as a human spirit. We just want to avenge his sufferings. We have no intentions of harming anybody else. I'll let Jack talk to you now," bin Laden explained.

"Yes, my friends. You are my family. I was one of you. Peter betrayed me and listened to that lying bitch. He thinks she loves him. She is a very cunning bitch. She is just using him for her own evil designs to rule the dog ghost world and other ghostly worlds. She will not hesitate to betray Peter also when the time comes. So be careful and rational. Think with your own brains and do not fall in her trap," Jack cautioned the dog ghosts.

"Don't listen to their rubbish," Peter exclaimed. "They just want to divide and rule us. You are mighty warrior dog ghosts. Don't you want to be the kings of all the ghost worlds? Wouldn't you like human ghosts serving us as we have been serving them and surviving on their leftovers? We always had to look up to them to throw some food to us. We had to play some stupid tricks in front of them to get some food. Stop listening to them and fight. Be your own kings." A dog ghost came running in front of them.

"Don't listen to Peter's rubbish, friends. Jack is right. Naughty Bitch used him and us. She has taken half of us who're loyal to her and fled. She is not coming to attack from behind. I've heard her telling all this to her loyal dog ghosts. She had planned all this long ago. She wants to be the powerful queen and rule all the ghost worlds. She made a fool out of Peter and us. We don't have any problem with the human ghosts, only Peter and Naughty Bitch do. So, my friends, I urge you to surrender," the spy dog ghost said.

225

"He is lying. She should be here soon. She can't do that to me. I'm not stupid," Peter growled in uncontrollable anger.

"She did, asshole, and I warned you about her," Jack said. "But you didn't listen to me and fell into her trap. She knew you will lose today and bin Laden will kill you. That's why she saved herself and her loyal army. By now she must have gone wherever she had planned. You're such a stupid dog. You never use your brain. Call her to attack us. We can give you some time. Send your dog ghost to check if she is waiting to attack. You will find out the truth."

"My dear friends, we have no enmity with the humans, so let's retreat," one of the prominent and wise dogs said. "I urge you. Let Peter face the consequences of his sins alone. We had also told him not to commit suicide, but he didn't listen to us."

"Yes, we all want peace. We will not fight. You can do whatever you want with Peter," loud voices came from the dog army. All the dogs raised their legs in support. Peter was left alone.

"You motherfuckers, you can't do this to me. I will not give up. I will prefer to die fighting bin Laden." Peter was a brave dog, although not very intelligent. The human ghosts gave him one hour to wait, but Naughty Bitch didn't turn up. Peter understood that he had been betrayed. He got ready to fight.

"Come on, bin Laden. I'm not going to surrender. You have to fight me to the finish. I'm not going down easily. If you're a warrior, fight me alone."

"Yes, I will fight you alone. As promised, I won't kill you. I'm going to beat the crap out of you first, and then I will insert my powersucker in you to get your energy. After that, I will take you to the human ghost world and humiliate you every day in front of the public," bin Laden said.

"Fuck you, don't waste my time. Come and fight. I'll tear you into pieces. I'm coming." Peter got angrier and pounced on bin Laden. Bin Laden fought back with full energy. Peter put up a good fight but was no match for the mighty ghost. He dropped on the ground, injured and crying, unable to bear the debilitating pain. Bin Laden penetrated his ass with the powersucker and sucked his energy out. Peter screamed and begged for mercy, but it was too late. Tears of happiness rained from Jack the child ghost's eyes. Bin Laden didn't kill Peter and ordered the other ghosts to carry him to the human ghost world. They didn't have enough time to go after Naughty Bitch. Besides, she didn't pose any immediate danger. Jack thanked bin Laden for avenging his sufferings.

"OK, friends, we will take this filthy Peter with us. We leave you in peace, and if you get any news about Naughty Bitch's whereabouts, please let us know. Don't trust her. She will instigate you all for her evil intentions," Jack said.

"No, we won't, Jack," one of the wise dogs said. "We would like to offer these twenty dog ghosts to guard and help in Peter's torture. They were all humiliated into submission by Peter and Naughty Bitch. This way they will be able to take revenge. They're very talented in spying and could be great help to you."

"Yes, we will take them with us. Thank you very much. See you all, and if you need any help, please let us know. We have to leave now," said Jack. Bin Laden and his ghosts left them to return to the human ghost world. Naughty Bitch and her army of dog ghosts fled into Mexico jungles to escape the fury of bin Laden. She used Peter to delay bin Laden's army from coming after her. Her plan worked and she escaped. She felt proud of herself, thinking she out-smarted Peter and bin Laden. She sent some of her dog ghost spies to keep an eye on bin Laden. As a precaution, bin Laden also left some spies in the dog ghost world to keep an eye on them. Peter was brought to the capital and tortured every day in public. The dogs from the dog ghost world were used for this purpose. They fucked his ass and humiliated him every day.

Bin Laden sent his spies to find the politicians' whereabouts. He decided to assassinate them before the monster arrived. One of his spy ghosts came back after a few days. He whispered something in bin Laden's ear. Bin Laden hurriedly followed the spy ghost. In another city, politicians and their spouses sat in a secret underground government facility. It was about 6:00 p.m., and they all seemed intoxicated. Empty alcohol bottles were lying around. The people still had glasses full of alcoholic drinks.

"Mr. President, I think we should make a very lucrative offer that bin Laden can't refuse. That is the only way we can feel safe and reach an agreement with him," one intoxicated politician suggested.

"And what could that offer be, you old ass?" another drunken politician asked. "He is a ghost now. He is not interested in any money. Why would he want to make a compromise with us? He is already enjoying all the privileges and immunities. He can have any American pussy he wants. And look around here. We are left with only old, fat, shaggy, and wrinkled pussies." After he used those degrading words, the women stared at him as if they wanted to burn him alive.

"Yes, you are right. I miss the young women in my office," another intoxicated politician said, forgetting his wife was also there. "Oh, what a good life I had. I miss all those tight asses, firm boobs, intoxicating smells of their delicious pussy and butt holes, and the creamy and fresh skin of their athletic bodies. I hate bin Laden. Because of him we are stuck with these old and ugly bitches. I wish he dies soon."

That politician's wife got really pissed and spilled the beans. "Look at yourselves first. We also didn't want your old and fat bodies and soft and limp cocks. We were putting up with you old farts just for the money and free parties every day. Behind your back, we enjoyed fucking your young bodyguards with strong and stiff cocks. We used your money to get fucked by strong and handsome young men. They could go the whole night. Fuck you all. I hope bin Laden comes here and fucks you all."

"Shut up, all of you," the president shouted. "Talk about something else. Don't remind me about my office. I'm already disheartened and feeling miserable. I will start crying if you remind me about the young women in my office again. They were so fucking hot. That's why I pretended to be working hard and spent most nights in my office." The president had tears in his eyes, imagining the young women in his office naked.

"But we are very happy here," another politician's wife said. "We have plenty of new and young bodyguards. We're still enjoying our lives. Fuck all you old farts."

"Don't feel sad, assholes. I'm here. You can all enjoy my cock now," came a frightening and dreadful voice. It was bin Laden. He immediately became visible. Seeing him, the politicians jumped out of their chairs. The intoxicating effects of alcohol took flight in their brains, and bone-chilling fear gripped their minds. Some of the male politicians defecated. They tried to flee, but bin Laden's ghosts surrounded them from all sides.

"Hello, motherfuckers. There is no escape today, and nobody is coming to rescue you. Your bodyguards are already dead. They can't do anything to me or my ghosts," bin Laden shouted. His ghosts had killed all the security personnel.

"Tie them up and take them to the capital city. I want to make an example of them," bin Laden ordered. The ghosts didn't waste any time and took the politicians and their partners to the capital city. Bin Laden sat on his chair while the politicians were being paraded.

"It looks like we have only half of them here. We need to torture them to get information about the others. We're lucky we have caught the president," bin Laden said.

"Sir, I'm not the real president. I'm a look-alike put there to hide the real president. Please believe me, sir. You can get a DNA test done to confirm it. They operated on my face to make me look like the real president. If I'm found to be lying, you can do anything with me," the guy who was mistaken for being the president pleaded.

"I don't believe you. Anyway, to satisfy myself, I will get a DNA a test done on you. We will use the DNA from inside the capitol building in the real president's office for comparison. Strip all of them. We want to entertain our viewers with the politicians' reality show," said bin Laden. Following the orders promptly, ghosts tore off the politicians' and their partners' clothes.

"Now ask all the males to wear sexy lingerie and makeup, and make them dance like strippers," ordered bin Laden. He wanted to humiliate them in front of the world. His ghosts did as he ordered, and in about twenty minutes all the male politicians were dressed in sexy lingerie.

"Turn on the music. Now dance like sexy bitches," shouted bin Laden. As soon as the music was turned on, the politicians started putting on a good, sexy dance show. They didn't feel humiliated. They were actually enjoying it. Everybody, including their partners, was surprised when the male politicians danced like real female strippers.

"Bloody hell, the motherfuckers are really enjoying their punishment. This is really weird. Turn off the music. We have to punish them in some other way," bin Laden said.

"Sir, can I say something?" one of the women partners asked bin Laden.

"Yes, go ahead," bin Laden replied.

"Like you, we also don't like these assholes. We had nothing to do with whatever decisions they made. This president is just a look-alike. You can see the marks around his face from the operations done on him to make him look like the real president. I've talked to all the females here, and they have agreed to leave the politician husbands and serve you. If you accept us, we can be of great service to you and provide you with whatever important information we have. We will do anything for you."

"I can spare your lives, but I don't want to have sex with old ladies," bin Laden said. "My deputies might be interested in that. Can one of you check the marks around the president's face to make sure she is telling the truth?" he asked his deputies. A deputy confirmed that she was telling the truth.

"Sir, we might be old, but we are very experienced," the woman said. "Just give us one chance, and we can show you how experienced we are."

"OK, I'll give you one chance, but there is one condition. I want you all to beat the shit out of all the male politicians and torture them whatever way you like. If I get satisfied from the torture, I will spare your lives and accept you as my bitches," said bin Laden.

"Leave that to us. We will gladly do that because they always cheated on us and fucked the younger girls in their offices. We are all hungry for revenge," she said.

"Fucking bitches, you all also cheated on us. How can you change so fast to save your own ass?" one of the politicians shouted.

"We learned it from you. You all do anything to save your own ass and misuse power to achieve your goals. If we can save ourselves over your dead bodies, why not?" another politician's wife answered.

"Get ready, hubbies. We have big surprises in store for you," another wife warned. "Look at your soft dicks, and you all want to fuck young bitches. You can't even satisfy them." The females asked the ghosts to tie the male politicians to the iron poles with their hands behind their backs. Encircling the male politicians, the females started giving electric shocks to the male politicians' balls and cocks every few seconds. The politicians' heart-wrenching screams fell on the deaf ears of their revenge-seeking and angry female partners. After stopping the electric shocks, the females picked up baseball bats and thrashed the politicians mercilessly. The politicians begged for forgiveness from bin Laden but without success. Turning into cannibals, the wives then bit off the men's nipples, which started bleeding. People watched in astonishment as the females turned into vicious killers to save their own skin. Even bin Laden and his ghosts were surprised. Tears ran from the politicians' eyes because of the debilitating and unbearable pain. The females then removed the males from the poles and lay them on the ground with their hands still tied behind their backs. They also used ropes to tie their legs. The naked ladies then squatted over the males, opening the politicians' mouths wide with their hands. Realizing what they were about to do, the politicians struggled to free themselves, but the ghosts held them. The females then crapped in the politicians' opened mouths.

"Oh, that's really disgusting. I didn't expect that," said bin Laden with an unpleasant look on his face. The viewers and the public watching also couldn't believe the females would go to such disgusting lengths to please bin Laden. With their mouths full of shit, the politicians gasped for breath. Their faces were covered with their partners' crap. Once finished, the ladies got up and cleaned themselves.

"That's really good and disgusting at the same time. Even I couldn't think about such smelly and dirty punishment. OK, ladies, now you have to clean their faces by licking them with your tongues," said bin Laden, surprising everyone watching.

"What. But si...r...r, you promised that you would spare us from punishment. We will be loyal to you forever if you don't punish us. Please, sir," one of the females said.

"I promised to spare your lives. You weren't loyal even to your own husbands. How can you be loyal to me? If someone presents you with an opportunity to punish me, you will do the same thing to me. I never trust bitches. Now, do as I say, and I will spare your lives. If you don't follow my order, I will give you a worse punishment than they received. I don't want to hear even one word more," bin Laden said and stared at the females with fiery eyes. The females had no choice but to quickly start licking their own shit from their partners' faces. They almost vomited, but the fear of the dreadful made them swallow it. Forgetting their severe pain for a moment, the male politicians started laughing at their wives from hell.

"Bitches, you really deserved this," the fake president said.

"I think there is some left on the left side. Do a good job and clean it properly," another politician said to his wife, who was licking his face.

"You all have done a very good job. Everything looks clean. You all look very professional in shit licking. I don't want to kill you all. You will repeat this every day in front of the camera for the rest of your lives," bin Laden ordered. The females didn't look happy and felt betrayed. But the males were satisfied that at least their wives got the same treatment as them. This kept going every day, and the politicians prayed for some miracle. Bin Laden interrogated them about the other politicians' whereabouts. He found out that most of them were not real politicians and were just look-alikes. After torturing them for a few days, he believed that they were telling the truth about not knowing anything. The Secret Service had properly planned it to safeguard the other politicians if one group was caught.

Chapter 10

The day of reckoning came. The American Indian holy man sat in a deep cave in the forest praying. He had only thirty more minutes to go. As he prayed, the whole forest shook with dreadfully frightening and creepy noises, as if there was a big earthquake. People felt it all over America and the surrounding regions. The capital city's skyscrapers shook. Animals and birds behaved in a strange and frightened way. Horrifying and bone-chilling fear sent shivers through the spines of bin Laden and his ghosts. Everybody knew that it was the day for the monster to wake up. Bin Laden's and his ghosts' fear grew as the noise got louder. The public burst into a rejoicing and dancing mood. TV and online channels informed the public that it wasn't an earthquake—it was the thing everybody had waited for. Watching the public enthusiasm and celebration scenes on TV demoralized bin Laden and his ghosts.

In the forest not far from where the holy man sat praying, the earth split and out came an old-looking pyramid-shaped building. Something inside the building roared to life. The holy man continued praying. He had only two minutes more left to pray. Curious army and CIA men who guarded the forest ran to see what it was that gave the creeps to bin Laden and his men. Helicopters flew overhead. They saw the newly emerged pyramid in the forest. As the noise became less and less, the forest became very calm. The army helicopters descended at a safe place nearby. As the soldiers came near the pyramid, they saw that something had already left it and was making its way through the forest. The men were disappointed because they just missed it. The pyramid appeared about two thousand to three thousand years old. The monster went through forest, flattening everything in a ten-meter-wide swath. Soldiers followed its path. The monster had gone to the holy man first and then went out of the forest. The holy man was standing outside the cave. The soldiers stopped to talk to him.

"Your Holiness, was that the monster you were trying to awaken?" one of the soldiers asked.

"Yes, he is. He came for my blessings and to thank me for awakening him. He has left for the capital city. It already knows where to go and what to do."

"You referred to him as 'he.' Is he a human?" another soldier asked.

"Sorry, fellows, I can't reveal any more details. Don't waste time. Go and look yourself. You will see him in action. If you don't want to miss it, go as fast as you can. Otherwise you will regret not seeing the extinction of bin Laden and his ghosts. Don't worry—he won't harm any civilians or your troops. He knows who the enemies are. Go now. I'm going there also," the holy man answered.

"Come with us, Your Holiness," one of the soldiers said.

"OK, I will. Be quick. We don't want to miss the real action."

"Let's go."

The soldiers didn't waste any time, and helicopters flew toward the capital city. When they reached it, the monster wasn't there yet. They waited outside.

"Where has he gone? Please tell us, Your Holiness," one of the soldiers said.

"Have some patience. He is visiting some of his old places. He will be here soon."

Inside the capital city, bin Laden gave up attacking anybody else and waited for the monster. Journalists had quietly sneaked inside the city for live reporting. It was unnecessary because the whole city was already online with cameras covering every place and street. But the journalists didn't want to take any chances in case the power went off. Bin Laden had brought thousands of more ghosts to combat the coming monster. He was putting up a brave face. But inside he was freaking out because of what the Afghan holy man had told him. His ass felt paralyzing and unnerving fear, as if something never seen before was about to ram it to death. Bin Laden started giving a speech to his ghosts over the speakers installed throughout the city.

"My dear deputies, don't worry about this coming monster. It's nothing but a media hype to scare us. It is another American government tactic to demoralize us. We have always fought and defeated our enemies. They brought President Benjamin's ghost before, declaring that he was going to finish you and me. Look what he does now. He is my servant and massages my cock whenever I want. We can fuck his ass anytime we want, and nobody can stop us. I've got his strength now, and nothing will be able to stand in my way. You just watch what I will do to this fucking monster or whatever they call it. We don't want to turn off the cameras. I want the whole world to watch the humiliating defeat of that monster. I'm going to suck the power out of this monster with my powersucker. Be brave and don't panic. Place your trust in me, and we will be victorious as before. We will fight and defeat whatever is coming. We will be the number one power on this earth. Nothing can stop us from achieving our goal. So be ready, and victory will be ours. Thank you," bin Laden said to infuse the fighting spirit in his ghosts. The whole city resonated with battle cries as soon as bin Laden finished his speech. His ghosts got ready to fight to the death.

"Something is coming. I think it is the monster," one of bin Laden's ghosts shouted. All the attention turned to the screens and outside the city. About eight kilometers away, something was dashing toward the city. Dust and dark clouds surrounding the thing made it impossible for people to see it clearly. As it came nearer, it became clearer. It looked like a long red giant about two kilometers in length, and it moved like a serpent. People held their breath as they watched their savior approaching the city. Bin Laden and ghosts felt nervous and scared. Fear even gripped bin Laden's ass. Whenever he tried to squeeze it to test its strength, it felt loose and without any power. His cock also shrunk to about one inch and became numb, as Benjamin's cock had when he tried to suck the power out of bin Laden. To test the waters, bin Laden ordered a battalion of his ghosts to confront the monster outside the city. His battalion unwillingly obeyed his orders. As they confronted the monster, bin Laden and everybody else wondered why the monster didn't kill them. The battalion ghosts came back laughing. The red thing also followed them.

"Sir, it is not the monster," one of the ghosts said. "It is Naughty Bitch and her army of dog ghosts. They have some kind of red powder on their bodies that has made them visible. There is nothing to be scared of. She is still in the dog ghost world. We couldn't touch her and her dog ghosts; otherwise we would have finished them off there. She knows that we have to go through the wormhole to do that."

"What is the bitch doing here? Doesn't she fear for her life?" bin Laden asked. Before anybody could answer the question, Naughty Bitch was already there.

"Hello, honey, did I scare the shit out of you? I wanted to surprise you and see for myself how freaked out you are. Your ass must be trembling with fear while waiting for the monster. I think you must do some ass-tightening exercises to make your ass tight and stronger. Just squeeze and let go. Do it about three hundred times, and it will work wonders on your ass. Don't worry. I won't dirty my hands by killing you. I just came to watch your ass being fucked by the monster. I have heard it's your last day." Naughty Bitch enjoyed scaring the shit out of bin Laden. She could smell the fear inside him and his ghosts.

Bin Laden got really irritated and angry. "Shut the fuck up. I will deal with you later. I will fuck the monster first. Don't run away. It will be your last day. I'm going to make sure your holes are torn into pieces by my ghosts."

"Don't you want to fuck me anymore? Oh, I know, because I'm not a virgin anymore you don't want me. But my ass is still virgin. Maybe you would love to have that. But it is too late now. Your own ass is on the line today. Someone is going to tear it into pieces, and we're all going to enjoy watching. I've heard the monster has a very big cock that he is going to put through your asshole, and it will come out through your mouth. That's really scary. I wouldn't want that monster cock inside me." Naughty Bitch looked very excited and over the moon as she tried to scare bin Laden to death.

"Fuck off, bitch. My cock is also capable of coming out through your mouth. I will show you later how it feels. You won't be able to escape now," bin Laden said angrily.

"Your cock won't be able even to tickle me now. Look how tiny it has become. Your shrunk dick is showing how frightened and terrified you are. The wormhole is one hundred and fifty kilometers from here. By the time you reach it, I will be gone one hundred and fifty kilometers in the opposite direction. But I'm not going anywhere until I watch your humiliating defeat and your ass get torn. I want to give you some advice: Wear shorts made of steel so you can save your ass for some time. You can also use some oil or cream to lubricate your hole. That way you will feel less pain. If you want, I can help you apply the cream on your ass." Naughty Bitch had sensed how scared bin Laden was.

"Can anyone do something about this bitch?" bin Laden asked. "Please make her shut up. I'm having a headache listening to her crap. Peter, I will let you go free if you can do something about her."

"Oh, I totally forgot about Peter. How are you, my king? Did you miss me?" Naughty Bitch asked sarcastically as she turned her attention toward Peter, who sat nearby looking very weak and depressed.

"Why did you betray me, bitch? If I've another chance, I will do worse to you than what happened with me because of you. If I hadn't listened to you, my life would have been different," Peter growled.

"As dogs are always after new cunt, bitches are after power and wealth. You had lost interest in me and fucked new bitches every day. Sometimes I felt betrayed and used because you stopped having sex with me. I couldn't say anything at that time because I knew you would kill me for a new bitch. I had to watch you fucking other bitches. From then on I decided to become powerful myself and fuck any dog I want. I was just waiting for a perfect opportunity to finish you. I couldn't do it myself, but bin Laden did it for me. I used you to let me escape. I was fucking the other dogs behind your back, and they all followed me and betrayed you. I went to visit a monk, who gave me the same ability as you to become powerful. I suck energy through my pussy from male dogs. I seduce them and fuck new dogs every day. I'm the most powerful among the dog ghost world now. I wanted to acquire enough power to fight bin Laden. But too bad, his end is very near. By the time I become that powerful, he will be exterminated. Don't make the mistake of attacking me ever. I will have no mercy on you. I'm not the same weak bitch you used to fuck."

"There is an end to everything. Don't dream big. There will be someone or something that will make you pay for your sins," Peter warned Naughty Bitch.

"Has Peter the Asshole become a philosopher? You don't have any brain, so giving advice to others doesn't suit you. Go lick your own ass and it might get healed, because it looks torn and shaggy," Naughty Bitch said.

"I hope bin Laden kills the monster today and comes after you," Peter said.

"Don't wish what is not possible. Once he is killed, I will take you with me and give you the same treatment every day that you get from him. Bye, I will come back later to fuck with your brain." Naughty Bitch walked away and went to look for bin Laden. He slipped away quietly when Naughty Bitch was busy with Peter. She saw him discussing something with his deputies not far away.

Bin Laden's ghosts caught the soldiers and the American Indian holy man while they were hiding outside the city. They brought them to bin Laden.

"Sir, we caught these soldiers and the holy man outside the city. They were hiding in the bushes. Upon interrogation they revealed that he is the holy man who has awakened the monster. We thought we can use him as a hostage to negotiate with the monster," one of his ghosts said.

"Well done, boys. That is very good. Bring him here and tie him up in that chair." Bin Laden was delighted. At least he had something to use against the monster.

"Why did you do that, old man? Didn't you fear for your own ass? You could have asked anything from me, and I would have given it to you. But you chose to go against me. Tell me if there is any reason I should forgive you," bin Laden said as he twisted the holy man's arm.

"I did what was right. I'm not scared of you. Maybe you will need me. Only I can kill the monster with my powers. If you do any harm to me, I will not utter a word and the monster will increase your sufferings. It will be here soon. Go get ready to defend yourself. Don't waste your time on me. I wanted to be caught—that's why I came here. If I want, I can disappear now and you won't be able to find me," the holy man explained.

"We have been waiting for it since morning. Maybe it got scared and ran away. If it doesn't turn up by the evening, you can't even imagine what I will do with you," bin Laden warned the holy man.

"You wish it ran away. It won't. It is coming, and I can sense it. Get ready."

Naughty Bitch again started giving bin Laden a hard time. "Listen to the holy man, you asshole. Go get ready to save your ass. Don't worry. I'll be right behind you watching your ass. Whenever I see any cock going for your ass, I'll clap and warn you. Keep it squeezed tightly. Do you want me to shave the hair on your ass? The hair might get in the way, and you will feel extra pain."

"You should shave your hair from both holes because when I'm done with the monster, you're next. Fuck off now."

"Is my honey angry? Don't be angry, because you need your brain intact to fight. Anger can make you do the wrong things. You might even take the monster's cock and put in your ass yourself. You can never know what mistakes you will make when you are angry." Naughty Bitch kept up her irritating behavior. She was really enjoying herself.

"OK. Old man, can you just tell me what it is?" bin Laden asked the holy man. "If you think it is so strong, you shouldn't have any problem telling that."

"Be patient. I don't want to ruin the suspense and the surprise. One hint I can give you is that when you see it, you will really freak out. It's very creepy and nobody has even imagined such a thing, let alone seen it. You will laugh and cry at the same time when you see its extraordinary powers. You will wish you hadn't lived to face such a scary thing. If you don't want to go through all that, you can commit suicide and save yourself all the pain and suffering. You won't be able to hide anywhere from him on this earth. He will find you," the holy man said.

"I think you came with this bitch just to scare me. Maybe there is nothing out there. It was supposed to be here this afternoon. Maybe both of you should commit suicide to ease your pain and suffering. You said 'he.' Is he a man? If you can sense him, what time will he be here?" Bin Laden had many questions to ask.

"As I said before, be patient. It is four more hours. Don't be so desperate to meet him. You will regret it later," the holy man advised.

"Maybe his ass is feeling horny and getting desperate for a big dick," Naughty Bitch chimed in. "Isn't that right, honey? Maybe you are gay and longing for an extraordinary cock to suck and fuck."

"Don't call me honey, bitch."

"What are you going to do about it then, honeyyeeeeeeee? Fuck me? Come on. I think you won't even be able to get a hard-on. Your cock is already shrunk with fear. Come on, show me if you can get it up. I can see you are too scared. I promise I will shut up if you make it stand up." Naughty Bitch was good at talking and manipulating.

Bin Laden got really angry and accepted the challenge. "You want to see it hard? Hey, girl, come here and suck it." He called over a very sexy girl who was standing nearby. "I'll show the bitch how big it is. It will make her run away. Come on, suck it and make it hard." The girl came at once and started sucking. But five minutes passed and his cock was still soft and small. Naughty Bitch was right. Bin Laden was really nervous, and the fear was taking a toll on his body.

"See, like I said, it won't get hard. You are too scared already. I suggest your other ghosts run away and save their own ass. Don't commit suicide for this soft-cock wanker. Don't depend on him. He won't be able to save his own ass, let alone yours," Naughty Bitch said loudly.

Bin Laden felt ashamed and desperate. "Bitch, you don't know how to suck." He hit the first girl and called over another girl to suck it. "Suck it properly. If you fail, I will kill you." She tried but didn't do any wonders. Bin Laden kicked the girl. She fell backward, crying in pain.

"Stop, it's not her fault, asshole. It's your cock. You're too scared and going to crap in front of everybody. Your other ghosts are like you. They have all freaked out and become impotent. You are all fucking cowards," Naughty Bitch shouted in order to divert bin Laden's attention from the girl. It worked, and he picked up a brick and swung it toward Naughty Bitch.

Bin Laden lost it. He forgot that he couldn't hit Naughty Bitch because she was in her own dog ghost world. "I'll kill you, bitch. You just fucking wait. I'll kill you. I'll fucking kill you. Get out of my sight, you nagging bitch."

"See, asshole, fear is making you crazy. You like to scare other, innocent people. Now see what it is doing to you? I'm really going to enjoy watching you being fucked. Come on, you want to hit me, fucking bastard. Fuck you." Naughty Bitch didn't want to stop. She really got on his nerves. Bin Laden again tried to hit her, but it was useless. He got frustrated and angry. His ghosts saw his reaction, and fear gripped their hearts more. They were all trembling, and bin Laden noticed it. He realized that Naughty Bitch was playing psychological games with him and his ghosts. She was really good at it, and she succeeded in demoralizing his ghosts and him. He stopped responding to her tricks and walked away. Naughty Bitch followed him, but he just ignored her. She kept on going for some time and then gave up. She came back to Peter to get on his nerves. Bin Laden went onto the skyscrapers to motivate his ghosts for the fight. They had no choice but to stay put and fight.

Bin Laden came down. Five more minutes remained, and everybody stared at their screens. The whole world stood still and silent. People left everyday chores to watch the ultimate fight and humiliation of bin Laden. People started getting anxious and worried because there was nothing in sight around the city. People even used telescopes to see around the city, but there was nothing. Only one minute remained, and nothing was happening.

"No one is coming this way, old man. You have just been fucking with me all the time. You have played the greatest hoax ever on the public and me. Now there is only one more minute to go, and where is your fucking monster?"

"I said be patient. He is already in the city and coming toward you," the holy man said.

"You asshole. You fucked with my brain for so many months by spreading lies. Even I believed the Afghan holy man. Now

I understand it. You're all part of a plan to demoralize my ghosts and me so you can make me leave America. That's why you're asking me to commit suicide. Ha, ha, ha, ha, ha. I'm an asshole to fall for your lies. It must all be planned by the CIA and the government." Bin Laden became very happy after the time was over and nothing happened. The public got outraged that the government and the holy man lied to them and gave them false hopes.

"Come here, you fucking asshole holy man. Who is going to save you now? I will make you scream when my monster cock fucks your holy ass. And my monster is real, not a fake one." Bin Laden walked toward the holy man.

"Stop there. Do not move. He is here, and he is touching your ass now. Behave yourself if you don't want to suffer too much. Do you feel him touching your ass? He is not invisible. You can see him and feel him," the holy man said. The public looked around bin Laden and couldn't see anything. They were really pissed off and cursing the holy man. Bin Laden felt a little tickling on his ass and moved around to check it. He couldn't see anything.

"Yes, I felt a little tickle. But there is no monster here. Stop lying, asshole," bin Laden shouted at the holy man.

"Check it properly. You can hold him. He is sitting around your ass," the holy man said. The public again got curious and watched their screens. Bin Laden touched his ass and felt something near his hole. He got hold of it and brought it in front of him. It was a very small creature about an inch in size. People couldn't see it clearly.

"Did anybody put this insect on my ass? You call it a monster. He is lucky I didn't fart—he would have been dead and burned by now. I can even beat him to death with my cock. It's a really tiny monster, people. Look at your savior. It is sitting in my hand and trembling with fear. If I want, I can crush it like a cockroach now, but I won't. I want you all to see it first. It looks like a tiny half man, half octopus. It's got a lot of tiny tentacles. Wait a minute—he is trying to say something. I can't hear him properly. I have to move my ear closer to him. Yes, scary fellow, what is it?

"Really? He says the tiny things around him are not tentacles. They are his cocks, and he is going to fuck me with one of these cocks. He says his name is Saint Cockfighter and he fights with his cocks. He says he has won many wars just fighting with his cocks. Wait a minute, he is trying to say something again." Bin Laden listened and repeated what the tiny thing whispered in his ear.

"He is asking me if I am scared of his cocks and whether I will be able to take one of them all the way inside my ass. You think I should be scared of these cocks that we have to use a microscope to see? Looking at his size, if I take him all inside my ass, he will be crushed by the tightness of my cheeks." Bin Laden made fun of him. People wondered what the thing was. On the screen it just looked like an ant. Bin Laden moved his hand near the microphone.

"OK, Cockfighter, you can talk through the microphone so everybody can hear you. They must be thinking I'm making all this up. Here you go." Bin Laden put him near the microphone.

"Dear public, you have to trust me. I'm really Saint Cockfighter. I have come to kill this asshole called bin Laden. He has just seen my big cocks. He hasn't seen my giant balls yet. When he sees those, he will faint. OK, bin Laden the asshole, my cocks are not erect. If you touch them, they can grow as big as you want. Then you can choose the size that fits your ass," Cockfighter said.

"Ha, ha, ha, ha, ha. I think if I masturbate and come on you, you'll drown in my semen. OK, don't say afterward that I didn't give you a chance. I want to be fair. These sexy girls will touch you. See how big you can grow. This is really funny. The thing that scared me for so long is smaller and weaker than my cock," bin Laden said.

"It won't be funny anymore when I put one of them in your ass," Cockfighter said. The girls started touching Cockfighter, and he really started growing. He got heavy in bin Laden's hand, and he threw Cockfighter on the ground in disbelief.

"The fucking thing really grows." Bin Laden looked astonished. The public also couldn't believe what they saw. In a few seconds, he grew about three meters in size, and the cocks around his body moved like serpents and elephant trunks. The girls got so excited seeing so many big cocks that they started touching and licking them more. More girls came running to suck the enormous and growing cocks.

"Stop, bitches, can't you see he is growing in size? I have to kill him to stop him from growing," bin Laden shouted.

"Don't worry about him, girls. I'm here, so keep on enjoying. If any of other girls want a piece of my cocks, come on. Come lick and suck my cocks to give me power. Don't be afraid of this asshole. My one cock is enough to fight him." Girls all over the world felt horny looking at those giant cocks. Those nearby came running and forgot all their fear. They indulged themselves in cock licking and hugging. The girls rubbed and grinded those extraordinary, out-of-this-world cocks all over their sexy and hot bodies. They couldn't put them in their mouth because each cock grew about three meters long. Bin Laden and his ghosts couldn't believe their eyes. One of bin Laden's ghosts tried to attack Cockfighter from behind, but he was flung in the air when one of the cocks hit him. The crowd cheered the girls to touch and lick the saint's cocks some more. Cockfighter's body had now grown to about twenty meters high. He had giant balls hanging between the two cocks he used as legs to stand on. The balls were almost touching the ground. Some girls went for his balls and licked them. Bin Laden didn't want to take any more chances and proceeded to attack him. But as he came near Cockfighter, one of his cocks grabbed bin Laden around the neck like an elephant trunk grabbing a log. He carried bin Laden up in the air. Bin Laden tried to free himself, but the cock was too strong. Bin Laden hung in the air, trying to kick the cock. The public all over the world and the crowd watching erupted in celebration. People in the city rushed toward the capitol building to watch the scene in person. Some of the ghosts attacked Cockfighter to free bin Laden, but they died on the spot from just one hit from a cock. The others didn't dare to come near and fled, leaving bin Laden alone. Even Jack, his loyal child ghost, fled.

"Is it big enough for you, asshole? You think you can take it all the way inside? Why aren't you laughing now? Have you lost your sense of humor? Did you forgot the saying to never judge a book by its cover?" Cockfighter asked bin Laden.

"Oh, that feels so good. Keep on licking and touching. Oh, girls, I'm coming now. Oh yes." Saint Cockfighter's cocks turned their heads toward bin Laden. Cockfighter came with a bang on bin Laden. His whole body got covered in Saint Cockfighter's slimy cum. Saint Cockfighter released his neck, and bin Laden fell on the ground. He wiped the cum from his face. His eyes and mouth were full of cum. Bin Laden got up while cleaning himself.

"Don't try to run. You take one step, and one of my cocks will be in your ass," Saint Cockfighter warned bin Laden. Bin Laden had seen his power and didn't move his feet. He stood there cleaning himself and trembling in fear.

"Are you scared? Why are no words coming out of your filthy mouth now? Sorry about all the cum. That was just foreplay to make you wet before I penetrate your ass. You also forgot to never underestimate your opponent. You thought if something was so small, you could crush it with your tight ass. Try it now. Do you want to test the tightness of your ass now? I will put one of my cocks inside your ass, and you can try to crush it, asshole," Saint Cockfighter said. Bin Laden was scared and at a loss for words. He couldn't comprehend that something so small could be so dangerous and terrifying. He was warned, but he didn't believe it. He felt very foolish and degraded. In a few seconds, he had lost everything. His power was nothing in front of Saint Cockfighter.

"Please forgive me. Please let me go now. I will never come back to America, I promise. I beg you, please let me go."

"Why the fuck you are begging? You like entertaining people online with live shows, don't you? Well, we're going to entertain the world by using you. You will see how funny it will be. The public will love it, and it will be the top-rated show of all time."

"I provided you with those girls to let you grow in size. Otherwise you would still be short. Please consider my generosity and let me go," bin Laden pleaded again.

"So you think I would still be short. I became short just to fuck with your brain. I can be any size whenever I want. That was just to entertain the public. OK, folks, play some pop music. I want to show him some of my powers and sexy moves. Watch this, asshole." Somebody turned on the music, and Saint Cockfighter started dancing. People couldn't believe it. It was so amazing. The saint could dance different styles using his cocks. He could grow to a few kilometers high, and he could shrink to smaller than an ant. His cocks moved like snakes and elephant trunks. His cocks could become hard like steel and break even the biggest rocks into pieces. The girls went crazy watching his abilities. They felt very horny, and a lot of them had amazing orgasms just by watching him and his cocks online. The girls there in person became so turned on by watching him that they experienced multiple orgasms. His eyes were intoxicating, penetrating, and seductive. Saint Cockfighter teased bin Laden with his cocks by touching his ass and body. The public couldn't stop laughing, and bin Laden felt humiliated and weak. He jumped and ran around to save his ass.

"Did you see that, asshole? You can choose whatever size you want in your ass. Now I want you to lick one of my cocks and suck it. I'll make it thin enough to go in your mouth. Another cock will be on your ass. If you try to bite or play any tricks, my cock will tear your ass like paper. So let's make the show interesting. We don't want to bore our viewers." Saint Cockfighter put one cock's head on bin Laden's lips and one on his ass, ready to penetrate in case bin Laden didn't follow the orders.

"Come on, try it. You will love it," Saint Cockfighter said. Fearing for his ghostly life, bin Laden started licking and sucking unwillingly.

"Oh, baby, that feels so good. You seem to be very experienced. Oh yes, right there. Now increase the speed. Don't be shy. It's all yours to enjoy. OK, I'll rub my other cock on your ass to make you horny." Saint Cockfighter massaged bin Laden's ass with his cock while bin Laden carried on licking and sucking the other one.

"That feels so good. Don't stop. You stop and my cock will go inside your ass and come out from your mouth," Saint Cockfighter warned. Bin Laden got scared and started licking and sucking faster. He didn't want his ass torn and his energy sucked out.

"Oh yes, baby, I'm coming now. Don't stop. I want to come in your mouth, and you have to swallow. Yes, I'm coming now. Oh yes, oh yes, oh yes." Saint Cockfighter came and bin Laden's mouth was full. He swallowed it all.

"Good man. That was a great blow job. I think you won't be hungry for a few days," Saint Cockfighter said.

"Can I've your permission to ask something?" bin Laden requested.

"Sure, go ahead. You're my bitch now. You made me happy just now, and you can ask anything," Saint Cockfighter said.

"I don't understand what kind of saint you are. You seem to be a very vulgar, horny, and sex-addicted saint. How come you have all these powers?"

"Oh yes, a great question, and it deserves a full explanation. The public also must be wondering about that. You see, centuries ago I used to live in a forest. I was the most handsome young man in my tribe. There were about one thousand people in our tribe. The tribe's chief had a nineteen-year-old daughter who had a crush on me. I always avoided her company because she wasn't very beautiful. A lot of other girls in the tribe were very seductive and sexy. It was the tribe's rule that the members could have only one sexual partner in their life. The couple had to get married and stay together. I was engaged to the tribal chief's daughter. The problem was that all the married and unmarried young and beautiful women wanted to sleep with me. I couldn't resist it, and I had sex with all of them. I enjoyed it very much. But it didn't last long. The chief's daughter found out and informed her father. All the tribal men were angry and thirsty for my blood. They tied me up and tortured my body for days. I was repeatedly hit on my cock and legs. A hungry dog was let loose on me. It ate my dick and balls. I became unconscious and was thrown near the beach. A holy man saw my body and took me to his place, which was just near the beach. My legs were infected. The holy man amputated my legs and saved the upper part of my body. Then the holy man caught a giant octopus about two meters high. The holy man cut the octopus's head off and attached his body to mine. I started swimming and walking using the octopus's tentacles and body. But I felt very depressed and disappointed without my cock. I asked the holy man how I could get it back. He advised me that in order to get back my cock, I had to pray and repent my sins for centuries. A holy man would wake me up when the time came. He said I could enjoy my cocks, but I had to listen to the holy man who woke me up. And if I did that, I would get extraordinary powers and all the tentacles would turn into cocks. He warned me never to have sex with married women. If I didn't obey that rule, I would slowly lose my powers and all of my dicks. I accepted the challenge and sat in a place to pray. It went on for centuries. People built a pyramid around me and worshipped me. I didn't open my eyes and continued the prayers. Slowly the pyramid was covered by trees and dirt. People forgot about me. I never gave up, and finally his holiness saved me and ordered me to come here and make you repent your sins. You know the rest of the story, or you can watch it on video," Saint Cockfighter explained.

"So there is a way to lessen your powers," bin Laden said.

"Yes, but it will take millions of married women to take it away from me. I have to have sex with them willingly; otherwise it wouldn't affect anything. It will give you something to think about and keep you busy. Good luck if you can find a way. I'm not worried about it. Please free the politicians now. Does anybody else have any questions?" Saint Cockfighter asked.

"Are you allowed to have sex with female dogs? I'm dying for it after watching you," Naughty Bitch said. The sight of Saint Cockfighter's cocks and their abilities amazed her.

"No, bitch. I wouldn't do that. Don't you have enough dogs already? You bitches are never satisfied. After a while you would get fed up with my cocks and want something new. It's always the case," Saint Cockfighter said.

"Sorry, I was just curious. But will you let me play with bin Laden for some time? I will come to his ghost world to give him a hard time," Naughty Bitch said.

"Sure, anybody who wants to play with him will have their chance. We're not going to kill him. We'll take away his powers and humiliate him every day. Without him, our show will be very boring."

As Saint Cockfighter talked to Naughty Bitch, bin Laden jumped toward a tall building and made an attempt to escape. He jumped to the sky and landed on top of a building. His powers still intact, he was very fast—but not fast enough to escape Saint Cockfighter. Saint Cockfighter went after him and inserted one of his cocks inside bin Laden's ass. He brought bin Laden back screaming in pain with his cock still in his ass. The public cheered Saint Cockfighter and spat on bin Laden.

"Please forgive me. I won't try to escape again. I'm very sorry. Please make it a bit thin. It's tearing my ass," bin Laden pleaded.

"There is no place on this earth where you can hide from me. You try it again, and I will keep it in your ass the whole day and expand it inside. I have to suck your energy out now so you can't attempt it a next time."

"Can I say something, Saint Cockfighter?" President Benjamin asked.

"Yes, what is it?

"Your Holiness is already powerful enough. Please let me suck out his energy. He took my energy before. If you allow me, I can be your deputy and look after things so you can be free to enjoy yourself. If I take his energy, there won't be anybody else powerful enough to fight me. So you can go wherever you want and I will manage everything in your absence."

"That's a very good idea. I will hold him down, and you go ahead and put your powersucker in his ass. I want to watch a cock fight." Saint Cockfighter laid out the terms for the cock fight. "When you have sucked fifty percent of his energy, I will ask you to stop. Then I will tie your and bin Laden's hands behind your backs. Both of you will fight only with your cocks. The winner will get the energy. To be fair, you will have an equal chance of winning. Come on and do it now. Don't be scared, I'm holding him." Bin Laden screamed in pain when Benjamin inserted his large cock inside. Because of massaging it every day with oils, Benjamin's cock had grown to twenty inches long. The crowd and the viewers all over the world enjoyed bin Laden's sufferings.

"OK, stop now," Saint Cockfighter told Benjamin after a few hours. "That is enough. Now get ready for the fight. Bin Laden, you can keep your energy if you win." He ordered their hands to be tied. But bin Laden's cock was too tiny and soft because of the fear and humiliation.

"Come on, get it up, otherwise you're going to lose even before the fight starts," Saint Cockfighter said. Bin Laden tried desperately to wake up little bin Laden, but it looked as if it had gone into permanent sleep.

Bin Laden pleaded with and begged his cock. "Please don't let me down. Please wake up. If you wake up today, I will reward you with thousands of virgin pussies. Think about all the sexy and hot American pussies you fucked. Please wake up. I'll cut you off myself if you don't wake up today."

"It's not your tiny dick who has to do the thinking, you moron," Naughty Bitch taunted bin Laden. "You think with your brain and send him the electrical signal to wake up. To help you, you can think about my sexy backside and pussy.

I still remember how hard it was when you tried to rape my virgin pussy."

"Yes, bin Laden, you do the thinking," Saint Cockfighter said. "Come on, girls, help him to get it up. Show him some sexy moves and suck him. We want the fight to be fair. If he doesn't get hard, we can't enjoy the fight." The girls sucked and seduced bin Laden for half an hour, but it didn't work.

"That is no good, Mr. bin Laden. Have you become impotent? These are hot and sexy naked girls sucking you. Even a dead man can become alive if they seduce him," Saint Cockfighter said.

"Sorry, sir, it never happened before. It seems today is not my day. Everything is failing and deserting me. My ghosts also have fled and deserted me," bin Laden said with disappointment.

"Can I try, Your Holiness?" the donkey ghost asked. "He used to fuck me three or four times a day. I always gave him a hard-on. He is too attracted to my backside."

"Yes, go ahead. Wait a minute—you can't touch each other, so how will he able to feel you?" Saint Cockfighter asked.

"Sir, I followed them when they went to attack the dog ghosts. I saw the wormhole and went through it. I'm in the human ghost world now. I was just waiting for a chance to have sex with him. I think now he can't stop me if Your Holiness permits," the donkey ghost explained.

"OK, that's good. Mr. bin Laden, let her try, and if she is successful, you have to fuck her every day. I'm not asking. That's an order. OK, donkey ghost, go ahead." The ghost didn't waste any chance. She asked that the music be turned on loudly. She danced sexily with her backside toward bin Laden. To everybody's astonishment, his member regained its feelings. The donkey ghost went to bin Laden and grinded her backside against his cock. It worked wonders, and his cock hardened like steel. It grew to about the same size as President Benjamin's cock. Even bin Laden himself was astonished.

"That's wonderful and creepy at the same time. What have you been doing in the Afghan mountains, Mr. bin Laden? What so many hot girls couldn't achieve, a donkey ghost has done successfully. Good on you, donkey ghost. You will have your reward every day, but please let them fight first. OK, begin the fight now," Saint Cockfighter said.

The fight of the hardened and erected cocks began. They hit each other's cocks like two mighty swords clashing. Bin Laden put up a good fight. The public was worried and didn't want Benjamin to lose the fight. The fight went on for an hour. Their cocks swelled from the hits. It was like two boxers fighting and punching each other. Finally bin Laden fell down. When he turned around to get up, Benjamin inserted his enormous dick inside and started sucking his energy out. After a few hours, bin Laden's energy was gone. He became an ordinary ghost. Humiliated and his ass mutilated, he lay motionless on the ground. He could hear the public celebrating and fireworks going off everywhere. The rein and pride of bin Laden was taken away.

"Sorry about that, bin Laden. I gave you a fair chance of getting your energy back. Now you have to stay here and entertain people," Saint Cockfighter said. Seeing bin Laden defeated, Naughty Bitch rushed out of the city to get through the wormhole and come back and fuck with his brain. The American Indian holy man also said good-bye to everybody and left for the forest.

"As you know, Your Holiness, my energy has gone. Is there anywhere I can get my freedom back? I pose no danger to anybody now," bin Laden said to Saint Cockfighter after gathering some strength.

"Oh yes, there is always a way. It is money, Mr. bin Laden. Money always talks. You can buy your freedom," answered Saint Cockfighter.

"How much? Please tell me fast. Money is no problem for me." Bin Laden's hopes of getting freed lit up his face.

"One billion dollars," Saint Cockfighter said.

"Oh, that shouldn't be a problem. When do you want it?" Bin Laden's excitement grew, and the public became angry. They didn't want him to be freed. They shouted in one voice that he shouldn't be free and looked extremely angry with the saint. They knew bin Laden could get one billion dollars in no time. Even the government officials became worried when they watched Saint Cockfighter becoming greedy.

"Wait, there is a catch-22. You should earn the one billion dollars. Since you don't have any job, you have to prostitute your ass for it. You have to beg people to fuck your ass. You can charge a maximum of one cent per fuck to your clients. You can't refuse any client, no matter who it is. Once you save one billion dollars this way, you're free to go. You can start now," Saint Cockfighter said. People understood and erupted in celebration again. They understood the saint used cunning tactics to humiliate and punish a disoriented bin Laden. Bin Laden promptly started counting on his fingers how many clients he would have to serve.

"But, Your Holiness, there are not that many clients on this earth." Bin Laden got confused and was totally left with a fucked-up brain. He was still thinking about getting freedom that way.

"Don't worry, you can ask your clients to come back again and again. I'm sure they will keep coming back if you provide good service."

"But that is going to take too long." Still, bin Laden didn't want to give up. "I'll try it anyway. I will earn my freedom." He started immediately and begged the men to fuck him in the ass. The first day, nobody came and he felt disappointed.

"How is your new business going?" Saint Cockfighter asked bin Laden in the evening.

"Not good. I've waited since morning and had no clients," bin Laden answered.

"You must advertise and present your services properly. Use your brain. Check some other advertisements and learn how people promote their products," Saint Cockfighter advised.

"Yes, Your Holiness, I will do that," bin Laden said. Saint Cockfighter went away to rest for the night. When he came back the next day, he saw bin Laden dressed in sexy women's clothes. He wore red high-heel shoes, G-string, fish-net stockings, and bra. He had a signboard put up near him. It read, "Come get cheapest fuck ever. Just for one cent enjoy my ghostly ass. You get a bonus for free—I'll lick your balls if you take my services today. For every five fucks, you get one fuck free. Full money-back satisfaction guaranteed." Men were already lining up. Even beggars and homeless men lined up for that price.

"Well done, you really know how to advertise. You look very hot and sexy. Keep it up. You will earn your freedom one day," Saint Cockfighter encouraged him sarcastically. The next day, bin Laden looked happy because he was busy the whole day and night.

"You look very happy. Business must be going great," Saint Cockfighter said.

"Yes, Your Holiness, I served one hundred clients yesterday and earned one dollar. Here it is, and keep counting. I'll get my freedom one day. It doesn't matter how many balls I have to lick," bin Laden said. It seemed he had lost his brain along with his power. Bin Laden saw Naughty Bitch coming back with her dog army. She had gone through the wormhole and entered the human ghost world. Bin Laden's face changed and didn't look happy.

"The bitch is back. She knows I have lost my powers and has come back to haunt me," bin Laden said to himself.

"Look who is prostituting himself to buy his freedom. I always had a fantasy of wearing a strap-on dildo and fucking a man ghost. What a wonderful and hot man. Can I pay one cent and fulfill my fantasy, Mr. bin Laden the prostitute? If you let me, I might marry you one day. I may accept the proposal you made to me in Afghanistan." Naughty Bitch never had so much fun before.

"Fuck off, bitch. I'll never let you come near my ass," bin Laden said.

"I think you're forgetting one of the conditions set by Saint Cockfighter. He told you that you can't refuse any client, no matter who it is." Naughty Bitch was on to him. She didn't let him find any excuse.

"OK, I forgot about that. Come, bitch, you can have your way with me. It is your day today. Maybe my day will come one day. I will not forget you." Bin Laden gave up. Naughty Bitch put on a really big dildo and mounted him, forcing the dildo deep in his ass doggy style. Shouting abuse at her, bin Laden screamed in pain.

"You see, I'm a good ass fucker. You are already moaning with pleasure. You want it hard. You want it all the way inside. Come on, enjoy it, motherfucker. You want some spanking and scratching on your butt? I know you want it." Naughty Bitch became violent and wild. She spanked him hard and scratched his butt with her sharp paws. Bin Laden screamed with pain, but she continued humping and abusing him. The viewers were clapping and laughing all over the world. Naughty Bitch dismounted after one hour.

"Oh, honey, that was a great fuck. I hope you enjoyed it. I enjoyed it very much. I'm all huffed and puffed now. I think I'll enjoy it every day. That's some very cheap ass for only one cent a fuck." Naughty Bitch went away, leaving behind bin Laden moaning in pain. President Benjamin came near him to sprinkle salt on his injuries.

"Did you enjoy that, Mr. bin Laden? She was very good at it, wasn't she?"

"Then why don't you bend over and enjoy it too?" bin Laden shouted.

"Don't be angry. You had forgotten that what goes around comes around. This is just starting. There is worse in store for you. I'm the new manager here now, and I'll make sure you never rest in peace. Beginning tomorrow, you have to massage my cock for two hours in the morning. Is that understood? Say yes, sir." The president kicked bin Laden in the gut.

"Yessss s…i…r," bin Laden said in pain.

"Now you can carry on your business." Benjamin left him to let him do whatever he was doing.

Bin Laden suffered in everybody's hands. People came from all over the country to take revenge. The politicians and their partners paid back the favor by defecating into bin Laden's mouth one by one. Janet and the vampires also came and took their turn torturing him. John took his revenge by raping him every day. Tom and Judy also came to see him. They seemed very happy together in the ghostly world. They also tortured bin Laden for a few days and then left to enjoy their own life. As each day passed, bin Laden became a little more disoriented and crazy. Sometimes he just talked to himself. He knew nobody was coming to help him and only suffering and torture lay ahead in his ghostly life. Benjamin always kept security guarding him so he wouldn't escape.

Chapter 11

Two months passed without any incident, and bin Laden's miserable life continued. His ghosts who had fled didn't dare to come back to rescue him. Fearing for their own ghostly lives, they ran away to Afghanistan. President Benjamin every day enjoyed a new girl in front of bin Laden to irritate him. Janet, John, the vampires, and Naughty Bitch kept up their daily torture routine. The donkey ghost also irritated him by trying to have sex with him, but his cock became permanently soft and unable to rise for the occasion.

One day Saint Cockfighter and President Benjamin sat in front of the White House, discussing what to do with bin Laden. Suddenly, an army helicopter flew above and touched down in front of them. An army general emerged and walked toward them.

"Your Holiness, you and the president have to come with us right away. There is an emergency," the general said anxiously.

"What is it, General? You look very scared. Is everything all right?" Saint Cockfighter asked.

"Not really, Your Holiness. Our two very populated cities have been surrounded by a lot of flying saucers since early this morning. They are something we have not seen on this earth before. They look very advanced, and one came down. Some strange beings came out of it. It looks as if they are from another planet. We tried to ask them who they were, but instead of replying they shot down our fighter planes. We grounded our planes, but the saucers are still flying over the cities. We think they're preparing for an attack. You have to come with us straight away. If anything goes wrong, we think only you and President Benjamin will be able to handle them. Please come now. We need you."

"OK, it sounds like a very serious problem. Let's go, Mr. Benjamin. I will go to one city and you go to the other one. Try to talk to them first to see what they want. If it doesn't work out, do whatever necessary to stop them. Don't worry about here. We will ask Naughty Bitch and the friendly ghosts to guard bin Laden. He is too weak now and won't be able to fight them."

"OK, Your Holiness, let's go." Benjamin and Saint Cockfighter went with the general. The helicopter dropped President Benjamin at New York and then took Saint Cockfighter to Los Angeles. TV channels broadcast everything live second by second. The government brought in big guns to fight the aliens. The aliens didn't respond to the government's friendly gestures. In both cities, the spaceships opened up and out came extraordinarily sexy and hot young women soldiers. With their big and juicy boobs and hourglass figures, they stood about two meters tall. Dressed in a special kind of G-strings and bras, the gorgeous goddesses moved in such a sexy way that the men of Earth couldn't resist their temptations. Straight

266

men got hypnotized by their beauty and hotness. The men's hearts melted, and they started daydreaming about having sex with the beautiful goddesses. The women of Earth were jealous and heaped abuse on their men for ogling the aliens. The aliens took over the Internet and TV channels with their advanced technology. One of them who looked like their leader started speaking in English.

"Hello, earthlings, I'm Miss Hot Pussy. We are from a planet called Pussy Paradise. It is about thirty light-years away from your planet. Our solar system consists of twin stars. Our planet is populated by women only, and they all look young like us. We also had a male population long ago. But when a woman became ruler, she effectively planned to eliminate them. She conspired with the other females and injected all the men with female hormones. They all became gay. Seventy percent of them accepted the free operations offered by our government and became women. Our ruler enslaved the rest of them and didn't let any woman bear a male child. Our technology had advanced to a stage where we didn't need men's sperm to produce babies. We cloned only female babies. Now there are no males left on our planet. We have a new ruler who is interested in Earth's men for entertainment and sexual pleasures. She wants to bring back the extinct males. We have come to take all the handsome and healthy men from Earth to our planet. They will enjoy as much pussy as they want. No questions will be asked, and our women are not nagging bitches. You won't have to work, and we will provide everything you want. You will get brand-new flying sports cars and ten women like these you see now to fulfill your every fantasy. When you're tired of them, you can exchange them for new ones. The greatest pussy pleasure is guaranteed. We plan to take only one million men at first. If you want to apply, please go to our website, which we have just created, and submit your details and photos. The entries will close at ten tomorrow morning. Go now. You don't have much time left. Your governments or military can't stop you. We're very advanced in technology and can eliminate your military in minutes. We just want to take what we came for. I will play a video of my planet. Bye for now."

The video showed gorgeously sexy and hot naked goddesses at the beautiful and stunning beaches of their planet.

As soon as she finished her speech, there was chaos on Earth. Soldiers dropped their weapons and ran to find Internet access. There were no male soldiers left guarding any place on Earth. Straight men fought like dogs to get their hands on any device to access the Internet. Men started shooting and killing each other to go to planet Pussy Paradise. Men left their wives and girlfriends and rushed to apply online. Their mates begged them to stop, but nothing was enticing enough to stop them. The wives and girlfriends promised their men a nagging-free and sex-filled life, but the men didn't fall for it. The government had to quickly resort to emergency measures to recruit women and gay men for the army. As the aliens had taken over the Internet and TV channels, the government's women soldiers had to go door-to door-for the recruitment. Angry women and wives wasted no time in joining the army. The women of Earth took the arms, and even gays joined the army. Newly recruited women soldiers ignored army rules and regulations and attacked men wherever they found them applying for Pussy Paradise. Some angry wives even cut off their husbands' cocks to stop them.

The government regretted its decision to recruit so many women. The leaders didn't think that women soldiers would get so emotional and disobey orders. The men fought back and joined hands in killing women. The aliens didn't have to do anything. Their beautiful and hot soldiers did the job without firing a single shot. Saint Cockfighter, President Benjamin, and the politicians tried to infuse some sense into the people, but it was too late. The Earth was full of bodies everywhere. A lot of men lost their dicks. To stop the carnage, Saint Cockfighter and President Benjamin attacked the aliens. As soon as they attacked, young women soldiers from all the spaceships surrounding the cities descended on Earth and fought with an extraordinarily sexy style. They had laser guns installed in their big boobs and in their G-strings. Within minutes, people fled the cities. Only President Benjamin and Saint Cockfighter were left to fight. Benjamin used his extraordinary ghostly powers and brought down some alien ships. But the exceptionally sexy and hot goddesses distracted his mind while fighting, and he avoided killing them. He even preferred to stay visible while fighting them. The alien soldiers and their weapons couldn't inflict any damage on the ghostly body of President Benjamin. They had no choice but to retreat. Their technology could harm only the humans. As President Benjamin continued fighting the retreating alien goddesses, an alien ship landed nearby. Benjamin couldn't believe his eyes. A middle eastern looking ghost came out of the spaceship. He immediately remembered seeing that face in the photos of dead American enemies. The ghost looked like a spirit of Saddam Hussein.

"Holy shit, another fucking problem has come back to haunt America." President Benjamin couldn't believe his eyes.

"Mr. Benjamin, stop being a pussy and fight with a man. Sorry, ladies, I'm a bit late. Leave him to me. Your weapons won't be able to defeat him." America's new nightmare roared to life. Benjamin stopped fighting with the alien girls and turned toward the new ghost. The alien girls stopped to watch.

"He is all yours, Mr. Hussein. We will just watch him getting fucked," the aliens' commander said.

"Oh, so you are Saddam Hussein. I watched some videos and read books about you. Have you forgotten how you hid in a hole to save your miserable life? Have you come to America to get fucked again?"

"I was betrayed by my own people. We will see who gets fucked this time. The Americans looked for weapons of mass destruction in my country. I'm the ultimate weapon of mass destruction. After I've killed you, I will enjoy destroying America in a terrifying and dreadful manner. I'll personally scare the shit out of every American. They can't even imagine what I will do with them."

"Don't get any false hopes. I'm here to defend my country. You and your alien friends will not be able to escape the onslaught of a ruthless killer of American enemies. My power will touch new heights after I fuck you with my powersucker. Don't be a fucking cunt and run away to escape," Benjamin said.

"I've heard very convincing stories about your powers. When the time came, your tiny powersucker couldn't even tickle an ass. I've also heard you're an excellent and professional cock massager. I would love to get my junior Saddam Hussein massaged by you. You would love holding my extrabig and thick powersucker. Let's get to business without wasting any time. I'm not going to run away. Come on," Saddam Hussein said. Two extremely powerful and dreadful creatures pounced on each other. Saddam Hussein's power surprised Benjamin. The fight became fierce and intense. Benjamin underestimated Saddam. He thought he could beat him easily because he had also sucked all the energy from bin Laden. But Saddam almost overpowered him. Benjamin's overconfidence cost him some injuries, but he quickly came to his senses and fought back with full force and extra vigor. Saddam also didn't expect his opponent to be such a skillful and awesome warrior. No one was winning the fight, and suddenly the aliens' commander shouted.

"Come on, Mr. Hussein, we have to leave now. Something else more dangerous is coming our way from the other city. We just received the information. We didn't know anything about that monster and his abilities. I do not understand how we couldn't detect his presence on Earth. You wouldn't be able to defeat both of them. And if we lose our ships, we won't be able to get back to our planet. Don't worry, we will come back soon to exterminate them."

"OK, as you say, but I could have exterminated this asshole. Get into the ships while I cover you all," Saddam said.

"You bloody cunts, why are you fleeing like sheep now? Stay here and fight to the finish," Benjamin roared. He rushed toward the spaceships to bring them down, but Saddam thwarted his every attempt.

"Come on, Saddam, we're ready," the commander said. "Hit him hard to buy some time to get into the ship." All the other ships were already out of Benjamin's reach. The one with the commander waited for Saddam Hussein to board. Benjamin dashed to take it down, but Saddam kicked him so hard that he flung away from the ship and fell about three hundred meters away. This gave Saddam enough time to enter the ship. Benjamin attempted in desperation to reach the ship, but it went up into the sky with lightning speed.

"Come back, motherfuckers. I'm standing here and waiting to kick your asses," Benjamin roared. He felt disappointed because the alien girls snatched his prey right out of his hands. He turned around when he heard a helicopter landing nearby. Saint Cockfighter stepped out of it.

"Well done, Mr. President. You're America's true hero. We made an excellent decision that time by letting you suck bin Laden's power. You've proved today to the American people that you really deserved the power. I rushed here to help you. I was scared that you might be tempted by the alien girls' hotness. Good on you, you didn't fall for their sexy and seductive tricks. But I'm very disappointed because they have managed to escape. I wanted to enslave those gorgeous bitches."

"Thank you, Your Holiness. Saddam Hussein's ghost was with them. I almost nailed the bastard, but it was his lucky day. Their weapons had no effect on me, but Saddam's ghost was equally powerful. I'm just wondering from where did he acquire all that energy? I know they will come back soon. It seemed they knew everything about me but nothing about Your Holiness. They seemed to be scared of Your Holiness's abilities. They couldn't detect your presence on Earth. That's what their commander said."

"We have to be prepared for next time. I think because I remained buried for so long, they couldn't see me coming. We can't underestimate them. They would find a way to eliminate us because they are extremely advanced in technology. I think next time there would be a big army of the aliens descending on this planet to control it," Saint Cockfighter said.

"What happened in the other city, Your Holiness?"

"The alien soldiers saw me fighting with my extraordinary cocks and fell in love with me. They offered me every privilege on their planet if I followed them. They were interested in cloning me. I refused and attacked their ships. I brought two down. They avoided injuring my cocks and wanted to capture me alive. They threw special nets on my cocks to entangle me. The nets were made of a material so strong that I got entangled and couldn't break free. I couldn't fight any longer and fell down entangled in the nets. Then I played the trick of becoming smaller than an ant and disappeared. The alien soldiers looked everywhere in desperation but couldn't find me. In an angry mood, they embarked on their spaceships and blew up the city. By that time, I was already out of the city. I quickly came here to help you because there was nothing left in that city to defend," Saint Cockfighter explained.

"We're lucky that we have damaged their two ships, which they couldn't fly off. Our scientists have to study them in detail as soon as possible, and we have to find their weaknesses," President Benjamin said.

"Yes, you're right. Let's go to the capital city. Let the authorities do their jobs," Saint Cockfighter said.

They got into the helicopter to go back to the capital city. The governments of the world were busy restoring peace. The women and men of Earth didn't see eye to eye. The women were left angry and sulking by the men's behavior. The aliens sent the selected men secret messages in their heads by telepathy to assemble at different places. The alien ships came back to get them. The government was unable to detect them. A lot of unsuccessful men came back to their wives and girlfriends and begged for forgiveness. Some women forgave, but a lot of men got beaten up and rejected.

As Saint Cockfighter and President Benjamin approached the capital city, they saw a lot of dog ghosts' and soldiers' bodies strewn about. Smoke and fire were everywhere. They rushed inside the city to check what had happened. City streets were full of dead bodies. One injured soldier was lying in front of the capitol building. Saint Cockfighter helped him.

"What happened here? Who did all this?"

"Sir, after you had gone, four spaceships landed here. We couldn't believe our eyes when we saw Saddam Hussein's ghost disembark from one of the spaceships. He introduced himself. He said he came from a planet called Pussy Paradise. The alien women of that planet took him there. He said he liked his new avatar. He was accompanied by the most beautiful and gorgeous women I have ever seen. I don't think there is any like them here. They came here to rescue bin Laden. They had been watching us. Before leaving, bin Laden borrowed one of their laser guns and killed as many as he could. We didn't stand a chance in front of the advanced weapon."

"Where are Janet, John, the vampires, the donkey ghost, and Naughty Bitch?" Saint Cockfighter asked.

"Bin Laden took Naughty Bitch with him in the spaceship to torture her. He killed all her dog ghosts who tried to defend her. He also killed Peter. But the donkey ghost, Janet, John, and vampires managed to escape. Bin Laden told me to give you a message that he will be back and you should be ready to defend yourself," the soldier answered.

"Holy shit, what are we going to do now?" president Benjamin asked.

"Start preparing, Mr. Benjamin. We don't know with what powers he will be back. We should have killed him. We were overtaken by pride and ego. I made a big mistake." Saint Cockfighter looked really worried. Janet, John, and the vampires came back the next day and felt sorry about not being able to defend the city. But Saint Cockfighter and President Benjamin understood their decision to flee. It would have been suicide because Saddam Hussein's ghost was more powerful than bin Laden's. Saint Cockfighter called an emergency meeting of all the experts, monks, vampires, and friendly ghosts to decide on the next course of action to face the horrifying and dreadful onslaught of bin Laden, Saddam Hussein, and the aliens.

Made in the USA
Columbia, SC
26 August 2021